SHE CAME TOO LATE

SHE CAME TOO LATE

MARY WINGS

The Crossing Press / Freedom, California 95019

Cover illustration by Mariet Numan.

First published by The Women's Press Limited of London, U.K.

Printed in the U.S.A. by McNaughton & Gunn of Ann Arbor,
Michigan.

                    Library of Congress Cataloging-in-Publication Data
Wings, Mary
    She came too late / by Mary Wings.
        p.   cm. — (WomenSleuth series)
    ISBN 0-89594-244-5 : $20.95.   ISBN 0-89594-243-7 (pbk.) : $7.95.
    I. Title.   II. Series
PS3573.I53213S5 1987
813' .54—dc19   87-21914
                                                    CIP

Thanks to Wendy Chapkis

The girls want things that make common sense,
The best for all concerned.
They don't want to have to go out of their way.
And the girls want to be with the girls . . .

Girls are getting into abstract analysis,
They want to make that intuitive leap.
They are making plans that have far reaching effects.
And the girls want to be with the girls.

One

'Hello, I want to kill myself.'

Many people think that's the kind of phone call we receive here at Women's Hotline. But no, the caller is usually very indirect and you can hear her struggling with all her self doubts, love for a man who is beating her, the inability to admit drug or alcohol problems and sometimes even a general self-hatred in the pauses before she comes to the point. These silences are harder to face than any person on the verge of self destruction, and I prepared myself for another day of work at the twenty-four-hour telephone service.

It was May 17, a Tuesday, and I didn't expect a particularly hard day. The women in our fair and not-so-fair city had weathered the weekend with and without traditional families, with and without alternative families and romantic conflicts. It was morning, and most women would be busily tending the laundry, or rushing to work, or settling down for a day with their children. The crises would come later as they stared at blank walls, or blanker husbands.

Our office is on a dingy side street of Boston; we don't need a public face, only a public phone number and a strong, clear, voice, but still the faded political posters, unframed and curling at the corners, depressed me as I sat in my little cubicle with my feet up on the desk. I was curling a piece of paper between my fingers and trying not to think about smoking. The Metropolitan Boston Transit Authority was having another fire today; that had meant driving to work and fighting traffic. It meant I was in a lousy mood.

The phone rang and I assumed the voice that was meant to erase the doubts of the vulnerable on the other end of the line.

'Women's Hotline'.

'Hi, um I was wondering what the process is in your organisation for validating the effectiveness of your support services.'

Okay. Another sociology student, this one without manners. Yet we weren't supposed to ask names; the rules were different in this game. I

1

gave her our line. I said that we tried to have our clients call back and follow up with their experiences at the social service agencies we had recommended. In addition we met regularly with other service groups, and – I went on for a minute reciting the blurb out of our pamphlet (why didn't she just read *that*) when she cut me off.

'Is this Emma Victor?'

I stopped myself. I was just supposed to be a voice on the telephone; our policy was to remain anonymous. Or was this a friend of a friend recognising my voice and unwittingly crossing the boundaries of social service into social life?

'This *is* Emma Victor, isn't it?'

'Yes.' I went for it. That was the first stupid thing I did. The voice was on the edge of recognition.

'Please, Emma, I just feel crazy – it's horrible – you gotta help me . . .'

'I don't *have* to help anyone. Just slow down a second. Catch your breath. Okay. If you'll just tell me . . .'

'Emma,' she was out of breath, 'Emma, I need you. I'm going to blow this thing to the moon. You can help me blow this thing open. Just meet me on the north end of East Lexington Street. Please. I'll smoke a cigarette and I'll be wearing a beige raincoat. Someone is following me already. There's one more person I have to talk to. Nine o'clock. Be there.'

'Hey . . .'

She hung up. And I was just about to explain our anonymity policy, our referral policy, our many policies and how we used this professionalism to help clients. Later I thought about how our professionalism helped us to protect ourselves. I wouldn't consider meeting this woman; I felt abused and I didn't want to be drawn into any high school dramatics. I'd already had enough roles in scenes like that myself. Besides my off hours were mine and other people's problems only existed from nine to five (my current shift).

I stashed the voice away in my mind as I answered other calls and effectively guided other women down probable paths to possible solutions. But the voice that called for me personally lingered in the back of my brain. It was only later that I realised that this must have been the woman we had discussed in the last meeting who had been repeatedly calling, engaging workers in meaningless conversations and hanging up. Not a hypochondriac but a searcher, and searching for me.

I was drifting towards that possibility (the phone wasn't ringing nearly enough) when Monica stopped by to remind me about the

2

city-wide women's services meeting happening in twenty minutes. Monica was a small, wiry woman, a red diaper baby, with a revolution in her chromosomes that seemed to guide her as she worked tirelessly at one and then another political project. She was a good co-worker, but with as much sense of humour as a cardboard box.

A volunteer arrived to relieve me and I showed her the outstanding features of my cubicle-desk; then Monica, Hannah and I went to the city-wide meeting to watch the death throes of some of the best service organisations for women in our city.

The YWCA had lent the meeting their largest hall, and the Y gals were there in full force directing a registration effort and organising work group meetings for special interest lobbies afterwards. They were doing their best, although they always seemed more at home out of doors and still would wear their flannel shirts and unbelievably sturdy woodsman's boots on the mere pavement of the city. Often very active Girl Scouts, with nowhere to go after their twentieth year, they found the YWCA, and all their associated camps, a wonderful place to use their skills in nature and with each other.

I smiled as a particularly winsome woman in a yellow (how daring) flannel skirt handed me a programme and directed me towards the main hall with the lightest of touches on the small of my back. I prepared myself as I opened the swinging doors.

Pandemonium. Our newly-elected female mayor was present and breaking the bad news. She needed our help in deciding what services would be cut. She needed to be let off the hook; could we please slit our own throats for her?

Everyone was there. The health services, the social services, our media, consisting of one small newspaper run by women overworked at their jobs, the women's radio station, in reality a few hours granted to women from an alternative left station itself on the brink of financial ruin, the battered women's shelter, always overcrowded and needing the most pathetic things, like silverware and sheets. Some social clubs were also present, coffeehouses for underage lesbians and a soup kitchen run by nuns who wore real clothes. All were up for the axe.

The third world women's groups made no pleas, they *demanded* funds; the infant mortality rate in the ghetto was shocking enough to be called genocide. The current administation had turned its back on minority groups, and women and children were the first to suffer in the land of plenty.

The alternative women's clinic, dealing often in herbs and psychic

3

body work and other such amorphous healing arts would probably be a lame runner. Everyone agreed, however, that our survival meant at least our physical survival. But where did we start, survival of black women and their children, women who were being beaten by husbands and boyfriends, or the Janssen Centre, where suburban women addicted to valium and streetwise sixteen-year-old junkies, now turning to prostitution, could kick the habit, once and for all, maybe.

I heard all these women speak, eloquently and with a fervour on the edge of self-righteousness. Our city was a sinking ship, women and children going down first. I also reminded myself that these were women who had made their careers and lives out of badly funded social work. Many were in their mid-thirties, had given a lot, were getting burnt out. The mayor nodded appreciatively at their desperation; it couldn't be easy for her either, but at least she was famous.

The other famous person was sitting prominently in the first row, taking unnecessarily copious notes. She whispered quick comments to a woman behind her; several messages were passed to her. She had the aura of importance: in the tense way she sat, in her attention being drawn to people needing her, lending them a fraction of ear while hastily scribbling on a legal pad. She had liberated us all with her speculum; her name was Stacy Weldemeer. She represented the Josephine R. Blackstone Women's Clinic. I knew something about the Blackstone Clinic. My sweetest, slightly alcoholic and best friend, Jonell Flax, volunteered there once a week, playing receptionist. She was crazy about Stacy Weldemeer and also about the Blackstone Clinic.

The Clinic and our phone service were about the only two organisations not in total panic. The Hotline had funding guaranteed for the next five years through a combination of private foundations and specific city grants. The Blackstone Clinic was a different matter. Beset by internal problems five years ago, the collective had decided to hierarchise the structure and of course the prolific Stacy Weldemeer had 'drifted' to the top position.

Stacy was a media hound, which in itself wasn't bad in such a troubled and poor city. She had made big news, nation wide, with one of the first clinics to inseminate single women who wanted to become pregnant. The publicity not only brought them clients, who paid on a sliding scale, but also generated controversy around single parenthood and lesbian parenthood particularly. We were finally grabbing the boys by the balls and a lot of them didn't like it.

So the Blackstone Clinic was doing fine, its tiled corridors and

4

upholstered waiting room swept away all thoughts about clandestine insemination. Its modern sperm bank and testing laboratories gave credence to our control over our own biological functions. We had arrived, and it was no small accomplishment with the New Right Bible thumpers working the same side of the street. Most clinics needed fresh funding and troops to exist from year to year; thanks to Stacy Weldemeer the Blackstone Clinic had both.

Because I was suspicious of Stacy O'Malley Weldemeer. She had a way of pandering to the powerful; you could see her at gatherings dropping a conversation as soon as anyone big in the entertainment field beckoned. She was nearly a media beauty. Fine features, cultured voice and the posture of a ballerina even with her large frame and big bones, made her a good talk show guest. She was usually encased in something called dressed for success; her rigid work ethic encased anyone who had even volunteered to lick stamps for the Blackstone Clinic. But there was passion underneath the shocking red curly hair, freckles and perfect teeth. I was afraid Weldemeer was not just working the media, but becoming a media creature herself. And she was making the field of women's health care her stamping ground.

She could chat cleverly with reporters; on the Luke Kelly Late Night Show she made artificial insemination sound like something for Bloomingdale's, at a Danish press conference she made it sound like the essential step in the dialectic of the women's revolution. Her face was seen twice in *Time* magazine; she didn't have to come out because she never had a steady girlfriend. Rumour had it that she was celibate, but her convent training made me suspicious of that. She was probably good at working a lot of closet angles. Publicly, she'd said that her own inability to have children led her to the field of women's health care. I doubted that: I thought Weldemeer was just ambitious as hell; which wouldn't be so bad if she didn't cover it up with a patina of shiny goodwill.

The meeting was winding down. The mayor was promising to organise a cadre of private funders to meet with groups in the future. A few angry voices shouted 'When?' The mayor looked directly at the crowd and said, 'This month, as soon as possible.' There were still grumbles as women broke into work groups trying to figure out new lobbying techniques, ways of pressuring the legislature. The mood was bleak; I felt like it had been raining for ten weeks.

I begged off and said goodbye to Monica and Hannah. Monica was already perusing the opportunities for her organisational talents with swiftly darting eyes; Hannah would follow. I made my way through the crowd which was jawboning about the mayor and complaining about everything. I noticed Stacy Weldemeer leading the pack, carefully crunching a note in her clenched fist, like a maniac waiter folding a napkin. Then I noticed who was walking alongside her and I kept on noticing her. A woman even my best fantasies couldn't touch.

Her mouth was too big, her upper lip curled slightly at the corner giving her almost a sneer except that her hazel eyes had a jaunty half moon shape. She had a rather stocky build, her jawline made a sharp corner leading to two tiny perfect shell ears. She stood with her feet apart and I let her presence burn into some part of my subconscious. She was beautiful and she was arguing with Stacy Weldemeer.

The woman was clenching her teeth.

'Look, you can't interview a hormone and get it to respond. This isn't the media, Stacy. We're talking about long-term, partly trial and error . . .'

Weldemeer said something to her in smooth tones designed to unruffle the angry woman. The woman with the mouth said coldly, with finality, 'You deal with the administration. And only the administration. If that's not possible, we can just put the baby to bed.' Not many people talked to Stacy Weldemeer like that. I looked at Stacy's face and thought all the freckles were going to jump off. She was furious, but she still listened to the woman telling her, 'The situation scientifically exists on a timetable . . .'

The rest of what she had to say was drowned out by a woman in overalls shouting, 'I don't care if their pricks have been pruned, I don't want men doing childcare . . .' Overalls was poking her finger into the chest of a tall, thin blonde woman who didn't like it. Their identical necklaces, linked double women signs in silver, grabbed some sunlight and sparkled on their tie-dyed T-shirts. Tall, thin and blonde didn't like being poked and pushed; her face filled with blood like her Gay Marxist Collective button. She put a palm on Overall's chest and moved her lips in an ugly way. Then there was a pushing and a pulling and I was shoved backwards with the Beautiful Mouth woman behind me. We slid down together, my back against her and her back against a steel doorframe. Then she was on the floor and I was in her lap. I turned and saw her crinkly eyes and realised that I couldn't get up. I thought we paused an unnecessary second before I stretched my arms to the floor, around her hips and pulled myself upright. I stood brushing my trousers and watching tie-dyes walk out the door, still sputtering.

'What's the problem, transvestites in toyland?'

'Apparently,' she answered. The skin of her lower lip had small wrinkles.

'Well, nothing like constructive dialogue about differences . . .'

'Better get used to it, there's more emotions than social services now.'

'I am used to it. Doesn't mean I like it any better.' We were fighting already.

'Well, no one is about to pull off a loaves and fishes here,' she said.

'Still, I'd rather not get ready for physical fights over it, thanks.'

She arched her eyebrows. Somehow she had an investment in being tough. I would have preferred not to play the pacifist myself, but she continued, 'Then you'd better figure out the quickest way to score drugs or pour yourself down a bottle because this is the game for a while.'

Whatever her vested interest in accepting the worst she put out a hand to straighten my collar. Manicured nails, short and no polish.

'Blackstone Clinic is doing okay,' I remarked.

'But nothing else is. There's a three-year waiting list for all the childcare centres now. Most single mothers are feeling pretty shoved around. You'd better get used to being shoved around too.'

'And winding up in your lap.'

She almost smiled. 'Sometimes we luck out.'

And with that she was swept out with the crowd and Stacy Weldemeer.

Two

I walked back to the Hotline office and picked up a book I'd left there. Seeing my cubicle, stuffed with notes and reference materials, made me illogically think of the phone call I'd gotten earlier that day. 'I need you, Emma Victor.' The desperation circus at the Y had almost let me forget that.

I walked to my big horsy Plymouth. It was a silly car, a large brown job, a gas guzzler; it was a road-hog; it even had cruise control. At least it didn't sport roll-up windows. It had been my father's car and he had died two years ago hiking in the mountains. He'd had a heart attack: I figured, except for the last two minutes, it was probably the best way to go. He left me a life insurance policy, which would keep me in vacations for a number of years, and a huge brown Plymouth. I got in and smelled the cream coloured leather upholstery, now getting cracked with age. He'd always taken good care of the car; I would take care of it and pour gas into it until it died too.

I was tired; I punched on a jazz tape on the system I'd had installed in the car, but it didn't smooth out the stop and go traffic. Finally, I got up a little speed, enough to feel the traction of the big tyres as I took a curve.

At home I stroked the cat, envied her briefly and reheated a rather good quiche I had made the day before for myself. I made a baroque salad which included walnuts and feta cheese and settled down for a nice meal. After dinner I opened a good book about fourteenth-century France, at the moment my favourite vacation spot.

I was becoming absorbed in the antics of penitential processions when the phone rang. It was Jonell Flax, the nicest person I know.

'I'm trying to give a party next Friday. Do you think anyone will come? Is there anything else going on? Will you bring some of those tofu cubes you made for Clara's barbecue last summer?'

'Glad to, Jonell.' Jonell was kicking booze at the moment and also a love affair that just sort of soured and dragged on too long. She needed some stimulation of a social sort. 'Be sure and invite those girls from Jamaica Plain, things have been coming down heavy over there with a few break-ins and I know there's nothing else going on. I'm sure you can pull it off.'

We rang off and I glanced at the clock. I suddenly remembered – eight-thirty and I had mystery woman walking up and down a dark street in half an hour. I didn't want to meet her; I didn't want her problems, but more than that I didn't want her walking up and down Lexington Street by herself. I thought I would be just stupid enough to join her.

The north end of East Lexington Street is perpendicular to two commercial streets, full of dead businesses and burnt out street lamps. The houses on East Lexington itself are the eastern seaboard brick family dwellings, transformed into big city urban ugliness by time and speculators. Skirted by porches and housing dining rooms with woodwork and plate racks, topped off by big bedrooms upstairs to house a growing family, they were relics of another age. The neighbourhood didn't use calling cards when it socialised, it was as likely to use small, easily hidden arms. The inmates crouched inside the dwellings now converted into two and three apartments. The bricks sheltered all varieties of singles and couples with and without children, and even nuclear families, squeezed into dining rooms now bedrooms and bedrooms now parlours with oversized kitchens if you had the downstairs and, if you had the upstairs, undersized kitchens from what was once a large walk-in closet.

It was a quiet street, too quiet, with almost nowhere to park. No one peeked out their windows as I slammed my car door and looked at the pools of darkness broken by inadequate street lighting, noticing all the little side alleys. I decided to put my ring of keys in my fist, keys between my splayed fingers, jagged tips ready for a vulnerable spot, if I had time to find one.

I didn't see anyone, and could feel the local lesbian bar, conveniently just around the corner, pulling me like a magnet. It was exactly 9:02 on my ugly little digital watch and I decided to walk once up and once back. I started down the street, feeling like a patsie. Twice I almost turned back. What kept me walking was that she knew my name.

She had wanted me, and had been calling the Hotline enough times to get me. It was quiet and dark, as if no one lived there, as if it was a desert and not a dark and dangerous city street. I heard muffled sounds, none too close. A car door slammed somewhere. All the houses had carefully opaque curtains. Occasionally a piece of stained glass would hang in front of a window, or a row of little crystals that would prism Boston sunlight entering cheerily during the day.

At night everything looked tight and uptight. Every car door locked, curtains closed against the dark, doors shut, and deadbolted and locked again, and first storey windows barred. Once down East Lexington Street, I had only to walk back. That would mean I had done my duty to the voice on the phone, or rather, to my own curiosity. Maybe it was someone using my vulnerability, snickering at me now from behind a curtain on a second storey window. A man whose girlfriend I had driven to the battered women's shelter, or the junkie who'd left her dealer-boyfriend who'd been hiring her out. They had split her salary a little too long. Splitting it once was already too generous, I thought. The boyfriend would have an axe to grind. I ran through possible motives and past clients, looking at the end of the street which was coming nearer.

Then I saw them. The feet, just like the feet of the wicked witch of the east sticking out from under the house of Oz. But this wasn't Oz and these feet weren't attached to a witch. They were sticking out ever so slightly from an alley off East Lexington Street. The feet had on red shoes and were just visible in the outer circumference of the indifferent light of a street lamp. I stopped and felt cold sweat run to my waist. I reminded myself that it was time to act if a life could be saved, and pushed the other questions out of my mind. She was wearing a trench coat.

I gripped my keys and started towards the dark alley. I didn't see anyone, didn't hear anything. I grabbed the wrist. It was warm but there was no pulse. Not that I could feel. I felt for a pulse on her neck, not trusting my fingers. She was a warm body and I was seeing little white lights dance in front of my eyes, as gravity swiftly pulled all the blood to my feet.

I stood and looked at her another second. Her face was to the ground.

I didn't want to know her. And I didn't want to notice the small black charred hole in the back of her trench coat. It meant the sticky black pool slowly spreading on the ground, was blood. I called out but my voice lodged in my throat. I saw her purse, more like a daypack affair, open contents on the ground. A bottle of pills, Empirin three. Codeine.

I cried out but only achieved a squeak. I saw an address book peeping out from the daypack. I grabbed it on impulse; my first thought – would my name be in it? All this took a very long stretched-out second. The white lights were becoming smaller, had slowed their dance before my eyes. I saw a passerby. I called out again; the breath somehow got past my lungs.

'Call the police, get an ambulance,' I gained my wind and my wits but I was losing my stomach.

The pedestrian turned. I saw it register on his face, he ran off to one of the shut-up houses. The door opened, chain in place, and the person inside ran, presumably to the phone. I leaned against the side of a brick house and threw up.

Then things began to happen fast. First a police car, then an ambulance, the logic of our city. Men stood over the body. Some of them shook their heads. Suddenly every curtain on the block had been pulled, porches were filling with people and the most curious ventured on to the street. I was just contemplating my quiche when an officer approached me.

'You discovered the body?' The body. So she was dead.

'Yes.'

'Name?'

'Emma Victor.'

'Address?'

Just then a van pulled up, and some slightly higher ups in the police department stepped out. I gathered they were already in the neighbourhood, chalking off another body shape on another sidewalk just a few blocks away. I saw them taking the photographs.

'Touch anything, miss?'

'No. Felt for her pulse. Neck and wrist.'

'Just passing by?'

The whole Women's Hotline staff passed before my eyes. The funding crisis. The scandal in the press, clandestine meetings, murdered clients . . .

'Yes, just passing by,' and I neatly compounded the errors of an entire day.

We continued with the formalities. Some of the neighbours were getting off on the excitement. Some were afraid. Having someone murdered outside your door was getting close to home, even with bars on your windows and chains on your doors. I noticed most of the people weren't speaking to each other. It was a neighbourhood of strangers.

They hoisted the lifeless body off the ground, leaving the chalk marks behind. They turned her on her back and an arm which had been lying across her chest flapped down and swung back and forth, dangling off the stretcher before someone replaced it. Her body had a tight conditioned look, even when limp. Then I saw her hair, cut medium and thick, it stopped just over her ears as they arranged her on the stretcher. Her face looked tanned and sunny, but she wasn't very dead yet. I walked towards the flood of street light which illuminated her body being laid out. Just before two ambulance attendants in white pulled a sheet over her face I noticed the pointed chin and the small shapely mouth above it.

Two long thin welts, puffy and red, were blazing across her cheek. There was snot running out of her nose. But even with the panic and the red welts it was a pleasant face. A face that had had a conversation with me, in a French restaurant, just two weeks ago. The night came back to me, like a bolt shooting into a lock.

Two weeks ago. It was May 3 and I was being a good girl. I had volunteered to do the statistics for our yearly calls. It was a job everyone hated, but it allowed an overview of our work for which the daily grind of voices asking for help only provided a background. I was tired and I needed those voices in the background, so it was pleasurable to count columns and make referral summaries without feeling any of the needs behind them. It was also pleasurable because I did this yearly work over a thirty dollar dinner, alone, on a peacock blue linen tablecloth. I had chosen the snootiest French restaurant in Boston.

It had a sunken dining room with lots of tables covered with thick blue tablecloths and wearing sparkling silverware. Dividers, sporting exotic greenery and cages filled with canaries almost protected the diners from one another. A cadre of waiters with starched white uniforms stood at attention in various doorways by the kitchen. They would bring the courses slowly, with enough time in between for me to count the ciphers that told of a city's worth of misery. But I wasn't the only oddball in the place, and I wasn't the only woman who stayed late.

In a big booth in the corner a woman sat alone. She wore her brown hair in a Dutch boy cut and it stood out thick and soft, like a giant brand new paint brush. It swung above her ears. She had a small heart-shaped face, a little nose, tan, and ruddy skin. And a small portion of mouth. She wore a light blue silk shirt with pen pockets over each breast. Her sleeves were rolled up and I could see a forearm with admirable muscle definition and a digital watch. She looked at the watch a lot and sighed. The watch beeped. Eventually the waiter came

12

with the telephone and she smiled and took the receiver from him. She made what looked like cooing noises into the plastic receiver, then she hung up and appeared satisfied.

The waiter bowed slightly and returned the phone. Then he came back and stood before her asking a question with his shoulders. The woman leaned back. She had a broad chest and the silk shirt was pulling slightly against her small breasts. Then she opened the menu and ordered in what sounded like very flat Midwestern. The waiter grimaced and took some notes. Then he walked away and I saw her settle down to wait for her dinner alone.

I opened up my notebooks with loose pages in them and began the task of separating the calls by category. I had a mechanical pencil with an H lead in it with which I could make fine numbers in the pre-drawn grid paper I had prepared earlier that day. I had just gotten through March when I looked up at the kitchen doorway. Two waiters were standing at ease, white towels hanging off their forearms and a bad attitude hanging off their noses. I looked around the dining room with them. Their only customers were two lone women, one making meticulous notes with a mechanical pencil and the other leafing through a magazine and staring off into space as if this were just a pit stop to grab a bite before heading off to work. Then a crowd of young noisy businessmen in three-piece suits and dates in wobbly high heels burst in.

The waiters went to work and assisted their seating which made the young businessmen nervous. They had forgotten to seat the ladies themselves. The waiters handed them gold tassled menus in triumph and returned to their portal to let them suffer through reading French, the only language that appeared on the menu and the only language that could describe their food.

I went back to my statistics and then put them away as the waiter appeared before me to do some arcane performance involving pâté and small slices of toasted bread. I sampled the pâté and thought about the eighty-three women who were in their homes being battered when they called. Sixty-seven of them went to the battered women's shelter, thirty-seven of them had stayed there for more than one month, twenty-four of them had found new addresses. Nineteen were on welfare.

I dawdled over the last crumbs of melba toast and thought about how simple my life was. I had no conflicts with my cat or co-workers. And I was in a French restaurant eating pâté. Life was streamlined and lonely and I was liking it that way.

13

The other lonely diner was liking it too. The waiter appeared before her with the pâté which he delivered with two spoons and a miniature stoneware urn. Then he dazzled her with a flaming meat dish and ignored her at the same time. She didn't care, she just let the dinner come to her.

After our main courses there was a pause. I was busy counting referrals to the crisis centre. She walked to the bathroom. We didn't look directly at each other. She had a broad build but she was toned. Her dangling earrings were the only femmy and self-conscious thing about her. She was graceful and confident. She walked through the big dining room like a train on rails and she was wearing faded Levi's in the best French restaurant in the city.

I continued cataloguing calls. I was all the way up to mugging when she returned to her booth and crawled into the upholstered seat. Her salad was waiting for her, and mine was just arriving. We ate our salads and spent some energy not watching each other and pretending to be interested in lettuce. After a while we were over coffee and I started feeling silly. I raised my finger at the nearest person wearing gold epaulets. He sauntered over and I enjoyed asking him to ask the lady at the other table if she would like an after dinner cognac.

He did and she did. When it arrived she raised her glass towards me, took a sip and tried not to grimace. Then she returned to the boring magazine but it appeared not to have gotten any better since she last put it down. Her eyes didn't move back and forth. Finally she put the magazine down, sighed and looked just to the right of me. I got tired of her getting the nerve up to come to my table so I walked over to hers.

'The cognac tastes a lot better if you hold the glass in your hand and let the warmth from your palms bring out the flavour.'

'Frankly, I just like drinking it.' She had a husky voice and quick smile. A nice combination. The kind of combination, along with the healthy look, that a few people would really fall for. Not me, particularly. 'Come on, sit down,' she said. I sat down.

Her complexion was even better close up than it was far away. She had not one enlarged pore around her nose and not a molecule of makeup on her short thick brown lashes. She had a narrow forehead and a small, thin nose that pointed towards a little chin. She shook her head and the brown thick hair went with it.

'So, you like to come to French restaurants alone, to chat with the natives?' I indicated the two waiters standing stiffly in their white coats performing surgery on a roast.

'No,' she laughed and tried the cognac again. This time she didn't

14

make a face. 'My girlfriend likes to chat with the natives. She speaks French.' She made it sound like her girlfriend liked to floss her teeth. 'She comes from the horsy set where French is standard equipment.'

'So, you're regular customers? That's a rich diet,' I said, thinking about the bill.

'She's a rich girlfriend.' She wiped her mouth with the thick linen napkin. Her eyes were green but not like dollar bills. 'Oh but that canard à l'orange was rich.' We groaned and she held her small tight belly. We made comparisons about our dinners and groaned some more. The young urban professional types were speaking quietly and glancing about the room. We all noticed the waiters at the same moment. They were gesturing in low tones towards our table. The maitre'd joined them.

The woman and I started to laugh. Then one of the pair of waiters strode over and placed an oval chrome object on the table and briskly moved it back and forth with an attitude as if to remind us that we were only interlopers, scabs in his house of high cuisine. He finished his job with the chrome crumb duster and without a glance returned to his station. At first I didn't dare look at my cognac partner, but when I did we both got giggle sickness.

We managed after some time to control ourselves and I finally swallowed a mouthful of cognac which had been threatening to burst out of my mouth and splatter the table. The urbanites at the next table were being dutifully respectful and I counted to ten to try and regain my dignity, which was less fun that the giggles, but at least I could get the cognac down. The woman was looking at me intensely. Too intensely.

'I know you! I saw you on TV. That folk singer who came out, Maya Russgay. You introduced her at the press conference.'

'That was a five-minute spot.'

'You also went on a talk show with her. Boston Good Morning, that was it.'

'I didn't say much.'

'You're memorable enough,' she said, but she wasn't flirting. 'But that's not the only place I've seen you.' Her earring dangled and caught some light. 'You used to work for that doctor who came out against the Vietnam war, late sixties, early seventies.'

'Yeah, another public relations gig. You do have a good memory.'

'I was young and everyone who sat on a podium at a rally was etched in my mind as a revolutionary hero, especially the women.'

'I'm scarcely deserving of that label. I forget that people remember me from that time.'

'Besides,' she continued, 'I used to do a bit of work for immigrant workers, organisational stuff, a bit of publicity. I wasn't very good at it. We tried to reach you once to get hold of your doctor, so your name was around. It fell through for some reason.'

'So now you're sitting with your revolutionary hero. Except these are different times.'

'Are they?' she asked.

'Well, Maya Russgay's famous future has gone down the tubes. It may help the cause along a bit, but I think coming out of the closet has trashed her career. She hasn't cut an album in quite a while. Her audience was the straight left, don't forget.'

'Well, we all have to give up something. I mean, you can't really live in the closet. You'll suffocate one way or another.'

'Maybe announcing your sexuality at a press conference isn't necessary.'

'She's a public figure. It's her responsibility.'

'Bullshit.' I sipped my cognac. It was just right. 'What do you do during the day?' I felt irritated with her idealism, even if I figured as a positive character in it.

'I work nights in a warehouse. And I have one gig teaching beginning tennis.'

'Where?'

'At a country club.'

'Horsy set?' I asked.

'French,' she said and smiled.

'So you'd have something to lose if you came out of the closet. The Mercedes crowd doesn't exactly go for locker room lesbians.'

'To be honest, most of them make me sick anyway. I'd just be repaying the compliment.'

'To fill you in, Maya Russgay seems pretty happy and doesn't have regrets.'

'It's the only way to go. It never makes any difference to the right people. And being one of the right people, I sometimes think my girlfriend has a lot to learn. She's still afraid to come out.'

'So what happened to her tonight?'

'She's a little sick and going to bed early. We had a date to have dinner here. Sometimes this is the only time of day I have to be with her, between tennis and work. I work nights, so I'm pretty busy right now. She just said to go ahead and eat without her. Why not? I have to eat somewhere.' She shrugged her shoulders in the tight blouse. 'When I finish my shift I'll head over to her house, I'll bring her some flowers

16

and rub her belly.'

'Sounds like a busy life.'

'Oh, it won't always be like this. Pretty soon I'm going to quit my job. We'll take a vacation and then come back and find an apartment together. Or maybe even a house with other women and kids. At least that's what I want.'

Doesn't really fit in with French restaurants, I thought and looked at the model of tanned beauty and health across from me. She was being distracted by a flaming pudding taking place across the room. She wasn't impressed.

'What are you doing these days?' she asked. I knew I wasn't going to impress her either. She looked at me eagerly and I wanted to tell her that I was busy waving flags with lavender stars instead of counting depressing numbers, eating in fancy restaurants and going home to an empty bed. Not even a sick girlfriend in it. My happy loneliness was going sour on her winsome puppy dog attitude and all I could do was feel irritated. I had been answering history; now I was answering phones.

'I work at the Women's Hotline. It doesn't have the flash of TV, celebrities or the days of the revolution. In fact it doesn't have any flash at all, just a kind of deadly dullness at the moment.'

'So why are you there?'

'The days of flash are over, or haven't you noticed. The best and only thing flashing is orange mohawks. I'd do it, except I don't have the nerve.'

She sat looking at me with too much green eyes and I saw myself fall off the podium. It was a relief.

'I don't think it was flash,' she said. 'It was more like the will to fight.'

'Then maybe I'm a coward.'

'Maybe you're just tired,' she said, shrugging her shoulders. She smiled. She wasn't just sugar. We had drunk the last of our cognac and we were looking at the bottom of our coffee cups.

'I've got to go to work,' she said and picked up her magazine and started to pull on a mustard yellow corduroy coat. There was a small stickpin stuck in the lapel. It was a pole with a little triangular flag that had a nineteen engraved on it. It sparkled with the warm flash of real gold. She looked at it, and at me and winked. Then we nodded to the epaulets.

'What's your name? I didn't catch it.'

'I'm Julie, Julie Arbeder,' she said.

'I'm Emma,' I said unnecessarily. I shook her hand. It was dry. It was a muddled moment, like the partings of strangers should be. The waiter came with the checks. We made payment rituals with trays and plastic cards. The waiter put the cognac glasses and coffee cups on a tray.

'Well,' we looked at each other and slid out of the booth.

'Goodbye, Emma,' she said. I said goodbye too, and she walked out the door. I stood there a moment, turned to go and heard a sharp crack. The waiter had gathered up the edge of the tablecloth and with a violent snap had pulled it out from underneath the salt, pepper and vinaigrette set on the table, leaving them as still as if they'd always been sitting there. Then he turned his back and marched away.

'See anybody miss?' said a cop with a close shave and a tired look. I jumped.

'No. No one. Officer, she was shot, not robbed. That's no street mugging, that's . . .'

'Handled downtown. Everything goes downtown, miss. You got anything else to add?'

I didn't.

They all went away. The police, the neighbours behind their locks and chains. The last cop said, 'Better be getting home, miss. You okay?'

'Yeah,' I mumbled and headed for the Plymouth. I still had my car keys splayed between my fingers.

Three

I woke up the next morning with a big headache. I was my own headache. I watched Flossie the cat trying to find a nice spot on me or around me in the bed. I wasn't cooperating. I looked at all the little patches in the quilt made by my grandmother. This one was my mother's apron, and didn't I have a shirt from that orange stuff with the pattern that looked like it had little grey hatchets floating around on it? I tried to let the memories and feelings of safety and security flow into me but this morning the quilt didn't work. I had lied to the police about a murder. I had agreed to meet a woman 'in crisis' outside the office. But I hadn't agreed. She had given me no choice. Except that I didn't have to go. She would still be dead. And she was dead. And the someone who killed her had followed her, or knew of our appointment. Someone else was there for the nine o'clock meeting. Someone who murdered her clean and fast with no sounds or signs of struggle. Someone who didn't want something to be blown to the moon.

I wanted to call Jonell and tell her. It was a lousy time for her to be going away on some Alcohol Abuse Meditation weekend. It was time for her to comfort her friend, frightened discoverer of dead bodies.

Suddenly the thought of Julie's address book sitting in the pocket of my jeans burned a hole straight through my stomach. I was also withholding state's evidence. I longed for the mundane problems of yesterday, boring job and simple loneliness.

I showered and put on a security outfit. Clothes that don't make a statement, old favourites, without colours that attract attention. The exaggerated cut of the pants, flaring out at the knee and in at the ankle, were fashionable, but also comfortable and the dark blue worsted wouldn't startle anyone. I debated on mascara, but thought I might be rubbing my eyes in nervousness today, giving me *Night of the Living Dead* eyes. Besides I wasn't out to charm anyone. I didn't know what the fuck to do.

So I went through the motions, like everyone does at crisis time.

Enjoyed making The Perfect Egg, taking two clever shortcuts to avoid the traffic, and finding a parking space near the office. Except for the dead woman's address book which I had slipped into my purse, I almost felt normal walking into the Hotline office. Perhaps if I had a crisis, I could call anonymously, later, myself.

It was, luckily, a routine day. I could refer battered women to the appropriate place, after I had reassured them enough so they could tell me what was going on. One woman obviously too drunk or stoned to take any immediate advice, was made to promise to call back the next day and agreed to read some material from the Janssen Centre. We also had a frantic mother whose children were apparently driving her up the wall and who couldn't make it out of the house to do the necessary shopping with baby, toddler and six-year-old monster. We sent someone over from a single mother's self-help group which might give her some longer term help and would at least get her grocery shopping done for today. We had a teenager who was too afraid to admit she might be pregnant, but wanted to check up at a women's clinic for 'stomach pains'. I was happily busy with these mundane atrocities when Monica came in and said, 'Did you hear, Julie Arbeder was murdered last night?'

And with that the whole evening came flashing back. So she was an acquaintance of Monica's.

As Monica recounted the scanty details I debated telling of my involvement. Surely stonewalling it, especially to co-workers, was self-destructive. I needed support, in the current psycho-babble, I needed to share my experience, especially because now it was about a comrade, someone in our community.

'Monica, I found her. I found the body. On East Lexington Street. Last night.'

Suddenly I started crying, and Monica, never being one to warm the soul exactly, was nevertheless holding me.

I pulled out of Monica's embrace and slumped on a chair. I hadn't realised how upset I was. It wasn't just discovering a dead body, it was the feeling of being preyed upon, of being too busy with other people's problems, of waking up to an unfriendly aloneness every morning. It was the feeling of being a victim and not liking myself for that. I pulled myself together. I would tell Monica about finding the body, but I wouldn't tell her how I got to East Lexington Street. It felt like it was still my private pain or, more correctly, my private problem. Julie Arbeder had wanted me. It was she who had said, 'Emma Victor, I need you.'

I was still crying. I let Monica professionally console me.

'Emma, you need a rest. Why don't we talk about you taking a leave of absence for a month or a few weeks anyway.'

I tried not to look at Monica's spindly arms. I was a comrade getting worn out, not a good staff member. I let her go on consoling me, but I thought she wasn't telling me the truth. I wasn't able to hack the harsh realities of the system. I was getting sucked down the dunghole just like our clients.

'Listen, why don't you just come to weekly meetings,' she went on. 'We've got plenty of volunteers at the moment. We'll figure out a way to get you a short paid leave.' She looked at me with what I thought was hidden disdain. I wondered at her own doubts, but, as usual, gave up. Monica's parents had raised her to make a revolution. It gave her a kind of strength, in place of dimension. I wouldn't have minded trading places with her at the moment.

'Shall I call you tomorrow morning? Think about it tonight, okay? Lynne is just about to take lunch, why don't you go with her?'

'No, no, I just want to go home, I think.'

'Okay, I'll call you.' Monica hugged me efficiently. 'I'll let you know about the funeral for Julie, if you care to go.'

'Thanks. I don't think so.' I didn't need to work out my grief. I didn't have any. Just a lonely numb feeling that someone had needed me and had gotten dead.

Four

I walked into the gentle New England sunlight outside and into the beige cell of the Plymouth. I was glad I hadn't taken the subway, the T would be dark, and on the surface of the earth traffic was light and nature almost seemed to win over bricks and cement. When I got home sunlight would be filling my dining room. I picked up three papers from vending machines on the way. A *Boston Globe*, a *Herald American* and a sensationalist rag. Then I wound my way through the tacky commercial area to where I lived, my little house perched on a lump in Somerville. I was lucky or unlucky to have a garden in the front of my house where my garden laziness was publicly displayed, but I enjoyed being set back from the street where I could see everything without being seen. I sat looking at the street watching the daily rhythm of my neighbours. It was almost reassuring to see the woman from the corner once again glance nervously about as her dog raised a leg and pissed through the rod iron fence on a rose bush that needed pruning. The black minister, now pushing a grand eighty-five years, strolling slowly up the incline, his small quiet white wife with a stolen shopping cart walking behind him.

I made coffee and settled down to read the paper. The *Globe* mentioned protests in Europe over the placing of US nuclear weapons. That was good. More fun was the sensationalist *Informer* whose headlines mentioned a chihuahua who could hypnotise parrots and a weekly cure for cellulite as well as foolproof sex-selection at conception (with the use of something that boiled down to magic necklaces). It also carried the same story as the *Globe* about the wife of a rich man named Glassman falling off a yacht after a supposedly cosy family dinner. The *Informer* used space throwing around some dirt that she'd been arguing with her husband. They referred to her as a golfing *enthusiast*. She couldn't be called just a *golfer* by the boys in the half-tone trade. They had to make her sound like a cheerleader, even in her obituary. Boxed items included other 'yacht-slip' accidents among the

22

rich and famous, and a biogenetic industry breakthrough in the invention of synthetic insulin. I guess a lot of diabetics were happy today but the thought of happy diabetics wasn't really cheerful.

Of course the Y meeting and budget cuts made poor news. I wondered where Julie Arbeder would be buried in the paper. Death among the ordinary and poor citizens never made such sparkling tragedies. I found her on page seven where there was a recounting of the everyday grisly crimes. She was described as a mugging victim, and the story ran three lines with a little round bullet next to it. The next round bullet began a story of three kids who played double dare with a .45 automatic, aiming at cars from a pedestrian ramp over the turnpike. They had pulled the trigger several times but apparently had had no effect on the flowing traffic below. There was also a bank robbery just down the street. A Charleen McKinney had been seriously wounded. I didn't know her. The phone rang.

'Miss Victor? This is Lieutenant Sloan, Homicide. Just a few questions to clear things up about last night. Could I come over to see you in a few minutes?'

'Yes. Of course.' I gave him my address again.

I haven't had much experience with police, aside from demonstrations where they had their special task squads, clearly the enemy. I supposed that this sort of cop wasn't exactly the enemy, getting to the bottom of crimes against citizens. I wasn't sure what to do, offer coffee, tea? I supposed one let them in, it would look suspicious if I didn't. I remembered the address book, and thought, can't I just give it to them? Say I took it, was confused. Then the doorbell rang and I realised my hands were perspiring, so I wiped them quickly off on my pants and went to the door.

There stood Lieutenant Sloan and another man. Just what I expected, raincoats, little notebook in hand. Lieutenant Sloan was a rather clean-cut type, but without the chiselled appearance of an FBI. His shoelace was untied. The other one, introduced as Officer Saomi, had a beefy face, pudgy hands and a distracted manner. Sloan gave me a hand to shake. Saomi tipped his hat.

'Just a minute of your time, ma'am,' and they strolled into my house. Saomi had eyes that didn't stop flitting about constantly over the entire room. I followed his eyes and saw every piece of woodwork where I should have done a second coat of paint. Was there still that cobweb in the corner? My house became shabby and I was the guilty party in the little beady eyes of Officer Saomi. But Sloan was meant to reassure me.

'Not a pleasant scene to come upon last night?'

'No, it wasn't.'

'And you didn't see anyone?'

'No, no one.'

'No car suddenly pulling away? No footsteps running?'

Here I was innocent, but even so, I felt ashamed not to have some detail to give them. Just to satisfy them, make them go away.

'Did you know the deceased?'

Why would they ask such a question? How many witnesses know the victims? And why didn't I want to tell them that I had met her in a restaurant and after two cognacs she'd told me about her love life and the woman who didn't show up for dinner? I felt more comfortable leaving her corpse in the closet. After all, whoever had been trying to ruin her life wasn't using her bedtime activities to do it. Julie Arbeder was ready to come out of her closet any time for anybody. I didn't want to think there would be any jokes about a dead dyke down at the station. I also didn't want to admit that I'd pocketed her address book.

'Know her?' he repeated.

'No. But I found out today that a co-worker of mine knew her.'

This apparently satisfied them. Something they could write down? Saomi was looking at the books, I was sure he had already picked out twenty left, feminist and lesbian titles from my bookshelves. The bright colours and words were just popping out from their spines at him. Julie Arbeder might have those same books. It would be illogical in this city if I had never heard of her.

'What do you think happened, officer? Was it a mugging, or –'

'We just do our best, ma'am. Not good to speak about a case at this point.'

'Do you have any' – what did they call them – 'leads?'

'We're working on a few things, ma'am.'

Saomi was watching me. Perhaps to see if I was scared? If I had seen the killer, would I cover up to protect myself? I wasn't scared of that, and it must have shown in my voice. Saomi turned away, and even turned his beady eyes off, he was through absorbing all the physical features of my home.

'Well, thank you ma'am. Here's a card, call me if you do remember anything.'

Sloan gave me another warm handshake, which I didn't greet with too much sweat. Saomi nodded and walked behind his superior, eyes flitting about occasionally, like a kind of reflex. They left. I walked back to the table and took out the address book. As long as I had it, and wasn't going to give it to the cops, I might as well look at it. I could always give it to Julie's roommates and they could say they found it in her room, why not? This was a happier thought, letting myself off the hook, – hand over the book and I would have Julie Arbeder mostly out of my life.

I opened the little book and found a rainbow of colours. Red, green and blue pens had scrawled in under 'W' presumably for 'work' a bunch of boy names. Ricky, Grant, and Tom.

There were three library call numbers written in tiny green felt pen. Some names were listed under last names, some under first names, several were listed under 'U' for union, and under 'N' she had numbers typed and taped on to the page. They included ambulance, police, university, university graduate adviser, a Joe, a Joanie and an Al. Al had two numbers, the first was crossed out.

I called the number written neatly behind the front cover.

'Hello.' The voice was understandably not a happy one.

'Hi, my name is Emma Victor. I was the person who found Julie last night.'

'You found Julie?'

'Yeah, I, well, it's been very distressing, I didn't know her or anything, but still – I wondered if it would be okay to come over and talk to you a bit about her, if you don't mind that is. I . . .'

'Sure, c'mon over. We're just sitting here, and god, Julie's parents just called, I guess they're flying in tonight.' The voice sounded monotonal, she was in shock. 'We're trying to think of what to do with her stuff.' On 'stuff' the voice cracked. I also didn't want to picture the personal possessions of Julie Arbeder.

'I'll come over today, okay?'

'Yeah, sure.' Then I realised I hadn't even asked her name. Two hours, I told myself, before I would go to Julie's house. I wanted those two hours to start cleaning, cleaning away all the things that Officer Saomi had noticed.

I started from the ceiling and that cobweb, then down to the unseen surfaces of booktops, high up on a bookshelf. Slowly the dust came drifting down, until the vacuum cleaner came and sucked it all up into a bag. I took an attachment and got all the corners of the woodwork, in case the dusting had missed anything. I shoved all the furniture around so no dust motes, no little Flossie fur patches would get stuck under the leg of a chair. Then I scrubbed all the floors with a harsh ammonia and detergent brew, water so hot it nearly hurt my hands through the rubber gloves. When I was done with that I rearranged the bathroom cabinet, wiping off the rings left by one potion or another on the glass shelves. After that I attacked my underwear drawer, making clear again the distinction between socks and underpants. Then I brushed Flossie's grey fur to a high gloss and poured a hot bath for myself. It was too hot, and still didn't break the spell, the nervousness of seeing that death mask turned toward the night sky. I dressed and pulled out the ironing board and ironed five shirts, not forgetting the inside plackets behind the buttons and buttonholes.

It was time to visit Julie's house. Should I bring something? Were they in mourning? Do we have a mourning tradition? All we ever talked about was 'sharing', but I had a feeling grief couldn't be shared, only witnessed. I would take the address book, get rid of it.

Julie's house was a tall, forgotten row house affair in the South End. It hadn't been broken up into apartments yet. Someone had made a haphazard attempt at a few begonias in the tiny grass plot in front. But dandelions, the terror of Massachusetts lawns, were already strangling the small maroon stalks which had the minimum of tiny pink flowers. A house waiting to be torn down; the stairs were starting to rot, and plastic had been put up on the windows denying light but saving on heating bills. The heavy front door, beset with bevelled glass from a former happier time, was opened by a small woman with stringy blonde hair. Swollen eyes were the main feature of her face.

'Hi, c'mon in. I'm Misty.' She turned her back and I saw her pull a raw, cleaned carrot out of her pocket. I heard a crack as she bit off an end of it. I followed her into the house.

We went into the living room which had an overstuffed, predictably green couch. A yellow puppy frisked about chewing on a corner of a rug that had seen better days anyway. Misty didn't ask me to sit down, but that was not because she was impolite, she just didn't know what to do. She put the carrot back in her pocket. I sat down.

'I was just upstairs, going through Julie's things,' she said by way of explaining her lack of direction. She shrugged her shoulders which made her thin arms move out as if they were only tied with little strings to her body. Then she sat down on the green couch too. I knew there must be another roommate; the house was too big for just the two of them, and there had been three names on the mailbox. I glanced up and saw a shape at the end of the room. Misty stood up abruptly.

The figure leaned on the woodwork of the hallway leading into the living room, not for balance but a gesture of pause. She took it all in;

Misty shifting her weight from foot to foot and me sitting on the edge of the soiled green couch.

In the darkness of the hallway, I could make out a frame with wide shoulder blades, like the architect decided to make a horizontal line to balance out the long neck. She had muscled calves, almost a knot that was silhouetted underneath the skirt. She walked out towards me from the darkness and I noticed that she was wearing a long navy-blue A-line skirt pleated on one side. The thick white cotton blouse above looked starched and it had a pleat in it also. She looked like a slightly butch librarian who was into pleats. Her shiny black hair had a natural curve at the ends putting it all away neatly under her ears. She didn't smile, but she didn't move her black eyes away. She worked her jaw from side to side. She had broad cheekbones that matched the line of her shoulders, a nose that would be long except it tipped in suddenly to her face, making a small hook. She had slightly acne-scarred cheeks. She walked towards me with a hand outstretched.

'Hi, I'm Sue.' And then she sat down on the edge of what used to be a pink satin chair. 'Sue Martinez.'

I introduced myself and I tried to think of a way to explain my presence. I didn't feel like making any condolences to this woman, she didn't look like she needed it.

'Sue, there's some more messages for you by the phone,' Misty said.

'Thanks, Misty,' Sue replied. 'Think I can read the numbers this time?'

'It's not that I write small, you probably have impaired vision.'

'Yeah, like a hawk.' Sue smiled and turned to me. 'So, you found Julie last night,' she said.

'Yes, her death must be a terrible shock for you both.'

She looked away from me and crossed one leg over the other and began swinging it fiercely back and forth.

'Yes,' she said, 'I'm shocked.'

Then she got up and walked to the window and looked at the plastic. She lit a cigarette, took a very long drag, and waited to expel all the air before she turned to me and said, 'I've got some questions about her dying.'

'I do too. Why do you have questions?'

'Why do you?'

'I found her, that's all. I just found her on the street.'

'Was it difficult?' She raised an eyebrow and I felt like an intruder, which was how she meant me to feel.

'It's not something that happens every day. I'd just like to know something about her.'

'Okay, I'll tell you about Julie. She was a fighter. She did a lot of things on principle. When she saw things go wrong she always had to do something about it. Sometimes she didn't have a lot of oversight about that.'

'What do you mean she didn't have any oversight?'

'I mean I think she was neck deep fighting some union busters, alone, at a place she worked.' She stubbed out her cigarette butt and looked at me. She had narrow eyes that seemed to go with all the other horizontal lines that cut across her long frame.

Misty who had been sitting quietly in a shadow, said, 'She was going to have a baby.'

'Baby?' I repeated. 'She was pregnant?'

From Misty's expression the tragedy was therefore doubled.

'C'mon Misty, she talked about non-sexist fairy tales and bought a book about Lamaze. That hardly makes her pregnant.' Sue addressed her as if she were slightly retarded.

'Oh, you're just against kids.' Misty blurted out the words like a little bomb that had been waiting to explode.

'Okay, Misty. We've been through this before. Stop romanticising everything. That's part of your problem, you know.'

'Well, Julie liked kids,' her chin butted out. 'She would have loved to have had a baby. Julie was a very caring, nurturing person.'

'But that didn't make her pregnant. And what makes you think being pregnant is so wonderful anyway? You're always going on about your sister-in-law and her bundle of joy. She was just lucky. For a lot of women it's morning sickness, bloating and postpartum depression. I'll be glad for the day it happens in a test tube.'

'It's a wonderful event in a woman's life.'

'Yeah and as overrated as the multiple orgasm.'

Sue and Misty sat with their silences on either side of the umbilical cord. I sat with my own questions and a developing crush on Sue.

'But did she actually buy the Lamaze book? Hardback?' I asked.

Misty nodded, the little strings of her hair bouncing along.

'It must have been a present,' Sue explained it away. 'Julie was enthusiastic about some living group, alternative family. She was searching for security. With other people. I don't think Misty and I fitted the bill.'

I looked around at the soiled furniture and the living room. A poster whose masking tape was giving up slid off a wall of indeterminate

28

colour. Little balls of dust gathered in a corner. Misty had on terry cloth slippers with a lot of threads hanging off them and the brown carpeting was coming loose. It was a matter of time before someone tripped on it.

'So, Julie was looking for a new living situation.' I wasn't asking. The place was cosy as a drainpipe.

'Well, yeah, she said she was going to move pretty soon. We had some problems about who was doing the dishes, stuff like that.' Sue laughed a little, flicked her cigarette in the direction of an ashtray and missed.

'Did she have any lovers in her recent romantic past?'

'Her romantic past wasn't recent.' Sue stubbed out her cigarette and began another one. She didn't look at me, she seemed blasé in a nervous sort of way.

'Are you sure about that?'

'Sure, I'm sure.' But Sue was watching the curtain.

'What about your romantic past?' I asked and got her immediate attention. Sue looked at me the way a woman looks at another woman who asks her a direct personal question. I wasn't her therapist, so I was either nosy, nervy, a dyke or all three.

'My romantic past is ancient history.'

'Pity,' I said, and then Misty cleared her throat.

'The police have already been here,' she said.

'Do they have any ideas?'

Sue grinned, 'If you could call it that. Their main idea is that women shouldn't go out at night, especially alone, especially on East Lexington Street.'

Sue stood up suddenly, excused herself and walked to the stairway and up the stairs. I heard a door close. That left me in a vacuum with the greyish Misty. She picked up a large wooden bowl from a small round table in the corner. It was filled with popcorn. She offered me some, I declined and she started slowly munching the cold kernels.

'How long did you two live together?' I asked her.

'Oh, about two months.'

'Did you know Julie before that?'

'No, I just moved here from Worcester.' From the way she said it it sounded like she had arrived on the train that afternoon. We sat there in the grey, plastic dimness for a number of minutes without saying a word. Eventually I heard a toilet flush. A door opened. Sue loped slowly down the stairs, one hand gently gliding along the stairway railing.

I turned my head to her.

'You said that Julie was involved in union work, fighting union busters?'

Sue looked at me like I'd just arrived on the train from Worcester too.

'Yeah. At her work. To be honest, I'm not really sure what was going on,' she drawled.

Sue lit another cigarette and flopped down in the chair, the knotty muscles in her calves loosening up. It seemed she'd left some bitterness and information up in the bathroom.

Misty rustled in the corner. She put the bowl of popcorn down, and excused herself in a whisper. She said she wanted to go straighten up Julie's room. 'Her parents are coming tonight,' she said softly.

'Don't pack anything yet, I want to look through some of her things,' Sue broke into Misty's grey exterior like a bullet into a lake. Her shoulders tightened and contained Sue's command. 'She had some books of mine,' Sue explained in a softer tone. It was probably not a jolly household even when everybody was alive. Then Sue looked at me from the chair. 'I think Julie was heavily into this union-busting thing. It's some outfit from down south – Burtell – something like that. They send in so-called personnel managers. There's a lot of stuff going on against unions, especially small outfits.'

'Where did she work?'

'Parts Unlimited, a warehouse down by the docks.'

'I think Julie was in trouble,' I began cautiously. 'She called me yesterday.'

'Yeah?' The lifted eyebrow, but now the eyes weren't darting any more.

'I work at Women's Hotline. She wanted to talk to me, meet me on East Lexington Street.'

'And then she was killed.'

'Yes. Can you think of any other reason why Julie should be in trouble?'

'No.' Sue sucked another puff of smoke all the way in, and let it slowly all the way out. We watched it curl as it hit the plastic-wrapped window.

'I don't know how high the stakes are for these union-busting guys. But the cops sure weren't interested. It would mean a lot of hard, extra work for them.'

'Did you tell them Julie was involved in union activities at work?'

'Yeah. They wrote it down. Period. They only want enough of a

30

solution to bury it in the right column of statistics, something that makes them look good. Hired killings and union bustings probably don't fit into their categories.'

'Would union busters kill people?'

'These days? I don't know. I used to do more work with unionising a while back. Like I say, they've got whole businesses keeping unions out of places now, they've got ways that don't necessarily mean violence.'

'How did you used to work for unions?'

'Oh, I was pretty active with the farmworkers. I'm a para-legal.'

'Not working today?'

'I'm on vacation.' She sunk deeper into her chair. It didn't look like such a nice vacation to me.

Sue yawned. She was a funny woman. One moment I saw tensed up energy in her long limbs, then she relaxed and looked like a cat lying in the sun. She even had that sunbathing sleepy look, except that her eyes were red from crying.

'I think I'll look into what was happening down at her work. You know any guys that used to work with her?'

'No. She did mention a few people, but the turnover rate was pretty high there once they started putting pressure on people to get out of the union.'

'I have her address book.'

'Yeah?' Sue didn't look surprised.

'Do you think I should turn it over to the cops?'

'Frankly, I don't think they'd do anything except stick it in an envelope,' she said bitterly.

'Well, I think I'll try and call a few people that knew her; maybe one of her co-workers is listed in there.'

'Hm-hm.' The puppy yipped and pulled on her skirt. She didn't look up.

It was time to go. I said my goodbyes, called up the stairs to Misty who mumbled a reply and I went out the door. Sue stood up and closed the drapes. It was still light outside.

I sat in the Plymouth for a few minutes. I felt better. I would do my bit for Julie Arbeder, maybe to assuage my own guilt for not meeting her five minutes earlier, or saying the right thing that would have kept her on the line. Two more sentences and perhaps she'd be alive today. Or maybe it was just a crank phone call from someone else entirely and a street mugging of a one-time restaurant companion, a coincidence on the north end of East Lexington Street.

Five

My third call netted me three co-workers of Julie Arbeder's living in the same house in a suburb in Chelsea. I figured I could make it back and find out it was all a dead end in time for dinner. As long as I wasn't moving with the commuters I could enjoy the ride over the Tobin Bridge and through the suburban sprawl, sprouting with spring, on the other side. Following the signs I turned off at Oak Leaf Knoll. Grant, the husky voice on the other end of the phone, had assured me it would be easy to find the house, and it was. Another family dwelling, but this one still had its newness and suburban sheen on the outside. Inside the house was all boy.

Grant answered the door. He was one of those red-haired people who resemble every other red-haired person in the world, as if they were from the same gene pool. Pale eyelashes and milky white skin that would never stand the hot sun in the brown suburban hills. Eyebrows nearly blonde. Even the scraggly beard he was trying to grow was popping out red. I offered him a hand; I like to shake hands with men. I can usually tell if it makes them nervous or if I can expect a friendly, equal footing or a display of strength. Grant would be okay, from his handshake. He smiled and showed me into the living room.

'Scuse the mess,' he said and kicked some dirty clothes I didn't want to notice too closely into a corner. 'Ricky and Tom will be home in a few minutes.' Ricky and Tom had also worked with Julie Arbeder.

Large speakers were adorned with pyramids of beer cans. 'Wanna brew?' he asked, which I assumed meant he was offering me a beer.

'Sure, nothing like a good brew,' I said. I sometimes like playing with boys.

He walked to the kitchen where I noticed a heap of dirty dishes in the sink. I hoped he wouldn't pick two glasses out of the mess and rinse them off. He didn't. He gave me a can instead.

'Shit. What a drag about Julie. Nice girl,' he said, tilting his head back for a long swallow.

'Yeah. Did you know her well?'

'Well, however much you can know anyone working on the floor. I got my quota, I gotta move. Julie, she stood on the line, packin' all the things I ran around and collected. Order filling's great compared to packing. She just had little boxes inside big boxes all day long.'

Ricky and Tom came in. Ricky looked like a member of the Ozzie Nelson family. In fact, the place looked like the Nelson family home with the parents on permanent vacation. Tom had big grey eyes and a black forelock. Ricky zeroed right in on me, looked me up and down and walked right over with a grin. Girl in the house, you could nearly hear him think when he shook my hand and he made sure that my fingers felt like a butterfly caught in a two car collision. Tom would be nice, he gave me a direct gaze and my hand a rest.

Grant grinned easily. 'Wanna line?' He brought out a plastic box with a hologram of a bald eagle on the lid. He lifted it up to reveal five small plastic envelopes containing white powder, a small tube, and a mirror.

'Hydraulic line,' he held up the silver pipe and smiled, 'from a Bell Helicopter.' He put some coke on the little mirror and started chopping. Like I said, I like playing with boys.

'So about Julie,' I wanted to get this over with, 'what's the story these days at Parts Unlimited?'

'Fucked.' Grant didn't look at his companions, so I could assume they all had the same attitude. 'Ever since we got this new personnel manager out of Atlanta, Yellentrauw, they've upped our quota for filling orders. They've got us running all day, and I mean zippin' along. What the hell, we snort up and then start dealin' to keep up the coke habit so we can work.'

'Did Julie do drugs?'

'Naw. Can't imagine why not though, she had the worst job, packing,' said Tom. 'The packers used to drive routes, got them some relief from the conveyor belt. But now they've jobbed out the entire delivery service. Once they break the union, driving will be part of the work load again, but now they're just giving away the work to scabs.'

'But how can they do that if it's legally part of the job?'

'Well, I guess our original contract wasn't so great. Certain areas were pretty vaguely covered. One day they just pulled up with all these vans, and a whole other company took over the deliveries.'

'I talked to one of the drivers,' said Tom. 'They're making $3.50 an hour.' He grunted and then snorted his line.

'What about your shop steward?' I asked.

'Rich? Rich Janinni. He just wants up the ladder. He turns his back every chance he gets. That guy's a real ass kisser. Well, hell, he's got three kids and family problems.'

'Did you ever call union headquarters, let them know what was going on?'

'Well, Julie tried to talk a number of times to Rich. We all did. And I think, yeah, she did try and go to the main headquarters, or call 'em up or something.'

'Yeah,' Tom said a little dully. 'The main man was always at a meeting. I guess she was gonna bring it up in some council meeting in a month. That's what they told her to do.'

'And this Yellentrauw?'

'Oh, he's pulling all the strings. No doubt about it. Minute he came on, funny things started to happen. Work speed up, job changes. All legal, all within the contract. But clearly designed to demoralise everybody. Push 'em to the limit. Meanwhile, lots of sweet talk to get you to side with management. Talk of new job categories, easier work if you side with them. Half the guys there are sellin' out. Fuck it, man, I'm going back to school.' He put the tube to his nostril and ran it along the mirror.

'And Julie? What was her position?'

'Shit, Julie was one tough broad. She was so pissed she went out there and spray painted the side of the building once. What'd she write, Ricky?'

Ricky was barely listening. 'Uh, lemme see now. Solidarity, yeah, that was it. Want some weed?'

I refused; 'It just gives me a headache.'

'Julie was great.' Tom spoke up and I looked at him; his voice actually betrayed emotion and wasn't that bored, affected, boytone. 'She went out there one night when they had parked those scab vans outside the warehouse. She got a bunch of chains and chained them all together. She timed it and everything. She found out when security would be on, and she had heavy locks . . .' he broke off suddenly and looked away.

'Yeah. It was swell,' said Grant, quickly turning his head to frown at Tom. 'But she could've gotten in a lotta trouble.'

'Trouble?' I was still looking at Tom. It seemed like his chin was trembling.

Grant kept going. 'Sure, these guys play rough I'll bet. And she was a girl. Hell, she shouldn't have been out there.'

'We should've,' said Tom. Sometimes I can appreciate chivalry.

34

'You could have done it together,' I tried to suggest.

'But what the hell, she did it, she wanted to do it, and she got it done.' I put my arm on Tom's sleeve. My comforting tone was embarrassing the other two.

'So, uh, what's your interest in Julie?' Grant asked nervously.

'I'm just following up for her friends, actually. They wanted to know what was going on at work. Actually they wanted to know if these union busting guys would ever off somebody who gave them trouble. Chaining vans together sounds like trouble.'

'Naw. They wouldn't do that. They got a whole system worked out. Nice and legal with a platoon of lawyers and sweet-talking smoothies that seduce all the workers before fucking them over. They don't need to off anybody. They just get half the workers to sell the other half right down the drain.'

It wasn't a pretty picture, but it made sense. Uppity employees would be professionally handled, and union-busting companies would find legal ways to dissolve worker solidarity. But I was glad to hear about Julie Arbeder out there with her spray can, chaining vans together in the middle of the night. It was good to hear she was a courageous woman, except that she was dead. I said goodbye, refused a line, and made my way back through the traffic and over the bridge. I wanted a nice hot bath, and a nice hot evening. I thought I'd hit Franca's later, the local dyke hangout.

Six

I walked into Franca's, pushing open the green plastic tufted doors. How I wished the familiar sight wouldn't greet me, with its long and empty bar, the lonely sound of a video game plying its wares to no one. It would be too well lit; lonely bars are never dark enough.

But instead the place was really moving: light filtered through a blue smoke haze, a bass beat thumped through the people, and plenty of glasses were being filled. The bar was doing well, I noticed. A very tall Scandinavian throwback loped forward with shoulders that must have been padded. She even had that Northern inscrutable look, everything looked bleached, skin, hair, eyebrows, I wondered how deep it went and what it was like after that. She was good at the bar too, avoiding all the customers' eyes but getting to them as quickly as possible, and then with her complete attention. She didn't say a word when I ordered whisky, but gave me her total presence to the brim of the glass. She had nice eyes too.

I felt a tugging on my sleeve and looked down. A purple crystal amethyst was being pressed into my hand. I looked down further and saw the hand-stitched black suede cowboy boots, then blue jeans under a caftan embroidered with a galaxy of tiny mirrors. Above it all were the too meaningful eyes of Sandy. I avoided her eyes to look at her chest, exhibiting portraits of a female Indian Guru and a local character named Shiti John. I looked up.

'It's for,' she paused, 'healing.' She bored her green eyes into mine. I looked away and reminded myself that Sandy was a person with Premenstrual Syndrome. It made her moody, manic and difficult to deal with. It wasn't nice for her either. It was rumoured that she also had psychic propensities according to her oestrogen level. It certainly was turning her hair prematurely grey. But that was the hook, the salt and pepper curls over the naive unlined face. Throw in the green eyes, the total was a stunning woman. Dizzying, too.

36

She had been a beekeeper when I had met her. Now she was a problem with a lot of cosmic consciousness. After a three-day affair I cooled off and she had taken to 'healing' me. I sometimes worried about the hidden aggressiveness of the feathers, stones and other natural objects she bestowed upon me.

'So how's it going?' I asked, wary.

'Well,' she shrugged her shoulders and tossed the stone on the bar when I refused it. 'I'm scheduled for a D and C next week. At least I'm having it done at the Blackstone Clinic, where they treat a woman right.' She twirled the amethyst on the bar. 'Of course, psychic healing would be the answer. But let's face it, my channels are just not that clear. Especially this time of the month.'

'What happens next week?'

'Tune in and find out.'

She told me when her appointment was and I said I'd call.

'Only if you want to,' she said and I smelt trouble.

She picked up her amethyst, tossed it in the air and dropped it in a pocket embroidered like a peacock's tail. I remembered that she had great eye – hand coordination.

'The Great Mother is giving you a call, Emma Victor. Don't forget to answer, she never misdials.' And with a tilted smile, Sandy melted back into the smoke and noise of the bar. I looked around the room and saw no friends, a few acquaintances and that was all. I noticed a nervous little group in the back, and a few 'visitors,' perhaps lawn bowlers with nothing better to do tonight. Finally, around the corner of the pinball machine I saw Miss Wonderful With The Mouth.

I watched her work the pinball machine, with her feet firmly spread and planted on the floor. She had real hips, real lady's hips, like two holsters hanging below her waist. I watched her push the machine towards tilt; she had been mad at the machine, now she turned and walked away from it as if it hadn't touched her at all. I met her midstride.

'Care to play again?' I asked and she silently turned towards the machine and walked back, but not before I saw a smile rest lightly on that face. I slid two quarters into the slot and pushed the button twice. The first ball rolled up from the belly of the machine; I just wanted to watch her play again.

Too soon it was my turn, and pinball has always defied me. I just get caught up in the little lights wanting it to make its bell sound, like Pavlov's dog getting addicted to the cue. I like seeing the little balls pop out of the holes, where they arbitrarily come to rest, since I never pay attention to the points or gates. I couldn't get serious about it and I finally let my last ball roll into the trap, turned around and couldn't think of anything clever to say.

'Hard day at the clinic?' I ventured.

'Yeah, we're losing the battle with yeast.'

'I can think of worse.' Pause. 'You're taking something out on this pinball machine.'

'Actually, I'm feeling lousy tonight. It's sort of complicated to explain. Tell me something about yourself. It's a better subject at the moment.'

She had eyes that were flickering at me. Her black leather jacket had just few enough zippers, and her shoes were actually pointed.

'I'm not such a good subject either. How about a drink?'

She drank straight gin, with ice, and after I had recovered from a second Scandinavian invasion at the bar, I returned to her for recapture. Her caramel-coloured hair had, with all the pinball movement, assumed very odd attitudes on her head. It was more like fur, or a kind of down. Pushing it hurriedly back on one side had caused it to nearly stick straight up on top, while in the back, a wind from behind caused it to stick out from behind her ears like two low horns. She turned quickly and I saw her breasts move as she took the glass from my hand. She still had those manicured fingertips. All the little white moons showed, evenly.

'How long have you worked with Stacy Weldemeer?' I tried for something more than a yes-no answer.

'Two years.' She looked away. This girl was difficult. But interested.

'Why don't we dance, before we get on to good books we've read lately?'

It was a smile there, spreading that beautiful mouth, and I tried to keep my balance as she twirled me into a fox trot. I'm no great dancer, I just hop on for dear life, like a freight train rider, and hope I can follow and not lose all my social graces. She was a help, her hand sort of pushing me close, and upward, her movements became something comprehensible and I found myself relaxing as she carried me along. There was too much pleasure here in being passive, so I was grateful when the music changed and I could break away and do some free style. I closed my eyes, getting lost to the music, wondering what she was doing across from me and afraid to look. I peeked; she was doing fine, with those hips, underneath the softly rounded shoulders that didn't move in spite of the fancy footwork.

The song ended. She stood behind me and guided me towards the

38

pinball machine, with one hand in the vicinity of my ass. It made me nervous and I couldn't wait to turn around.

'Come here often?' I tried again.

'Yeah. I like it. I like when it's quiet because I can talk to the bartender and I like it when it's busy so I can watch women. Since I spend all day listening to complaints about cramps, crabs and diaphragms I want to see what everyone does besides itching and fucking.'

'Well, no one is wearing diaphragms in Franca's.'

'I wish some of them would. I've gotten some surprise patients lately. A het roll in the hay is the lesbian taboo. I've seen it at the clinic. They're thinking. "I'm not really fucking. I just thought I'd check out my vaginal memory." That's okay by me, but I never thought I'd be giving the women at Franca's lectures on birth control,' she laughed. 'Yep, lesbians get swept away and straight women come to dyke bars to get picked up. It's a weird world. Check out those two women over there.'

She beckoned towards the two 'visitors' twisting around in their seats to get a good view of everyone. I could see it was a matter of time before little baby butch Chris would try them out. They giggled nervously and resumed whispering like children at a grown-up party.

'Well, they probably still have their diaphragms in,' I remarked, noticing their fleshy pancake makeup.

'Don't count on it. I've seen some real adventuresses in here lately, and they score. This place is becoming a real amusement park for the ladies from the suburbs. The male strip joints they show on the tube are all for gay boys anyway, and the gals are getting tired of hard on soft anyway. It only leads in one direction.'

She raised an eyebrow, and I was ready to go for soft on soft any time. 'I've seen a lot of these women walk out of here with some of our best talent. I wouldn't say it goes much of anywhere. The country club life of Beverley Farms is hard to give up when dyke reality promises heaven between the sheets and struggle on the streets. Much nicer to be a housefrau with all the trimmings and get the goodies at night. I even saw, what's her name, that heiress that fell off the boat, in here once. The golfer. She had the triceps that go with the game. She was with the volleyball crowd, tennis shoes, tanned and alligators on the left breast. Now she's on the front page, dead. That's where frustration gets you. Dead, one way or another.'

'So, what's your frustration? Let's save a life,' I suggested.

'That I don't know how to ask you to sleep with me tonight.'

'It doesn't take asking, it only takes knowing.' I was glad to have the last word, and I was glad, after a long time, to really want someone.

Seven

I awoke the next morning to a stream of sunlight, my body happy, having been loved and loving the whole night. Dr Frances Cohen had left my bed at seven a.m. I slept through it. I felt like I was on vacation and she was part of it. I let my thoughts linger on the evening before. Those funny awkward moments when you've both given it away; you've decided to sleep together, have said the Thing. I like you; I like you that much. And suddenly you're letting each other into the beginning of all the secrets. One beginning was her soft, round body. She had breasts which were larger than I expected, with tiny brown nipples, and muscles in her shoulders and arms that gave a wondershape to that leather jacket. She had left her doctor's hands at the office. These hands weren't testing, but they had been tentative, asking, is this what you like? Sex was never fantastic on a first night, but the willingness to show someone those parts, to hint at other things not seen, that was everything. And as we held each other through the night I could feel myself falling into her.

So I was happy. Flossie mewed plaintively and I tried to massage away her loneliness. Oh, pet object, you are second best.

I strolled to the kitchen, noticed Frances had made herself coffee and left a wonderful little mess of coffee grounds in the sink, except I never think messes are wonderful. A bad sign. I better stop getting mushy I decided, and sat down to a simple breakfast. Today I would neatly tie up the Julie Arbeder affair. I was sure after my visit yesterday that the union was a dead end. I would make a few phone calls for that woman staring at the plastic-covered window, working her jaw; give her the answers that wouldn't answer anything, but might put her to rest about the union stuff anyway. Then she could be left with complicated anger at an unjust world.

I dialled Local 72, Warehouseman's Union. A woman's voice came on the line.

'Local 72. Can I help you?'

I identified myself and settled down to trying to make my way towards Mr Hendricks, Local 72 president, through the maze of secretaries and meetings.

'What is this in regard to?'

'The Julie Arbeder case.' She was a case now. If she was a problem to be solved I figured she would warrant more attention from the secretary.

'She was murdered two nights ago. She was an active union member and I'm following up on the report.' The report part was bullshit, but I figured people who also made reports would want to be in them, in a good way.

'I see. One moment.'

Mr Hendricks came on the line. I must have pushed the right button.

'Hello, what can I do for you?' a growly voice said.

'I'm checking out some leads on Julie Arbeder's recent activities. She worked at Parts Unlimited, the warehouse on 42nd. She was murdered two nights ago.'

'Oh, yes, terrible thing.' He had never heard her name.

'It is true that the management was busting the union there, is it not?'

'Well, they're giving us a lot of trouble, yes.'

'And recent personnel in management positions have been imported from Atlanta, Georgia?'

'Um, I belive so, yes.' He didn't know what I was talking about, the words came slowly through the phone. It made me mad.

'Mr Hendricks, Burtell Company from Atlanta runs a successful enterprise busting unions, particularly in Massachusetts. A Mr Yellentrauw is at this moment harassing union members in the guise of personnel manager. A Rich Janinni, the shop steward, has rolled over totally and is playing dead. You've got scabs walking in and out of that place, and you've got union members taking action without the knowledge of their shop steward because he's a candy ass. You've got one union member, Julie Arbeder, dead on the street after a week of action I won't go into here on the phone. I suggest you find out what's happening, what lengths Burtell Company is going to to bust your union, where this Mr Yellentrauw has worked before and with what results. Let's hope Julie Arbeder wasn't one of them.'

'Yes,' he drawled out his answer playing for time. 'What's your name again?'

'Emma Victor.' I wanted to get something for my efforts. 'Mr Hendricks, I'm enquiring on behalf of friends of Ms Arbeder's. We simply want to know the breadth of Burtell's activities. Are they employing, let's say, people who might use violence to get results? Have they been implicated in any violent crimes, or using provocateurs during strikes? How long have they been in operation? These are things I can't look into, but you could. Find out if other unions in this state know about Burtell, and what the story is.'

'Ms Victor, I certainly will.'

'On the level?'

'Yeah, on the level.'

It wasn't a brush off. The guy really didn't know about Burtell. What the hell was that shop steward doing anyway? 'I appreciate you calling. I mean it.' He did mean it. 'I'm going to get on it right away. Frankly, Parts Unlimited is a small outfit, we haven't been keeping up on it, and information isn't getting to us through members either. We've got our hands full with a huge mail order firm on the other side of town, but I want you to know this information won't get stuffed in a file.'

'Thanks. Can I call you back tomorrow morning, and get a run down on Burtell, Yellentrauw?'

'Yeah, I'll give you everything there is. And, thanks.'

We hung up; I made myself a sandwich and cleared up the morning dishes. I dialled Julie Arbeder's house. The still quavering Misty answered and I asked for Sue.

Sue had regained an edge of brightness. She related that Julie's parents had flown in; they had all had breakfast together. The funeral was tomorrow. A little sad parcel was getting wrapped up.

'Well, I've been checking some stuff out about the union. Union headquarters doesn't know much about the situation. As for Burtell, I can't see any company going in for premeditated murder. Neither can the guys who work there. Still, it stinks that Local 72 didn't know what was going on. Maybe some heat will come from above on to a shop steward's head. Maybe Yellentrauw will watch his step. Maybe some people will start watching some other people.' It wasn't much to give someone who'd just lost a friend.

'Well, thanks.' Her voice had the thud of resignation.

'Sure.' I wanted to do something for her. I wanted to distract her, take her to a film. I didn't think I wanted her to see *Norma Rae*.

I was just contemplating which film to see when her doorbell rang and the moment was gone. She excused herself to answer the door. It was a floral spray from Local 72. We rang off.

It was time to go into Boston for the staff meeting. The sun was peeping out from behind a fast moving cloud when I walked into the dark hallway of Women's Hotline. I was feeling pretty chipper. Frances Cohen had put spring in my spirits and a hot flush between my legs. The spectre of Julie Arbeder was fading. I had followed up all the leads and found out that Julie Arbeder was hot-headed but in spite of that and not because of that she got dead. I felt safe enough to spill the works at the staff meeting. We worked our way through another agenda. There was a pause and I knew that I was the business at hand.

'You all know I've been a bit upset. I discovered a dead woman on the street the other night; Julie Arbeder, some of you might have known her.'

The circle of heads sat watching me.

'But what you don't know is that it might not have been a coincidence.'

The eyes riveted. A wrinkled forehead. Monica's mouth tightened.

'I received a call here on that Tuesday afternoon, May 17th. A woman said she wanted to meet me on East Lexington Street. She started by asking a few questions, then she asked me, by name, if I would help her. She knew it was me; I guess she recognised my voice.'

I let this sink into the naked eyes around me. Monica's face was a gathering storm, but I knew she'd keep a lid on it until the right moment. When she had me alone.

'I didn't think about going there: I had forgotten about it. She had just hung up the phone before I had a chance to explain our policies. She didn't give me a chance to refuse.'

I watched them watching me try and cover my ass.

'But I went anyway, at the last minue, to East Lexington Street and discovered the body. It might have been Julie Arbeder on the phone, it might not have.'

I paused.

'Anyway, the cops came; I said I didn't know who she was, I didn't say anything about the phone call, or Women's Hotline.'

There was a silence in the room.

'I was flipped out about finding a corpse; I didn't want to put the Hotline in jeopardy, there's enough funding hassles and bad press about social services and movement activities as it is. Anyway, maybe I really screwed up. I don't know what else to say.'

After a moment there was a babble of voices. My co-workers sympathised with me, my position. It was suggested we needed a better process about phone calls that got too personal, that perhaps I empathised too much with the voice on the phone –

'Empathise, shit,' I said. 'The woman asked for me. She wanted me personally, and that's what I heard. I was just egoistic enough after supposedly helping people around this place for how many years now, to think that I was her personal calling card to safety. And I found myself tripping over a dead body, having a few sweaty days, a few ugly nightmares, and putting the Hotline into jeopardy.'

'Well, you must give yourself space for . . .'

I didn't want to hear the rest.

'Look. I figure we're all in danger of thinking we're saints or becoming martyrs while working here. The rest of the time we can get awfully depressed just hearing the stories this city upchucks every day. Between the two extremes is an endless number of possibilities. I was just leaning toward the saintly side, that's all. In reality there would have been nothing I could've done for Julie dead or alive.' But I wasn't sure.

Monica agreed. Sometimes I liked Monica. She would never have hugged me at a moment like this.

'Emma's right. As a service organisation serving people who are in a crisis we need always to be aware of clients drawing us too far into their personal situations, especially when we don't expect it. And,' Monica looked at me, 'all calls must go into the registry. Even when the caller breaks the connection themselves.'

We all decided to lay me off without pay for a week, not as punishment but as a vacation from stress. I thought it was a great idea except I still had to show up for meetings. I hoped my savings would hold me.

So that was settled. I received a circle of nods and I got back into my car to head over towards Somerville. The traffic crawled until the river where it let up. I was driving home watching people starting their vegetable garden preparation. I was wondering if Frances liked vegetable gardening. I was wondering if she was thinking about me as much as I was thinking about her. That was a dead end. So I thought about Sue. She seemed like such a competent woman, a bit mysterious. Those long sinewy muscles must be the result of some intensive workouts, or labour. She was idealistic enough to work for the farmworkers and cynical enough to suck in all the contradictions of a roommate's death without a protest. I thought about her sitting in that chair, on her vacation, dismissing the squirrely Misty with her tone of voice, and still ironing her Catholic girls' school white blouses. I thought I'd stop in and see her once again.

I saw the exit which led to the house and drove past the plastic

45

windows. Sue answered the door herself. She looked tired and a bit droopy as she willowed over me. She was wearing the kind of clothes that would rumple if you didn't iron them. And she hadn't ironed them.

'C'mon in.' Again we went into the living room. The sunlight did not stream in through the plastic. It sort of smudged itself into the room. On one of the windows the plastic billowed in and out. I could see that the window was broken.

'Better have that fixed,' I said. She nodded rather listlessly. I began to feel uncomfortable. I wasn't sure why I had come, and Sue wasn't going to help me find out. She smoked a cigarette and looked distractedly at the billowing plastic, swinging her leg. There was a sudden yelping noise coming from outside.

'That's the puppy. She gets stuck under the fence sometimes.'

All this was said with no apparent concern and Sue didn't hurry in response to the puppy's anguished cries. The shock of Julie's death must have numbed a lot of surface reactiveness. She pulled herself out of the chair and dragged her long limbs toward the kitchen. After a minute the phone rang. I called out for Sue and got no answer. She wasn't in the house, so I picked up the receiver.

'Sue there?' An imperative male voice.

'Yeah, just a minute.' I went through the kitchen and leaned out the back door and saw Sue struggling with the panicked, small dog.

'Phone for you.' I said, and saw the puppy set loose. All its fears forgotten, it started romping around Sue's feet. A woman who didn't like puppies or whiney roommates was becoming less attractive.

A frown crossed her mouth, then quickly disappeared. She hurried in through the kitchen door. I heard her go to the phone and as I walked into the living room was in time to see her take the phone into another room, the extension cord dragging behind her. She closed the door just as I heard her answer, 'Yes? No, no one. No.' The voice faded as the door closed.

I sat in the living room on the green couch. The puppy ran in and we both sat there being out of place. Except that the puppy didn't know it and I did. I stood up and walked to the bookshelf. Sue and Misty had a lot of books on fund raising, grant writing, lots of leftist analysis, some interesting tomes of labour history in the US. No lesbian books, none of the feminist classics, nothing on the Middle Ages.

I could hear her on the phone. The tone of her voice hadn't changed from the shocked monotone. I wondered how long that would last. I looked at the telephone table, cluttered with messages, some still for Julie, I noticed with a sinking heart. Usual household memos written in Misty's cramped script, black felt tip pen, dried raisins upon the page. It was comforting to see 'Bananas, oranges, pears.' Another scrap said, 'Call Glassman.' So they would get the window fixed after all.

I looked at the stairway with the faded flowered carpet. I decided to walk upstairs.

The voice went on behind the closed door. I found a hallway with four wooden panelled doors facing me. The smallest door would be the bathroom. One door was partly opened; I could see clothes flung over a chair. Another door had a 'Thank you for not smoking' sign, New Age left-handed politeness. I turned the knob and opened it.

The clean white room was a nice change from the second class hotel style of the downstairs. A streak of south sun made a rhomboid shape on the pine floor in the white room. Someone had put too many coats of verathane on the floor, it had darkened and yellowed, but it still shined. The room had just been painted and still had that naked look. That was also because someone's possessions were being moved out of it.

Bookshelves hung suspended on walls, lonely without books. Boxes were on the floor, haphazardly packed with objects and books together. I stepped inside. A few posters were curled up, already gathering dust in the corner. I uncurled one slightly, a silkscreen poster of two women on horseback soaring through the sky. 'Amazon Music Festival', it read. Another poster showed two women in a bed, quilts, kitties, all the comforts of home. 'Lesbian Love is Beautiful', it said. I opened the small closet door.

Inside the closet was a nylon rainbow of brand name sports clothing. New Balance, Nike, all were represented in a glow of brand names, little logos resting on corners of shorts and breasts of jackets. At the end of the closet a lot of boxes had a few balls squeezed into them. Playground balls, soccer balls, poof balls and volleyballs took up a lot of space. A map of Oregon and Washington was tacked with two thumbtacks into the repaired plaster of the closet wall. The map was still new, the memory of its folds made the lower half float off the wall. Behind the doorframe was a small pile of books. *Coming Out Stories, Sappho was a Right-on Woman*, a few other lesbian classics. These books clearly wouldn't be packed. What would Julie's parents do with them in Ohio (or wherever they were from)? Clearly Julie's lesbian past would remain in this room. It couldn't have been such a long lesbian past; one didn't keep posters up on the wall asserting one's sexuality for long, although the Amazon Music Festival poster had merit beyond its message.

I heard a noise in the hallway and turned around. Sue was standing there, shifting her weight from one foot to the other.

Eyes scanning the boxes and me.

'Might as well donate these books to the women's bookstore,' I said. I bent over and swept the small pile of books into my arms. 'That is, if you're not going to give them to her parents, or read them yourself.'

'Good idea,' she said, visibly relaxing. So she wouldn't be reading them herself. Maybe she was worried I was going to let the corpse out of the closet. Maybe she had mixed feelings about Julie herself.

'You knew that Julie was gay.' I didn't really make it a question. 'Was she, uh, active?' I made it sound like the Elk's Club.

'I think she was just playing around with the idea,' Sue said guiding me towards the door.

'It's not an idea anyone plays around with,' I said.

'Yeah, uh, sorry,' Sue said and I could feel myself becoming a member of a minority group. Well, when one woman comes out in a house with two straight women weird things happen, people say things they don't mean and mean things they don't say and feel things they don't feel because they're afraid to admit to themselves that they're just curious, or intrigued or personally scared to death. Hell, they could work it out for themselves.

I put my hand on Sue's arm. She didn't jump. 'It's all right, I don't expect you to know about lesbian life if you don't live it.'

I smiled, she paused a second and gave a nice little rolling laugh.

'How long did Julie live in this room?'

'Two months. She used to live in an apartment house by herself. She worked for the Latchkey Programme, the after-school programme for kids whose parents are still at work when school gets out. Then she decided she wanted to make more money. She moved out of her apartment, quit Latchkey and took on the job at Parts Unlimited. She was going to quit in June and take the summer off, she said.'

'What were her plans after that?'

'Well, after our last fight she said she'd be out of here as soon as possible.'

'What were you fighting about?'

'Oh, just crappy household stuff. But hell, you don't break up a friendship over who leaves the cap on the toothpaste.'

'But you can sure break up a household over it. Ever live with someone who insists on having a separate refrigerator and labelled food in the kitchen?'

'Yeah, Misty. She used to be anorexic. She really has a food control thing. She also puts ads in personals to broaden her non-existent social life. Except that I usually end up entertaining them because at the last minute she runs away to pick up her laundry at the laundromat or some excuse. Gees, the last time she left me with a guy who sold slaughter-house equipment to the cow butcher factories. He wasn't so bad except that he wanted to take me to Emmanuel II.'

Somehow we'd lost Julie in the conversation. 'Come on, let's get out of here.' Julie's pretty room had gotten suddenly cold. I picked up the unwanted books and followed Sue's long, swaying figure down the stairs. Her shoulders were tense.

'I'm so glad you checked out the union thing, Emma. I've just been too upset to think about it.' Her voice had a sing-song quality, like she was already back in the office, this time answering phones.

'I'm checking back with a Mr Hendricks this afternoon. He'll tell me if he's come up with anything shady about Burtell.'

'Thank you so much for doing this.' A warmth had come into her, perhaps artificially inseminated. But I wanted to give this up and down woman the benefit of the doubt. So I gave her my warmest smile and asked her for dinner. She gulped noticeably and said, 'Sure.' I noticed the pretty tilting shape of her eyes again.

I thought about how it was when I came out eleven years ago and my roommate, named Prudence of all things, discovered me in bed with my first friend. Sarah and I had the same hair, long bushy brown curls. Prudence had come into the bedroom to tell me about a phone call and I never forgot her face as the mass of brown curls separated on the pillow to reveal two heads. I don't think Prudence ever got over it either: two months later she was married.

But Sue was standing there with a kind of wise-ass grin, agreeing to go out to dinner with me, and her eyes weren't red any more.

'I'll pick you up at eight.' Then I got in my car and drove home.

My house looked to me as it sometimes looks. A house in transition. The house knew something was going to happen. I hoped it would be Frances Cohen, but I didn't want to think too much about it.

I called Mr Hendricks, or rather his secretary, who surprisingly put me through to him right away.

'Mr Hendricks, this is Emma Victor calling again about the Parts Unlimited situation.'

'Very interesting that you should bring this up. Pretty dirty situation. This Burtell outfit goes for the small outfits in big cities first. They're getting pretty good results, even where the union is strong. But the main tactic is worker demoralisation. There's been no violence associated with them anywhere down the line. I talked to union reps, who'd be the ones to know.'

'So, no way the Julie Arbeder murder would figure in it at all?'

'Impossible to say for sure. But they don't look like a strong arm organisation. Not yet. But we're going to look real good into the situation there. We're on to the shop steward, at least. I'll let you know if we come up with anything.'

'Well, thanks Mr Hendricks.' I hung up. I felt relieved, happy, and guilty, all at the same time.

Eight

When I pulled up in front of Sue's house I didn't have to ring the doorbell. She came right to the car.

I reached over to unlock the door on the passenger side to let her in. 'Hi. Windy night,' I said.

Her hair had been blown about her head like a spiky black tumbleweed. She had on crisp black pants and a red leather jacket, which, because it reached below her hips, made her look unbelievably long waisted. She brushed some strands of hair from in front of her face. She looked at me a little breathlessly and said, 'So where is this place?' She was wearing eyeliner, a thick black line that hung heavy on the edge of her eyelid. It accentuated the almost Asian look of her eyes.

'It's in the Chinese neighbourhood, not far. I think they're the only Italians on the block.'

I concentrated on the heavy flow of Friday night traffic. I always wondered what people were doing, where they were going, as I saw the faces briefly illuminated by passing headlights in the streaming freeway. Most people were alone in the cars, which made me think they were going to meet someone. It was not altogether a lonely thought, sharing the road with people on their way to meeting someone. It's just that I knew what the weekend staff at Women's Hotline were dealing with. Weekends were the busiest, ugliest times.

We reached the ample parking lot of 'Alfonso's Italian Family Dinners', and walked in. It was a dimly lit place. Dim enough to need the candlelight from the white net covered red glass candleholder to read the menu. The waiter came bounding up like a puppy dog.

'What can I do for you gals tonight?'

We ordered the family dinner, plugging in our own choices where appropriate, and sent him grinning away.

'This is a funny place. Half the people who work here are Chinese,' I pointed out.

'Reminds me of my own mixed blood,' she said.

51

'What's the mix?'

'My mother was Hungarian. My father was a wetback. He'd just crossed the border when he met my mom.' So that's where she got those black eyes, I thought. And also the Indian nose with the slightly pushed in end. But the white complexion stretched over the broad cheekbones was definitely European.

'My mom was in various internment camps after the war. She was technically a German living in Hungarian territory before Hitler. Most of those refugees landed in East Germany and remained there, or in Bavaria where they were treated like dirt. She had a cousin in America, pulled a lot of strings, I don't like to think how. The quotas were real low for refugees. You can imagine, she hadn't much in common with my father, just that. She spoke high German, Hungarian. He spoke Spanish.'

I was trying to follow the picture of the two people meeting together, her history, his probable history as an illegal alien from Mexico. It was like two people you couldn't imagine dancing together.

'So what happened, besides you?'

She seemed to fade for the ending. This woman was just like an ebbing tide.

'Oh, they didn't get along too well. It was sort of Babel of different tongues and terrific arguments. She died. He split.'

'And you?'

'I taught myself English. I made sure it was good English. I didn't try for law school; I do a lot of research as a para-legal,' she sighed.

'How did you meet Julie?'

Her eyes glanced away quickly. I thought people wanted to talk about persons close to them who were deceased. The printed word is sometimes uncomfortably wrong.

'Julie, yeah. Well, we'd worked together.' Her jaw started flexing again.

'Where did you two work together?' I couldn't drop it.

'Oh, at the Immigrant Workers Union Centre.'

'What did she do there?'

'She organised things, meetings, demonstrations, press conferences. Anything. It was just one summer.'

'Was she good at it?'

The body tensed. I couldn't tell if it was my question or just Julie.

'Look, Julie was a hothead. She'd get obsessed with something and pour herself into it. She did stupid things sometimes.'

'How stupid?'

'Oh, I don't know.' She sounded irritated that I had asked.

'She just went off and did things you know. Like at Parts Unlimited.' She looked at me and I felt that she was using my own information against me.

'You know about those things?'

'Well, I knew something was going on.' Her lips pressed an ending to the sentence. So, she knew something was going on, and they lived in the same house, but they weren't good enough friends to share it, even though they had worked for a union organisation before.

'I called Mr Hendricks today from Local 72. He said Burtell doesn't figure in anything violent, historically, or logically.'

'Yeah, well,' her eyes shifted away. 'I guess that's that, let's drop it.'

Our waiter bounced back and with too much show opened a cheap bottle of wine, poured it for us, and waited for a real reply. He had me taste it, I guessed I was playing the butch that night. I nodded and he went away.

'Sue, don't you feel bad that the murder goes unsolved?' I wanted to prick her feelings about this. I had the feeling she was shoving it all under a rug in her mind. Sue needed a friendly lesbian aunt to talk to; or maybe I was just being egoistic again. She looked at me; she looked scared and then she looked at her lap.

'I don't want to talk about it. Julie's dead and that won't change. Everything will be okay.' She tried to look at me steadily.

On that cheery note our dinner, family style, started to arrive. The soup was a little watery, but the pasta was great. The veal was perfect tenderness, but the vegetables were soggy. Sue pushed the food around on her plate and talked about the movies, and the weather, in a rather excited way. She still had a lot of food on her plate when she suggested we ask for the bill. The waiter came over, I asked for the check, we split it. I was glad she wasn't the type to make a lot of calculations. We both put some money down on the tray. She excused herself and went to the bathroom. I cleaned all the spaces between my teeth with a toothpick. Eventually she came back and we walked through the parking lot to my car.

On the way home she opened up the car window. It was a bit cool, but the evening air off the Harbour was excellent. I got off at her exit and stopped the car in front of her door. I didn't want to go in. I didn't think she'd ask me.

Very suddenly her head was on my shoulder. She giggled, something I didn't think she was capable of doing. Something I hoped she wasn't capable of doing. Then she put her mouth on my mouth. It was very soft, very warm, but I don't like being kissed without the intuition first. Also, I was ninety-nine per cent sure she was straight. I don't like it if straight women suddenly come on to me. I always think it's cosy if two straight women try it out on each other first. At least I like it when it's for real. This wasn't. I pushed her head away.

'Listen, don't worry,' she started with a honey voice that went with the giggle.

'Is that what you say to guys when they can't get a hard-on?' I asked.

That could have been an easy line to get pissed at, except that she wasn't.

'Aw, c'mon, don't be like that,' she said.

'Look, I'm sorry our evening is turning out like this.' It was true; I was sorry. 'I just wanted to distract you from your roommate's death, and I thought you were a nice woman. But I don't think you need distracting, and I don't think you're nice any more.' I watched how she took it. She shrugged her shoulders. She turned her face to me again. I reached over across her approaching lap. I opened the car door on her side. Before she slid out I caught a look at her face in the streetlight. Her black eyes were too black. They were so dilated that the pupil just ate up the iris into a glassy black circle that went very, very deep and didn't end.

Nine

I went home and tried eating a piece of bread to get the bad taste out of my mouth. I felt cheated; I wanted Sue Martinez to be another kind of woman. I thought that somewhere she still was. Also Sue, having been around feminist circles for any time, should know better than to come on to a lesbian like that. She had as much chance as Rhett Butler courting Scarlett O'Hara with a baseball bat. Or maybe Sue never had a chance to put the moves on Julie and she was making up for lost time in the wrong way. Whatever she was stoned on shouldn't have made that big a difference. It didn't let her off any hook, it just left a few more questions.

I tried feeding Flossie next. Then I went into my little bedroom and turned off the lights and looked upwards. My last lover had pasted tiny fluorescent stars in constellations on the walls and ceiling. They all lit up immediately when I turned out the lights. Once they had reminded me of the magic of that first, sweet, naive love. Now they just reminded me of outer space.

I made a list of all the things I would need for Jonell's party tomorrow. I mentally started my shopping trip; the stars presided over me and at last I fell asleep.

The next morning I went the planned route, first to the Japanese produce store where the man sat and sprayed a fine mist over the vegetables all morning. Then I went to the second Japanese produce store where they had firm tofu. I ended up at the health food store and bought some ingredients to make a marinade sauce. I came home and was busily preparing all these things when the phone rang. Jonell was nervously checking on me, and I assured her I was busy cutting tofu.

What with all the loose ends tying themselves up I began to look forward to the party tonight.

I found some navy wool pants folded flat in a drawer. They had a pleat in the front and a little steam made them fall just right. I had a cream-coloured cotton shirt, with little flat white buttons on two breast pockets, and a matching cream knitted tie which I loosely tied and tucked under the collar. I looked in the mirror, and put a foot on a stool and snapped a towel on the top of my black leather boots. They shone. I put on some eye makeup and after a few minutes and several products I changed my mind and washed it all off.

I pulled up to Jonell's house and was surprised by all the little candles she had placed throughout her garden. Small paper tubes kept the candles from blowing out and reflected poinsettias that were still blooming. I could hear the gaggle of voices, some thumping music and one outrageous high laugh above the crowd. I opened the door, which had a no smoking sign on it, and found the room filled with known, pleasant faces, and no smoke.

It wasn't a crowded party and the table of chips and peanuts hadn't been touched. I put the tray of shish kebab down and planted myself by the calories. Everyone was talking. Jonell stalked about the room in long black tights, skidding to a stop by various conversations. Then she'd swish the ice in her drink around, the cubes clinking as she tried to measure small sips for herself. She had a Chinese red silk sweater hanging loosely over the tights: the whole picture made me want to hug her and take the drink away. I saw Patsy the financial officer of a downtown bank back to back with Sally, famous for splitting and selling property parcels while they were still in escrow. There were a few of the Y types looking claustrophobic.

Then I noticed Sandy, who hadn't noticed me. She stood with an indian rubber plant in the corner. I reminded myself how much I had liked her when she was a beekeeper. I reminded myself that ill health had pushed her into cosmic solutions. After she fell in love with me she sold the hives, got unemployed and endometriosis. All bad luck; I hadn't given her any of it. I had even discouraged her from being in love with me, and I found it hard to understand why she persisted. She looked up and I was tempted to run in the other direction. Instead I was drawn to her, wondering if it was ovulation I was seeing in the flush in her porcelain face.

'Hi,' I tried for an upbeat.

'Hi.' Her eyes slid away.

'What's wrong?'

'Nothing.'

'Liar.' She screwed her features slightly to the left, a habit that never failed to irritate me. 'Come on, the other night you were trying to heal me, now you're hating me.'

'You know what it's about. Don't play with me.' Her puffy lids narrowed over the leaf green eyes I used to like so much.

'I didn't think I was.'

'Come on Emma. You're not taking responsibility for our closure. I think you have to come to terms with what's happening.' Her green eyes glistened and made me feel defensive.

'Okay, what's happening then?'

'You're following this tragedy script, investing yourself in emotional attachments and then denying your vulnerability,' she explained.

'Well, I didn't end it clearly, that's true. I hoped you'd sort of fade into the landscape.'

'Of what, your former lovers?'

'That's not such a pretty picture,' I admitted.

'Wonder why.' Part of her mouth made a little grimace, the other part still had a nice shape . . . I thought about ruffled potato chips and how I could almost hate Sandy's self-righteousness.

'Well, I just can't be a recruit to New Age religion,' I said.

'Hey, I never tried to recruit you. It's my thing. You know what a mess I was six months ago. I'm feeling a lot more centred.'

'If you become any more centred you're going to turn into a black hole and vacuum yourself up. Get it together Sandy. Do something.'

'I do a lot of things. Why do you think I'm into this shit anyway?'

'Because you're unemployed and depressed.'

'Is answering phones your solution?'

'You've got me there.' We looked at each other from across the little river of hostility and then we both laughed, like we usually did after we hit the impasse. She had good colour in her cheeks and I remembered how she knew all the latin names of trees.

'Emma you've got *so* much potential in that energy.'

'Sandy, please don't pick a fight with me about this. Let it go.'

'Come on Emma, it's not just that.'

I felt myself falling into the familiar pit where I always stubbed my toe. The party noises picked up around us.

'I guess . . . I guess, I just don't love you as much as you love me,' I shrugged. 'I guess that goes without saying.'

She looked at me with scorpions for eyes. 'That never goes without saying,' she said and stalked away. She always did it to me; I felt myself walk into the kitchen; I hoped she had a lousy meditation all next week. Then I remembered that she was scheduled tomorrow for a D and C.

There was a steady ribbon of Minnie Ripperton floating through the air, and I was prepared to float with it. Instead I backed on to a wall by the kitchen doorway. A woman in beige pants and thick hips slid past me. The kitchen had a keg of beer and I could hear laughter as foam hit the floor. I saw my old friend Clara laughing and lighting up a dingy corner of the room. The story was that Clara was getting rich these days running an office and house cleaning service. Every now and then I thought I'd join her in the mop and bucket game if answering phones got to be too much for me. I reminded myself to go hang with Clara later; now she was talking to a woman with a lot of pink hair.

I moved from the doorway and drifted back towards the dangerous Sandy area. Then I heard a slightly hysterical voice say, 'You're *defending* rent-a-womb?'

It was a cool Stacy Weldemeer who answered her, as if she had planted an hysteric in the crowd so that her words of wisdom would be the contrast and relief that everyone would want. I wanted the science end of the Blackstone Clinic duo, Frances Cohen. I looked around and didn't see her.

'Yes,' Stacy said. 'There is rent-a-womb. And there will be worse than rent-a-womb. Biogenetics is a capital intensive high technology industry in a patriarchal world. Every eye will be on profit. But biogenetics just exists, objectively. Let's try to be objective about it and see what the implications are.'

'Lousy.'

'Well,' she turned to a woman with corn rows and a striped sweater, 'we can't just complain about it. We can't afford to. How lousy is it? And how lousy can it get? Let's make projections, keep up to date and work against the things that will harm us. And let's be creative enough to see all those things which could work *for* us.'

'Yeah, like what?' someone drawled and an ironic smile crossed Stacy's lips. She took a sip from her drink and I saw the black face of her large watch. It had no numbers. 'Let's not get in the same position that people did who argued in favour of the horse and buggy and against cars.'

'What happened to them?' I heard someone mutter.

'Car accidents,' someone laughed, and another voice said, 'Turn-pikes'. One person disappeared in to the kitchen, the foam and the giggles, and another voice said very quietly, 'Turnpikes happen to everybody.'

'Exactly,' Stacy bent from the waist to set her drink on a low butler table. 'And that's the point,' she said. 'Let's not just let history happen to us. Let's make some of it for ourselves.'

A small woman in a black suit and pointy black shoes nudged her way into Stacy's delivery space and the big group melted down into a bunch of couples. Then I defected to the kitchen, the source of a blinding fluorescent light and a floor covered with the spilt foam of beer.

'. . . red star vacations. Coffee harvesting in Nicaragua.'

'Placing your privileged, first world body, with a US passport stuffed in your pocket under CIA reconnaissance planes says *something* . . .'

Then I noticed Angela. She was from Texas and you could go to Galveston and back in the time it took her to make a point, but we always waited.

'Why are we always, always, so eager,' she paused as we pondered 'eager', 'to put our energies into *other* people's struggles?' She spread her hands out from either side of her barrel chest. 'It's simply a metaphor for how we, as women, are always, always putting other people's lives,' she pronounced it 'laavs', 'before our own.' The kitchen fell silent. Then the bubbly soprano giggle escaped from behind her massive, flattish breasts. 'Actually the S.C.U.M. Manifesto *did* make its point.'

Nicaragua walked away. The conversation turned to Alvin Toffler and milliseconds, the latter topic I find almost as frightening as looking at the Milky Way. Maybe Sandy was right and I should be a little more cosmic in outlook.

'. . . everyone says its her worst book.'

'Only if you read the words.'

'What does it mean?'

'It's gonna be a movie.'

'Whaaat? Fan*tas*tic.'

'You know who'll be doing the album . . .'

'I heard Rita Mae say the train systems were going to hell . . .'

'Especially if you have to get somewhere. Did you go to the concert last night?'

I could have almost hung out with *Lesbian People* magazine for the chance of hearing something about the wonderful Rita Mae, but I probably never would have heard what she thought about trains.

I took a turn down the little avocado green hallway which led to Jonell's room. I opened the foil wallpapered door and found Jonell lying on her chintz bedspread. She sat up, pulled her red sweater down and put her black-tight feet on the floor and smiled.

'What are you trying to be so brave about?' I asked.

'I guess I was nervous heading for a crisis with the sauce. So I decided to have one, and now I'm deciding not to.' She looked flushed.

'Nice going.'

'Yeah, well, I'm not having any drama tonight. I can't,' she took a shaky breath, 'afford to.'

'Easy choice.' I said and realised I would spare Jonell the literal details of finding Julie Arbeder dead on the street. But death was on my mind.

'So how are you Emma? You look a little drawn. Is everything still on the up and up? I mean you really went through the gloom and tomb period after your Dad died.'

'You don't get over it, you just get used to it,' I quoted someone or other. 'It's just the general fatal direction of life.' I walked over to Jonell's dressing table. She was the only woman I knew who had one. I played with some silly little bottles. One held some perfume. I smelled it. It was Chanel No.19. 'Have you ever thought that the deaths around you are a kind of clock, ticking off your own life?'

'That's pretty morbid isn't it?'

'Well, first your grandparents die, or rather maybe they live long enough to see the second generation. Then your parents die, and then your friends start to die.' Next to the Chanel was some hand lotion. I tried that too. It smelled like almonds. 'Have you ever thought about whether you would want to go last and save your friends all that grieving, or go first, so that you don't have to go through grieving over them?'

'Emma, honey, you really are morbid. Come back from the dead, girl. It's life, it's time to live. You know your parents wouldn't want you to be sad.'

But I wasn't thinking of my parents.

'I have some news.' Jonell looked at her black nylon feet and rubbed them together. 'I have a crush on somebody.'

'Tell me, tell me.'

'It's . . . Stacy Weldemeer!' Jonell brought her black nylon limbs back to the bed and crossed her knees. I noticed she had bad taste in bedspreads.

'God, Jonell, don't you think you'd better take it easy? You and Marion broke up three months ago after seven years, you have a shiny new house and bad taste in bedspreads. Don't take on anything else right now.'

'Emma, you never change,' Jonell laughed. 'But I'm not taking Weldemeer on. It's just fun from afar. She rarely notices my work down at the Clinic.'

'She should. You do it for nothing,' I sat down next to her, sinking in the soft bed, and rubbed Jonell's back, covered with bright nubby silk. 'Do you know Frances Cohen? Is she tight with Weldemeer?'

'Let's say she notices Cohen's work more than mine. But I don't think they're really tight. They just confer a lot. Frances has been doing a lot of work in the little lab; I don't see her too much. 'But Stacy seems to be everywhere,' Jonell continued. 'She's the kind of person that runs the show and never shows it. I think she has a real sense of vision, Emma. She may be, I don't dare to say it, one of the great people of our time.'

I heard myself make an involuntary grumble.

'It's important Emma. These are scary times.'

'I know, I know.'

'Anyway, being around her kind of cures the cynic in me.'

I patted her broad back, 'Come on, you're not a cynic.'

'Why do you think I have a drinking problem?'

'You enjoy it.'

'I enjoy being a cynic too.' She stretched her leg out and placed a foot on a little flowered slipper chair by the bed. Then she reached a hand out and curled it around her toes.

'You're in great shape for an alcoholic cynic.'

'Emma, these are really dangerous times for the female species.'

'What else is new?'

'Listen, they're developing technology to ensure a male offspring. They're figuring out how to *market* it.'

'Did Stacy tell you that?'

'Stands to reason doesn't it?' It did.

'I mean female infanticide in China, India, who knows, Indiana. What a great solution, "No need to off the baby bundled in pink, just use the handy XY condom and keep the pants in power." '

'Please, stop.'

'Imagine, women bearing male children and only enough females to continue a male population.'

'And Stacy Weldemeer is going to halt the fatal course of human civilisation? That charming, she's not. And that nightmare isn't going to happen. It's just her way of ensuring an enthusiastic support group.'

'I think you don't take it seriously enough,' Jonell said.

'And I think you're taking it too seriously. Come on, this is a party, let's have fun.'

Jonell took her foot off the upholstered slipper chair and we slid off the bed together, opened the door and plunged into the music and

61

noise of the party. We passed through the little hallway. Jonell seemed to have inherited her grandmother's taste in furnishings while adopting Liza Minelli's taste in clothes. It was weird and one of the reasons I liked her so much.

I passed by Stacy Weldemeer. She appeared to be drinking and laughing, just like an ordinary person, which she most likely was. What she had told Jonell made sense, but I was leery of the drama. I was also frightened of her visions, or jealous, or both.

'Jonell,' I touched her elbow, 'I think I'll go deal with the tofu.'

'You are a great person,' she said and nuzzled a kiss in my neck. Chanel No. 19.

'Let up with the great person stuff. Save it for your latest crush. Just kiss me some more with your Chanel lips, I love it.' She did and sailed into the living room whilst I went through into the kitchen.

I picked up the plate that had the metal tinfoil covering the lumpy shapes of shish kebabs. I balanced it on the flattened palm of my hand, kicked open the door leading to the deck and walked outside.

The small deck had a spreading apricot tree hanging over it. Jonell had put tiny twinkling white lights on the branches. Two sides had high fences, California redwood style, and the fourth side showed the door, part of a picture window and a small high window.

It was a beautiful night, the stars in the inky sky and a background of party voices. One excited voice floated over the rest for a while, until I realised it came from the small high window next to the large plate glass affair.

'There just isn't any more money. You'll have to complete the process yourself.'

'Well, I can't do it alone. It takes two. You know that.'

'I'll do my best.' It sounded like a couple's therapy that was bombing out.

'Aw hell, let's just skip it . . .'

'We can't skip it. This may not be so important to you, but it is to me. It's my life.'

'If it's your *life* then something's wrong with your life.' I recognised the voice. It was Frances Cohen. I dropped a stick with cubes of tofu and green peppers on the redwood deck. Something which looked like kitty litter was sticking to the tofu as I picked it up.

Her voice continued, rising, 'Don't get your undies in a bunch, after all you haven't gotten your fingers dirty yet.'

Then I recognised the other voice as Stacy Weldemeer. I put the spoiled food to one side. I wondered why Stacy's undies were in a bunch and exactly what Frances' fingers were dirtied with. I started assembling more shish kebab. I was turning the skewers around trying not to get spatters on my shirt when I saw Frances leaning against the door frame. She was wearing red jeans, with white stitching, a beige cotton blouse with a tiny red silk bow tie. Her fluffy hair managed to lie flat on her head. The thought of dirty fingers had kept me busy with the skewers and made me lose track of time. She didn't seem to mind standing there because she kept on doing it without saying a word. Just before it was getting to be rude, no matter how exciting it was, I said, 'Why don't you turn a skewer or two. I could use some extra fingers.'

'Sure,' she grinned and came over. I liked that she didn't pretend there was nothing between us. I felt all the familiar questions after a first night with someone. It seemed like a good idea to keep my wits about me, but I wanted to see how close I could come to throwing my wits away at the same time. It was a heady emotional roller coaster ride.

'What have you been doing?' she asked, one hand on hip, the other flipping the skewers.

'Oh, I've been investigating a murder.' I was ready to say anything to cut through her smouldering attitude. Actually I'd been spending the bulk of my time cleaning, driving and sitting in the hot and sticky subway.

I told her about Julie Arbeder, discovering her body, the police detectives. I told her about the union work Julie had been doing. I didn't tell her about the phone call that came to Women's Hotline or the codeine capsules in Julie's daypack, or the black opaque pools that were Sue Martinez's eyes.

Suddenly the noise of the party picked up. Someone was getting drunk; I could hear her voice slicing through the crowd.

'I'm afraid I may have been the last person to talk to her,' I told Frances. 'Being the last person to hear the words of a dead woman almost feels like a responsibility. But maybe I wasn't the last . . .'

'Don't you think maybe you're over dramatising it a little?' a voice asked. Stacy Weldemeer and all her red curls were standing quietly, not far from my right elbow.

'You scared me.'

'I'm not surprised; that's what happens when you play Nancy Drew.' She took a draw on her foamy beer. It didn't leave any head on her mouth.

'Stacy.' I heard a screech from the doorway. The attention of Stacy

63

Weldemeer was sucked away by a fan. 'God, I didn't think I'd find you *here*!' she screeched. Stacy departed to the enthusiastic hugs of a surprised admirer.

'So, you've had a busy couple of days then?' Frances asked me as the parade walked away.

'I haven't been really busy, just absorbed. I talked to a few of her friends, the people that worked with her. I guess I just have the feeling that she died in the middle of something.'

'Everybody dies in the middle of something.'

'Not like she did.'

'And you have to finish it? Why, Emma, the woman is dead. Try and get past it. There's nothing you can do about it.'

'It seems like everyone I talk to takes a lot of trouble to tell me to stop troubling myself.'

'Maybe if they go to so much trouble you should listen to them,' she put an arm around my waist, 'you can't change it Emma. Just give it some time and it will go away. Get busy with something else.'

'Is that an invitation?'

'If you want it to be.' She kissed me full, open, on the mouth.

'Do you think I'm uncentred, denying access to my vulnerability?' I touched her lightly above the hip bones.

She laughed. 'Will you give me until tomorrow morning to find out?'

That slow grin was growing across her face and the shish kebab were beginning to burn. I let go of her hips and we started to arrange the skewers on a platter.

'Let's get out of here for a while,' she said. 'I'm not in a party mood. What would you say to driving over to Boston?'

'That would be fine.' I left the food and the party and went out the back gate following the shape of Frances Cohen down the hill to her car.

Ten

Her transportation was an old four wheel drive jeep and I was pleased. A motor cycle would have pushed her tough style into affectation. She opened the passenger side door with a key and let me in. She used a manual choke to start the thing and did a U-turn to head up back into Boston.

'What do you use this for?' I asked.

'I like to go into the wilderness. I drive in as far as I can and pack as much stuff on to my back as possible and try and last a week in relative comfort. If I really want to stay, I can hike back and pick up more supplies from the jeep. I like the high places best, high desert, mountain timberline.'

'You do that a lot?'

'As much as I can. I like to see how things on the edge survive. Plants, animals, with little water, rough conditions. Every little mechanism is beautiful. I don't like to study it, I just want to sit with it.'

'Is this a response to seeing sick people all week?'

'Sick people, hell. The most illness I see is a vagina with a pH imbalance. And that's okay by me too.' She smiled very directly at me. 'Where do you want to go?'

I didn't have any ideas. She suggested live music. 'I know some musicians in town,' she said. 'On nights like this I just want to hear some good, clean old-time jazz. Jazz. No horns, just strings.' And she knew right where to go. She took us to Passim's, a club that was a great excuse to show off good musicians.

I listened carefully to the tunes as they wove their way around and through the scales. It was all very impressive technically, but except for minor and major keys a lot of the numbers sounded the same to me. Frances seemed to follow it all and leaned back and clapped her hands whenever some riff took an unexpected turn. The musicians seemed sweet and appreciative of each others' solos. Frances gave me some background on the history of the instruments, she seemed so honest in her enjoyment of the happy tunes. After a particularly frisky number the musicians called it a night. We finished our cider and left.

We stood on the sidewalk outside and separately contemplated the future of the evening.

'What was your tiff with Stacy?' I asked, and immediately regretted it. I didn't want any extra information, especially if it was romantic: my intuition was that it wasn't and I was right.

'My tiff with Stacy is how she is running that clinic, and trying to run me.'

'It's a hierarchy, right? So it's clear she has the power, isn't it?'

Aw hell, Stacy's okay. And I like my job. And Stacy's good to me, shit, half the time she thinks I'm Madame Curie.'

'Are you?'

'I start to feel like we're playing with plutonium down there.'

'Oh yeah? Are your sperm donations glowing in the dark?'

'I should know, I'm spending enough nights there.'

'Spend this one with me. I'll glow for you.'

She grinned an agreement and we went to her place.

Her house was on the second storey of a converted family dwelling. It was on an incline, but not on a hill. It was close enough to downtown to have trouble finding a parking place. We walked a block to get from the car to her walk. There must have been fifty stairs cast out of concrete leading up to the house. A hallway led up some steep stairs to Frances' small apartment. It was essentially one large room. The owner hadn't bothered to install walls to make it a bona fide second dwelling but it was better that way.

A large bookshelf dominated an entire wall. Books were stacked every different way on top of other books jammed into rows. A rag rug of pale blue-grey was on the floor. She had painted the floor white. An expensive beige couch was nearly the only furniture. There were detailed drawings of a rather sad looking woman on the wall. It felt like Frances wasn't in this house often, but when she was, she was comfortable. A small divider kept the kitchen in one corner. In contrast to the rest of the house, it was a mess. The remains of several nights' dinners left their evidence, a breadboard and a knife with crumbs sprinkled around it.

The entire back wall of the house was glassed in; it had once been an upstairs porch. The windows overlooked a tiny ravine, totally dark at night, but a fresh green smell wafted up through an open window.

A draughty corner housed a high bed with a soft white coverlet on it. A bedstand next to it was littered with newspapers, magazines, a book on genetic engineering. A geometric lamp over the bed shone a triangular-shaped light upon the pillows.

I sat on the bed surrounded by windows, listening to the creek and looking up at the constellations. Frances appeared with a bottle of red wine and two crystal glasses. We were too embarrassed to toast anything. The wine was good. She leaned over me and put her mouth on mine. I felt her exploring my mouth, taking it, drawing me into her. I would have been afraid except that I felt her warm hand on my back reassuring me. Then her hand found my breasts and began to find all my reactions. I couldn't stop a funny squeaking sound from escaping. She had my hands clasped over my head with one strong arm and her other hand went further and further pursuing all the boundaries, taking me so far along in the excitement it was nearly pain. And she went on and on, almost methodically except that I felt her own breath rising in response. I fought with the passivity but it was only fun to fight it. I let her go wherever she wanted. I let her find things I didn't know were there. I was so wet, with her hand between my legs. Her finger slipped inside me and my body rose. She held me for two minutes or ten minutes. Then it was my turn.

Eleven

We took a thirty-six hour vacation. It was that kind of vacation where you don't go anywhere or make any plans in advance. We unplugged the phone and stayed in bed so long that when we stood up I had forgotten how tall she was. Shorter than me.

I made acquaintance with every part of her body, the tiger stripes on her hips, the changes in her aureolae, the shape of her big toes. We told each other our personal histories: she was the working-class Jewish girl become doctor with all the attendant aches and pains of living down, fighting for, and embracing her background. She had only one long relationship in her busy, academic past, the Big One being punctuated with a recent spate of Uncommitted Situations.

I was the Unambitious Orphan ignoring Self-Realisation by enjoying life; except that I wasn't these days. My Big One had ended in disaster which I didn't mention. It was the kind of disaster you have when you say all the forbidden words like 'forever' and 'destiny' and believe them. When I lost that one I knew the future would always feel like a sort of compromise. Or maybe not. I had made love twice with Sandy, but felt like that didn't count. Aside from that no one had touched me in thirteen months. I didn't mention that either.

Frances was going to be problematic because she was too interesting to be uncomplicated and because I could tell that that wasn't going to make any difference.

Suddenly it was Sunday.

In the morning Frances made coffee in the small messy kitchen.

The voluminous Sunday paper had arrived at the bottom of the hall and we quietly worked our way through it. I found myself getting restless.

I decided to say goodbye. I wanted time to decide how interesting she was; I thought I had enough evidence. I kissed her warmly, but I broke the embrace first. She noticed. She had drawn on a white cardigan sweater, very long, with a design of small red trianges in one corner.

'Do you knit?' I had to ask.

'Yeah, in med school I figured out how to knit, purl and study at the same time. I got a degree and seventeen sweaters in three years.'

Then I knew I was in love. I walked outside and hit the world. It was like walking out of a Sunday afternoon matinee, everything was too bright, too shiny, too hard-edged. Frances' bed had been the kind of heaven only a movie could promise.

I closed the door and prepared myself for a bout of Sunday morning public transportation to get back to my car where I'd left it two nights before by Jonell's house. It was a clean exit, just kissing Frances, walking out the door and getting on a Mass Ave bus.

One hour and fifteen minutes later got me back to Jonell's house and the monster Plymouth looking like a pimpmobile next to all the politically correct American compacts and Toyotas on Jonell's block. I sat in the Plymouth for a few minutes. Any thought about Frances seemed to register immediately between my legs: it was disconcerting.

It was also a beautiful day. The water was white on the harbour with little fleeting sailboats. It would be nice to have a sailboat to get into that postcard; I would have to settle for roller skating in the Commons. It had been a perfect thirty-six hours and I wanted to have a perfect Boston Sunday. It would have been, except for bumping into Sue Martinez in the park.

I was just strapping on my skates when I saw her shiny black hair. It was so thick, with that little curl at the bottom; from the way the long shoulders hunched up, I knew it had to be her. It was hard to believe, with all the city's residents, families with young kids, even Japanese tourists, kite fliers and jugglers that I was running into a South End resident, or rather, watching the back of her head. She was talking to a man on a park bench. What interested me was the interaction. She wanted something from him. He was acting bored, disaffected. This is sometimes a moment when violence occurs, as I've learned from the Women's Hotline, because the men are never bored, never disaffected. The ultimate threat is that women will put their emotions on the line, and eventually the men will too. It is never pleasant to watch, and even worse to anticipate. But this time it didn't turn out that way; I saw his hand move in her direction and she suddenly stood up and walked away from him.

'Sue!' I came limping over on one skate. Perhaps she hadn't heard me. She kept walking. She had on a long green coat over beige pants. She walked so quickly the coat flew out a bit behind her.

'Sue!' I pushed my one roller-skated foot ahead, my other foot hopping behind it. I reached her and touched her arm. 'What?' She spun around as if she knew it was me, as if we'd been in the middle of an argument. My hand was pushed off her arm by the force of her turn. I had a feeling she meant it that way.

'Last time I saw you you were offering yourself on a platter,' I remarked, irritated. She wasn't even going to look at me. 'Well, you weren't just putting the moves on me.' I was going to be angry very soon. 'You assumed I wanted you because I'm gay, didn't you?'

Sue watched some leaf on the ground and looked up at me with a bored, exasperated sort of sigh.

'Let me tell you something,' now I was mad. 'I know when I want somebody. More or less. And I expect them to know that about themselves too. More or less. What you pulled didn't have anything to do with knowledge or attraction.'

'What do you know about what I want?' she said coolly, a different person from the previous week.

'I'd say it's painfully obvious what you want. And even if I had any you wouldn't have to turn into a coquette to get it. Speedballing gets a person gathering no moss pretty fast.'

'Well, it's none of your business.' I saw her glance nervously back at the park bench. 'Listen, I'm fine now. I don't need your help. I appreciate what you did, finding out that stuff about Julie, but now I just want to forget about it.'

'Sure, glad you're cooled out about your dead roommate. Just put her on ice and see if it goes away.'

'Leave me alone.' She accented every word. Then she walked quickly away from me, stirring up a few leaves on the ground behind her. I stood there wondering how many about-faces a junkie could do. That was something no one had the answer to. And I wasn't convinced she was a junkie either.

I hopped back to the brown car and smoked a cigarette. Then I put on my other skate, and skated hard, racing in between little children, shopping carts and puppy dogs. My Sunday afternoon was spoiled.

70

Twelve

The next day I was going to go back to work.

I like Monday mornings when I have skilfully prepared for them on the evening before. That Sunday evening I had. After skating I returned and did a bout of washing and hung it in the May sunshine to dry.

I looked through a museum catalogue of kitchen utensils of the Middle Ages. I read a story in a magazine. Then I watched television and ironed four blouses. If I had a coke habit I could probably take on pleated skirts too. Then I paid three bills, and reviewed my agenda for the coming week. A tardy letter to an aunt who was my last living relative completed my tasks. The aunt would reply with tales of cooking seven dozen Danish cookies for a party in her farm community three thousand miles away. If I was lucky she would send me the recipe, if I was luckier I wouldn't be eating them alone.

The week followed smoothly. I went to work every morning battling traffic or waiting for MBTA trains. I made myself a few great dinners, I enjoyed the solitude because I was alone with the person I could be most sure of, myself. I consumed three good books. I answered calls at work, I calmed a panicked female populace and was a very good girl. Which is how it should be. Only one evening my mind went fishing into the history of the last week. I didn't think I had been consciously avoiding it. Sue had closed a big heavy door on the whole mess which happily coincided with my own wishes. It was just that I didn't want Sue to be the character in the story she turned out to be. I wanted to see the energy flow continuously through those long limbs. I didn't want her encased in a plastic house. I didn't want her to giggle. The puppy probably wasn't even hers.

An unrelenting, silly maternalism made me concerned about her. The only three drugs I knew that dilated the eyes that much were angel dust, which she was too smart to use, LSD, which we were too old to use, and cocaine, which a lot of smart people used before they found

71

out they weren't smart enough. I wondered if drugs had left their little footprints on her arms. I decided to call her house, if only to make her angry.

The querulous Misty answered the phone.

'Hello?' When some people answer it's always a question.

'Hi, this is Emma. Is Sue there?'

'Sue? No, she left town this morning.'

'Left town? Where to?'

'She went to visit a friend. She has a friend in Tijuana?' The woman could hardly make a statement. I wondered how real facts passed her lips. 'She's taken all her things. She took a taxi to the airport.'

So much for Sue. I hoped she got away from the current drug of her choice south of the border. It wasn't likely. I also wondered how she paid for a trip all the way to Tijuana. I hoped she got stuck in the tunnel on the way to the airport and missed her flight.

My favourite vehicle of the week was a red jeep that pulled up at my office around lunchtime on Friday. I was standing in front of the door of Women's Hotline. Frances stepped down from the high cab and had two armfuls of red tulips which she held against a white cotton coat. She put them into my arms.

'I'm trying to buy you off with tulips,' she said. I wanted to kiss her.

'Wait a second, let's get out of the doorway.' Part of me is still in some kind of closet, usually my lips on a public street outside my own office.

'I'll take you to lunch,' she said and whisked me into the nearest quiche culture joint. It was almost next door. She found a table by a window. I helped her off with the white coat. Her light brown hair followed a static electricity pattern as I lifted the coat off her shoulders and hung it up. I sat across from her and had to pat the straying hairs down. It is difficult to talk to someone when hairs are standing out at right angles from their ears.

She took both my hands in hers. She leaned over earnestly. At least she intended it that way.

'You're buying me off with tulips,' I reminded her.

'Yes. And lunch and three good books of your choice. Except I have one right here.' She reached into a square blue canvas bag and pulled out *The Dancing Wu Li Masters*.

'But what if I'm not interested in new physics?'

'Oh, but you will be. It's a great book, it's . . .' She stopped herself. 'Emma, I think you are a wonderful woman. I want to see you a lot more. But there's something I have to do this weekend and all next

72

week. Maybe next weekend too. And I don't want to lose you and I don't want you to get any wrong impressions.'

'But you want to put me on ice? That's not a bad impression?'

'Yes.' She didn't make excuses. She looked at me with hazel eyes. They didn't match her navy blue sweater. The navy blue sweater was handknitted.

'What are you doing anyway? Moonlighting?'

'I'm working in a lab. It's a place where I worked last year, before I came to the Blackstone Clinic. It's good bucks and great equipment.'

'What are you doing there?'

'It's complicated to explain.'

'I'm a smart girl. Fill me in.'

'I can't just yet. I really can't.' She looked like she really couldn't.

'Okay. You want to put me on ice for a few weeks. And you like me very much. And you'd just as soon I didn't get involved with anyone else. I should sit home and read books and watch a small fortune in tulips die.'

'But they won't die! They're just budding now. You'll see them bloom. And I'll send fresh ones.' She stopped cheerleading about the flowers. 'I'm serious about you, Emma,' she said.

'I'll wait,' I replied. Then I kissed her hand. It was corny but the only appropriate thing to do across a table. Then I ate a beautiful lunch she bought me and went back to work. I saw her to her jeep but I wouldn't really let her kiss me goodbye. I didn't mind being bought off, but I hated waiting. This would call for some intensive ironing and I wondered if I would stoop low enough to iron underpants.

Thirteen

I didn't iron any underpants but I found myself enjoying the time anyway. I didn't have a social life and I liked it that way. I worked, I ate, I worried, I took the subway to work. It would have been perfect until my pre-sleep foreplay was interrupted late one evening. It was Sandy, being omnipresent on the phone.

'Hi Emma.'

'Oh, Sandy, how are you?' I suddenly remembered about her D and C. 'I forgot to call you, I'm sorry.'

'Well, I wasn't exactly a barrel of laughs at Jonell's party. Forgive me?'

'Yes. Okay. How are you feeling now? Sounds like the old hormone balance is in shape.'

'You do read me well, Emma.'

'How did it go?'

'Well, the women at the Blackstone Clinic were great. They explain everything, and generally made the whole experience bearable.'

I wanted to ask about Frances, but didn't. 'But was it painful?'

'Painful doesn't even come close, Emma. It was a total pain experience.'

'Ugh.'

'And that's not all. I was on the table, feet in the stirrups, and then they gave me the local. It wasn't like any other feeling I've ever had. There's no nerve endings in the cervix, but suddenly you get a cramp like the worst cramp you've ever had. Pressure building up inside of you, like someone was blowing up my uterus like a balloon. Then I realised I was being burned.'

'How awful.'

'There was this moment, when I thought I smelt something, and suddenly I projected right off the stainless steel table; I was floating up into a corner of the room. I could see myself lying there. The room became longer and at the far end there was a big window. I could see

74

little twinkling lights outside of it, and yes – I know what it was now. The John Hancock Tower. I was floating on the ceiling of the Blackstone Clinic, looking out at the John Hancock Tower. Weird, huh?'

'And did you feel any pain?'

'No, I was just suspended, outside of my body. And then, don't take this personally Emma, I heard your name.'

'But Sandy, we don't have that kind of relationship anymore.'

'Tell it to the Goddess, Emma. A whisper floated into my space, "Emma Victor," it said. And then the pain stopped completely. But then the monster came.'

'I knew it, my name brings on dreadful ogres.'

'No, Emma, it was really frightening. Suddenly I felt a hostile force enter the room; I was slammed back down on to the table, like a giant hand swatted me flat on my back again. I looked up and saw the para-medics, the physician and then I felt a presence; I looked back and I saw a terrible little hunchbacked man enter the room. He came to me and leaned over. I looked up around me but the women weren't even noticing. I looked back to see if he was still there, and I felt his breath on my face. Ugh. Cheese. I looked into his mouth and saw slimy, infected gums. I wanted to scream but not a sound would come out.'

'What happened then?'

'I fainted I guess. Then the next thing I remember was being aroused by a para-medic. She said that it wasn't unusual to have hallucinations. The women there are so nurturing, so *caring*. I felt much better, and now I have a clean bill of health.'

'Glad to hear it.'

'Emma, you wouldn't want to come to a seance up in New Hampshire next week?'

'No, I wouldn't.'

'Didn't think so.'

Sandy paused and I began to feel that uncomfortable vacuum in her character again. I could feel that the cosmic force wasn't filling it up either.

'Emma, I still care about you.'

'I know but it's getting to be an expensive fantasy for you, yearning after me. Why don't we just call it platonic and I can have the benefit of all your visions. Get my feet off the ground, a little vicarious astral projection.'

'I think you're just afraid of my big tits,' she said.

'That's one way of looking at it. I like the approach.'

'Okay, I'll keep trying.'

'You're incorrigible, Sandy. And I have to warn you, I have something new on the horizon.'

'Don't worry, cosmic insight gives me an edge over any materialist competition.'

'I wouldn't count on it.'

'Goodnight, Emma.'

'Goodnight, Sandy, I'm glad things are going better for you.'

I thought I was quite rested by the time Frances got around to calling me twelve days after the tulips. She wanted to come over and spend the night after working late one evening. I surprised myself by agreeing, but I wasn't really agreeable.

Frances bounded in at a decent hour, obviously trying to control some enthusiasm. She had bright red cheeks and an almost hysterical expression. In jeans and a workshirt she was the picture of health.

'You look happy, where's the party?'

'Oh, things are just going along nicely.'

'Okay, don't invite me. I don't like going to parties alone but apparently some people do.'

'Look, I'll tell you everything when I'm ready. Don't cramp me.' She picked up the evening paper.

'Cramp you! Hey, Miss Big Science, my living room is not your pit stop. What amazes me is that you think your presence, reading the paper, is enough to keep me waiting.'

'I didn't ask you to wait.'

'I think these after-work dates with you aren't working.'

'You're right. I'm sorry.' She put the paper down on the couch next to her. 'What now?'

'You wanted to come over here. You must have some idea.'

'Hey, I'm just a little tired.'

'So go home. I'm tired of you being tired and busy and tired and mysterious and egoistic.' I was crossing over into an anger that was going to be hard to come back from.

'*You're* the one that's mysterious. So we're both involved in other things. I've got this real important shit going on . . .'

'Great. Take it home and recover from it there. My living room requires interesting conversation and love scenes. You can't be cast in either role.'

'C'mere. C'mon.'

76

Of course I went to her, I let her earn my affection bit by bit. 'What role, if I could be allowed to appear, would you cast me in?'

'If you can't converse, I'm going to do everything possible to make your body scream for me.'

'That sounds pretty passive on my part,' she said.

'Totally. But I think you can easily handle it tonight.' Then we went to bed and I made very slow and careful love to her.

'You know, I like you a lot,' she said afterwards.

'You like me because I won't let you control the shots.'

'Are we in that much of a power struggle?' she mumbled against my breast, softly.

'It only looks that way when we're out of bed.' I pulled her head close, wrapping my arm around her graceful, brown shoulder. We floated off into that quiet world which love made possible because the power devils had been admitted and therefore banished.

'Do you know what I saw today?' she murmured out of her daybed-dreams.

'I wouldn't want to guess, my crazy scientist.'

'I looked into a whole body microscope.'

'What's that?'

'A whole body microscope – well, it looks like a body scanner.' Her voice rose. 'Do you know how exciting that is?'

'No, tell me.' I patted the downy hair on her scientific head.

'It means that you can see whole tissues – living tissues.'

'I don't get it, what's so special about that?'

'Before, if you wanted to examine something under a microscope you had to cut out a piece of tissue, and examine the dead cells. Maybe the only exception is a rabbit's ear, which is so fine that you can stick it under a conventional microscope. It helps if the rabbit cooperates, too. But now, with this thing you can put a human being under the lens and see the whole mechanism. It's fantastic.' She pulled herself up on one elbow, her breast hung down, brushing mine.

'Where did you see this?'

'At Genocorp. I worked there this morning. I don't really know what they need it for down there, but they've got some huge capital base right now so they're investing it in equipment right and left, like rich kids with a sweet tooth in a candy shop. And they're going to get richer, I'll tell you that.'

'Do they pay you well?'

'Yeah, I get paid well, senior technician scale, even though I'm only working part time. But it's the experience, the equipment. God, looking through that microscope was like witnessing life. It was beautiful.'

'Your world seems so far away to me. I hardly understand it,' a lump started to rise in my throat. 'My idea of high tech is a two-dimensional postcard.'

'Hey, baby,' she crooned softly, 'if I could get you in to look into this microscope you'd know what I mean. Even without technical knowledge you'd be knocked off your feet. It's the blood pulsating, the juices of life. It looks incredible.'

'You make it sound really attractive.' I looked into her eyes, and fell in. 'I love your inspiration, Frances. I could never have a girlfriend who didn't have it.'

'Inspiration, but not obsession, right?'

'It's a fine line.'

'I know.'

'You won't be moonlighting forever, will you?'

'No, but I don't like talking about forever.'

'Agreed. Stricken from the vocabulary we use about our relationship.'

We sat in the silence of our agreement, the word 'relationship' hanging in the air, admitting to a commitment because we admitted to boundaries. Suddenly, we existed as a couple.

'Your work at Genocorp,' I broke the silence, 'do you have political questions about it?'

'Entering the medical profession is being socked in the face with ethical problems the rest of your life. The only trouble is the AMA tries to give you all the answers beforehand.'

'Do you have all the answers?'

'No, I just try and never stop asking all the questions – that's the important thing . . .'

'But Genocorp . . .'

'Don't ask me to defend it, Emma, please.' She wasn't pleading, and again I felt her take the upper hand. She looked at me for a moment, her pupils were aiming into mine.

'Are you afraid moonlighting at Genocorp is making me a rich Frankenstein?' she asked.

'No, I just think you like those high tech toys.'

'If I can get you a security clearance I'll take you in one day and show you everything.' She put her hands under my back and suspended her chest over me. 'You can put the lens next to my heart and see my every cell, every tissue.'

'You're not that transparent.'

'Oh, yes I am.' She leaned down and circled me with her brown arms. She pulled me towards her and our breasts touched. 'You don't need a super-duper microscope to see it, either.' Her mouth travelled down my belly and it happened again.

At three in the morning I woke up in my empty bedroom. The fluorescent stars had already lost their glow. I smelt a cigarette being smoked in the living room. I heard a voice in low conversation. The voice said, 'Don't get your hormones in an uproar!' The stress was on 'your', then I fell back to sleep.

I woke up with Frances holding me and bright sunlight on the wall. I had to leave for work earlier than she, so I brought her coffee in bed. I explained how to lock the house automatically and I left her sitting up in my bed against some pillows. That gave me a better feeling.

I didn't hear from Frances for five days. It was not a particularly pleasant five days. I went to work and found that two of our most trustworthy safety nets had died – a battered women's home and a day programme for women alcoholics. The battered women's house should have gotten state and city support; it had died a slow death while bleeding its staff members' time into unsuccessful concerts and rummage sales. The day programme for alcoholics bellied up when funds which paid the salaries of therapists and day care workers were chopped off by some congressman in the middle of a fiscal year. Without agencies to refer these women to I felt like an empty voice, soothing some panicked soul and giving no more comfort than the pleasant and false tones of a TV commercial. I was also pissed. I went home every night angry.

Friday night and the promise of a weekend wondering if Frances would call didn't put me in a happier frame of mind. I stepped hard on the accelerator. The thought of going shopping in Franca's lesbian bar wasn't appealing, and I didn't have the energy to drum up a dinner party, balancing out friends and food, wine and conversation. A traffic jam, up ahead, and I looked in the rear view mirror and slowly squeezed on the brakes.

This was the mood that brought me home with all the other sweating suckers not anticipating their weekend. I looked at my little brick house like it was a prison. I looked at my garden which felt like hard labour. I looked at my front door and it was open.

Fourteen

Open front doors usually mean one of three things. There had been a burglary, or there is still a burglary in progress. Or I had been stupid enough not to lock my front door when leaving the house and going to work in the morning. I had actually done that once.

I listened inside for the sounds of professional burglars ripping electrical wires out of walls to make a quick getaway with the stereo. Daytime burglars aren't particularly quiet, they're just fast. They also weren't likely to pull a job at five thirty on a Friday afternoon, when millions of people in the greater Boston area were getting home from work. I wondered if the job had already been done, and walked into the hallway of my home. I still didn't hear any noises, so I proceeded up the stairway to the dining room. Sweat dripped to my waist.

A small white man was sitting in a chair by the dining room table. He had a dark green parka on, dirty shapeless brown pants and work shoes. He was clean shaven with short black hair and he was very, very nervous. He was also very angry.

'What are you doing in my house?' said my voice, I hoped without a tremble. My mind started racing through all the procedures I knew. Pretend your giant brother is outside. Pretend you have a gun. Oh, why hadn't I finished that karate class?

'Who are you? What are you doing in my house?' I asked again and thought about how far away the telephone was and the emergency number to remember except that I was getting it mixed up with the Scotland Yard number from a late night movie. 'What are you doing here?' He didn't say anything.

'Go on! Get out!' I cried. I sidled towards the phone which was sitting peacefully on a small maple stand. He didn't stand up. His pants were old bellbottoms, too long, frayed and dirtied on the bottom edges. I kept walking towards the phone but he didn't stand up.

'You, you . . .' he began stuttering as if shocked to see a human person before him. I knew then that he wasn't going to hurt me.

80

'Who are you?' I asked.

'Don't you know? You go around questioning a man's life. Call people, big people, in big organisations, a union. Don't you care when questions ruin a man's life?'

'You're Rich Janinni. The shop steward from Parts Unlimited.' The blood was draining slowly out of my face and I leaned against the woodwork and noticed a neighbour in her window two houses down. The mouth that was in such an angry line relaxed. He looked away.

'You know what kind of trouble you got me in, lady? Y'know what's comin' down on my head?'

I shook my head. 'It better be a good story, mister. We're talking breaking and entering.'

'You've got Yellentrauw fixin' to boot me out. And if that ain't enough I got some outfit in Atlanta, Georgia making ugly noises at my wife over the phone. I got a whole line of packers who hate my guts and order clerks trying to run me over at every aisle corner.'

'They had a union, remember? They were losing everything and you were selling them out.'

'Aw, hell.' He stood up. I flexed my body. He moved around the room, walking in a small tight circle. His head swung back and forth. He stopped and looked at the ground. Then he showed me two blue eyes that looked broken, but in a scary sort of way.

'Lady, I got a wife who's nervous. She imagines things, y'know. I love her, I gotta stay by her. We got three kids and it's all we can handle. She got a mother with a heart condition. Her ma drives her up the wall. We can't have her in the house. We'll never make it. We gotta think of the kids too. Esther, she's gotta keep it together. We had to put her mom in a nursing home. The place costs a fortune and still stinks like an old diaper. But we *can't* have her ma in the house. Esther'd never make it. Everything drives her crazy as it is . . .'

'Your fellow workers aren't doing too well either.'

'Aw, shit. I know. I was doing okay for a while. Then the company called in this Yellentrauw and he was talkin' circles around me. I couldn't tell if he was threatening me or what. I didn't know what to do.'

'You could have gone to your union.'

He didn't answer. He looked at the door.

'What's going on, Mr Janinni? You didn't sell out just because some smoothie made ugly noises at you. You got more muscle behind you than that. What gives? Or what gave?'

'Look, just leave it alone, okay?'

'Julie Arbeder is dead, Mr Janinni. Either she made some people very nervous or she got real unlucky in a curious way on East Lexington Street. You look very nervous to me.'

'You can't pin a murder on me.'

'That's something we both know Mr Janinni. I just don't like loose ends, and I'm in a crummy mood and I don't like coming home and finding an angry uninvited someone sitting in my house on Friday afternoon. The last man in my house was a Lieutenant Sloan from Homicide. He likes to ask a lot of questions. I have the feeling he might not always be polite, and he certainly won't care how nervous your wife is. He might even figure it makes *his* life easier. So, why don't you just tell me, as the price of admission for breaking into my house, what are you in it for?'

He slumped down into a chair, his shoulder hunched over. He didn't look at me.

I waited for a few minutes.

'What are you in it for, Mr Janinni?' I used my gentle telephone voice.

'Yellentrauw worked it so my health insurance pays for my mother-in-law's nursing home. He's worked out another job description so I can get different coverage.' The man sighed.

It was a big secret, a big petty ugly secret and I hated all the Yellentrauws, all the sneaky companies that put the squeeze on their workers, using their personal problems against them. It was sometimes called employee management, and some places even gave courses in it. And some courses were just a little uglier than others. Cost effective: break up a union for the price of a bed in a nursing home.

'Mr Janinni, why don't you go to your union? At least you've got some information to give now. The union could use it. Don't sell yourself out, it just makes more problems.'

But I couldn't tell him what to do for his nervous wife, or his mother-in-law. I didn't feel like playing social worker. I just felt tired and I wanted to be alone and have a nice weekend with my own problems.

'That's easy for you to say, lady. You try sitting in my position. Five people depend on me. I'm getting used right and left, by the company, by the union, by the insurance. I'm looking out for my family because nobody, I mean *nobody* else is. And I'll do anything I have to to keep us afloat; I will rob and cheat and steal. And if I have to I'll sell my buddies down the drain. I don't like it, I don't like the taste it leaves in my mouth, but I just spit and try and get on with the day.' He walked towards the chair where his poncho was lying. 'It would be a lot easier if people would keep their noses out of my business. I've got to handle it my way, so you just stay out.' He put on his poncho and picked up a dark cap that was lying on the table. He couldn't have had a real purpose in breaking into my house. He couldn't scare me and it wouldn't make any difference if he did. He was just a lonely sucker up against a wall with no one to be angry at.

'You should get a better lock on your door, lady. That one can be opened with a credit card.' Then he turned around and walked slowly down the stairs and in a moment I heard a car door slam and a noisy car engine start, throwing some rods around inside some cylinders.

It was not a pleasant prospect of an evening. I tried reading and I tried eating. I tried not waiting for the phone to ring. I tried opening up some Hotline mail, my job to prepare some things for the staff meeting Monday. There were some bills, some advertisements, three pitches from other organisations for money, a letter of commendation from the mayor timed for us to use when the foundations started up their application acceptance programmes in February. There was also an announcement of a funding fair organised by the mayor to help needy organisations get in touch with sponsors, foundations. It was a homey effort to keep her city's wounds bandaged, but it was going to be a drop in the bucket. The list of participants was impressive, some brokerage firms, they would need to give money away, a few corporations that didn't already have fixed philanthropic activities, Vanguard, the left foundation, American Express, who had recently set up a 'socially responsible investment service', the Pilford Fund and the Glassman Foundation, both family operated trusts. Unfortunately the invitation had arrived late and I was looking at it two days later than its arrival. The event was scheduled for tomorrow night. It was a good thing Women's Hotline didn't need the bucks.

I put the post away in two folders and threw the ads in the wastebasket. I looked at the phone and I stared at the ceiling. I thought about the last three weeks, about finding a dead body and a girlfriend who was a workaholic. I thought about all the people who called me for help, about a nervous woman who couldn't live with her mother, about a junkie with a broken window and a shopping list that read, 'bananas, oranges, pears' and who scored in the park. And I felt sorrier for myself than for any of them. I went to bed. The stars on the ceiling irritated me.

Fifteen

I had no problems waking up. I had been dreaming about puppies and roller skates, about golfballs and volleyballs, Foundations and broken windows. The dreams didn't lie, they made a strange kind of sense. I sat up on the edge of the bed, not bothering to bask in the stream of sunlight. I got out Julie Arbeder's address book. I looked under 'N' for numbers. Strange system. Someone who only calls a few numbers, a lot. I found the entry. 'Al, 823-6111.'

I looked at the quilt for a moment, fallen on the floor. I looked at the address book. I had a busy day ahead of me. I ate a light breakfast of coffee and toast. I put a chisel in my handbag and headed my car down to the public library, downtown branch.

It was a big, old fashioned building from the twenties. A hangover from an Egyptian fad in architecture with concrete art deco embellishments, a decorative time, before Bauhaus wiped out the curves with the right angles of steel girders and glass. I went to the pleasant reference room with dark tables, high windows and busy young staff people. I put in my request to see annual reports of private foundations and received the hardbound paper volumes from the young Chinese-American man who put them in my arms. I didn't get much information there, so I walked up the tiled stairway to the 'City History' section and found a good story to read. A quick trip to the microfilm section netted me reams of society columns, where the names were fortunately always in bold type. Upper-class women were often called 'Bootsie' or 'Muffy' by their fellow in-crowders. It was as if the women all became mascots of each other, replicas of their own white poodles. It was a weird world.

But I only found Allison Glassman in the society columns three times. She was from Los Angeles, and had the kind of sunny good looks that usually indicates a sun-fried personality. Wavy, thick blonde hair, she could probably get it to shine with a detergent

84

shampoo. She beamed and dimpled her way through a (group) deb ball and an engagement photo. She was smiling for her wedding photo, even though she was getting married at nineteen years of age. Then she disappeared from the newsprint for three years and started showing up on the sports pages. There she beamed and freckled her way through twelve golf tournaments and she started getting used to holding a trophy. You could almost count the seasons by how Allison Glassman went from lighter to darker as the year progressed. She wore a lot of ordinary wrap around skirts and showed a lot of tanned bicep in sleeveless cotton blouses. She had probably worn out a lot of low cut socks with the little yarn balls at the heel. Her shoes always had spikes. She looked happy in crowds of older women, who looked healthy, rich and wrinkled.

Once a reporter asked her if she wanted to turn pro. She laughed and beamed at the camera. The caption said that she said, 'Actually I'd like to get into volleyball!' That would get her out of the eyelid tuck crowd fast.

Then she dropped out of the sports pages for nine months and appeared again in social dribble column. There was a picture of Allison Glassman and her husband at the Geranium Gala Ball. I never liked geraniums myself and wondered why the upper class would choose such a plebeian flower, but apparently it gave them the excuse to wear a lot of cerise and red. The Sunday supplement photo boys got their pictures printed in four colours, the tans of the rich coming out with too much magenta making them all look like they were suffering from heat stroke.

But Allison Glassman had chosen black and had a lot of it wrapped sideways in silk around her. Her tanned and freckled arms didn't look right coming out of long and inappropriately white gloves. She was stepping down a wide marble step with the help of hubby who cradled her elbow. She had her hair on top of her head but it wasn't sprayed or lacquered. It did its thick, natural thing, springing out of a jewelled band in long wavy strands, ending in hay-like tips. She looked like Tinkerbell hitting *Vogue* magazine. She didn't pull it off.

She was wearing an earring that looked like a big black saucer. She looked about as happy as anyone who was wearing a big black saucer could look. From the stiff way she held her arms you could tell she would be happier holding a nine iron. Stanley Glassman was a different animal. He looked tanned and happy in a dark evening suit, a tux shirt without pleats and with little pearl buttons outlined in silver. He and his blow-dried hairdo took the marble step with grace and power, he looked like a male model, but without the blankness. He didn't so much walk with his wife, as steer her, and his white toothed grin had a clenched look against a sun tan. He looked sinister to my suspicious mind.

That was all for the social history of Allison Glassman. Stanley Glassman was a different affair. There were all sorts of assorted bull and public stunts he was dishing out.

Stanley Glassman was on the board of a university, a public utility and two banks. When he took a piss a city's worth of plumbing probably flushed in deference, his big hit was juvenile drug addicts. He'd found a few fourteen-year-old junkies as causes and used them to whore his way into some articles. Nobody ever got really interested: there aren't so many fourteen-year-old junkies to save and it was a city full of voters getting stupefied on one thing or another themselves. But Stanley got a few years' worth of mileage out of it and no controversy. The press was a one-way ticket into political life, that and all the money behind it. But Glassman hadn't made his big move yet. He was, at the moment, courting the favoured candidate for DA and probably pumping enough money into his campaign to float the interest on the national debt at least a few days. Stories with a human interest angle crept regularly into newsprint, Stanley opening a museum, Stanley heading a project to help ex-cons, even hiring a few himself. According to the article, he'd sprung a woman from a half-way house to work on his personal staff. Mrs Stanley Glassman, Allison, never appeared at these public events. She must have been too busy with the gals, first on the fairway, then at the net. Not so philanthropic, but honest. Meanwhile, a low profile brother, Hugo, was occasionally paraded out. Low Profile never said anything, and had a much flashier way with clothes.

I returned to the current newspaper stacks and found the article about the drowning of Mrs Stanley Glassman. The family secretary described a 'normal family dinner' with 'personal staff in attendance'. Photos showed the body in lurid detail. Allison hadn't dressed for dinner, she was wearing blue jeans and a large white overblouse laid in sad sogginess on the pavement. Apparently family events didn't inspire her to dress up anymore. The maid was in attendance and was being interviewed by the police, the family chauffeur had just arrived to pick up the maid when the photo was taken. Stanley Glassman explained that they were just about to take a little cruise. It was a tragic beginning to their vacation, said the paper unnecessarily, and went on to explain that through various divestitures and mergers in utilities

Stanley's worth had suddenly skyrocketed, making it a better tragedy for the tabloid trade.

The police ruled that it had been death by accidental drowning, after Allison, in a slightly intoxicated condition, had slipped and hit her head on one of the rock pilings just as the yacht was leaving the pier. An autopsy revealed that she was three months pregnant. The sensation rags got a lot of mileage out of her boozed up condition. They could peddle a lot of newsprint on the premise that ordinary people love to know that the rich are miserable enough to get soused up, and fucked up enough to die in spectacularly ugly ways. One columnist on the scene asked Stanley Glassman if he was aware that his wife had been drinking on board the boat. When he declined to answer she went for the jugular by insinuating to the reader that the Glassmans had been having a trial separation. 'If Stanley Glassman ever wants to run for mayor,' she cautioned, 'he'll have to make sure this doesn't become a campaign Chappaquiddick.'

Then I turned to this week's Tuesday edition with the special society section. The recently widowed Stanley Glassman was preparing to entertain in his bereavement.

I returned the microfilm rolls to the desk, gathered my notes and walked back to my car. I had a fifteen dollar parking ticket. The Glassmans were more interesting than I had expected.

I went to a small mom-and-pop hardware store on the way home. A white man showed me a variety of deadbolts. I chose a brass model with a heavy sliding bolt. I also bought a circle bit for my drill to make the correct size hole in the door. Then I had the man sharpen the chisel.

Then I walked next door to a lingerie store. I looked at the stockings: it had been a long time since I had thought about stockings. I kept going deeper and deeper down the aisles, lured on by diamond patterns, clockwork embroidery and the smooth plastic ankles of mannequins. A pair of black sheers with a seam and two small diamond triangles appliquéd on the heel caught my eye. I bought them.

I was anxious to get home, to put on my work clothes and install the lock. I had a lot to think about. I found the step-by-step carpentry work relaxing and conducive to thought. I had just measured out a neat little square where the bolt would slide into, and was making a matching indentation in the wood with the chisel when a red jeep pulled up. I kept on working while Frances took time organising things in her car. She ran rather breathlessly up the stairs to where I stood, surrounded by curls of wood still falling at my feet. I kissed her to be polite and returned to my chiselling.

'I was in the neighbourhood.'

'You don't have to explain yourself.'

'I've been real busy . . .' she started.

I hated her for being so sure of herself, so sure of me.

'Look, Frances. I don't want interludes. I want to decide if we're going anywhere. If we're not, that's the way it goes. But I have a feeling you're stalling me.'

She looked at me with a serious face. I liked her big mouth, which didn't look tight or angry. It looked sad. It wasn't fair that she was enigmatic and acting helpless at the same time. Maybe she had a mother-in-law in a nursing home who was a part time Frankenstein. I longed for the plots of Charlotte Brontë. Someone honked the horn in her car. Competition always rouses something in me. I slipped my hands under her jacket and found a silk shirt. She was wearing a bra. I kissed her on the forehead and some furry fine hair fell down.

'I'm busy tonight. Keep in touch. Call me, okay?' She nodded and walked a few steps towards the car. Then she fumbled in her pocket and walked a few steps back. 'I almost forgot, here's my housekey,' she said, 'I had an extra copy made.' She pressed a key with a blue plastic top in my palm.

She walked down the sidewalk and back to her car and slid in. The car headed back towards town. I watched the two grey shapes inside of it and I allowed two tears to well up into my eyes and fall. Then I wiped them away: I don't like the taste of tears.

I stood chiselling until I had the shape just right for the bolt. I fitted the metal plate over it and marked the spots to drill the holes. After drilling I inserted the screws. It took a comforting amount of pressure to screw them into the wood. I swept up the curls of wood at my feet, and put the tools in the hall closet. Tomorrow I would install the lock section; I didn't think tomorrow would be too late.

Sixteen

I looked at myself that evening in the mirror. I looked at myself too much and too long. If I looked at myself anymore in that mirror I was going to wear it out. I decided I wasn't worried about the funding fair. It would be peopled by well dressed down young execs and badly dressed up social worker types. The execs would hope that it would get over earlier so they could get back to their boyfriend's or girlfriend's for some homemade pasta, check up on what was missed on the VCR and have a last line of the day. They would be bored and look concerned when appropriate. The social worker types would be trying to figure out each and every way they could make their programme fit twenty different foundation's guidelines.

I wasn't dressed for any part. I didn't need to be, and besides the event I was looking forward to was private and I was going to have to earn an invitation. I smoothed down the carefully ironed black dress. It had a beautiful bias cut in the skirt that I had to iron every time I came near it. It was second hand and there was some evidence of fraying which could be concealed with a quick shot of steam. The forties must have been a time when people sent their clothes out to have all those intricate folds and lines steamed into shape. Even the professionals who did the ironing probably had their clothes sent out. It was that kind of time and those kinds of clothes.

But the dress had seen better days: pressing it flat was like trying to iron an origami bird. And the press didn't set; just as I completed one shoulder, I'd be wrinkling the other. Once I had it on I was afraid to sit down in it. I might as well wear a paper envelope.

I put on the black stockings, and some stilettos completed the disguise. When I noticed little black hairs poking through the stockings I peeled them off and sat on the edge of the bathtub and shaved my legs.

I had no conceivable jacket to complete my ensemble. So I shrugged on my leather flying jacket, the battered brown skin feeling appropriately silly above the flaring skirt. I felt like Joan Crawford wearing a dead cow.

Before I went out I checked in the full length mirror on the closet door. The ankle of one stocking picked up light and flashed its diamond triangle at me. I pulled off the jacket and lifted myself up on my toes and twirled. High heels make you do that sort of thing, the feet don't think for themselves anymore. The dress circled out slightly with the movement, the platform shoulders were balanced by my fluffy hair. I saw it was good. I was a girl.

I sauntered to the Plymouth and opened the door. It was a short ride to the gym where the gathering was held. It was a very big, bright room, like a swimming pool filled with fluorescent light. It didn't do a lot for my dress or my makeup. The goosebumps on my arms were defined, but cast no shadows.

It wasn't very busy, the mayor hadn't done a good publicity job. Young, restless execs sat behind folding tables, upholstered in expensive sweaters and designer jeans. I noticed two nervous and tense women from the Battered Women's Shelter hunched over in conversation. Then they walked straight to a table where Jonathan Menck, an activist turned six digit earner, was sitting. I had seen him fronting for one corporation or another, in a philanthropic role. Corporations found the single, WASP faggots well-suited to corporate life. It kept Jonathan in good restaurants and I once ate on his expense account while I was in the press business. It was a good lunch and a pitch I wouldn't take. That was several years ago. He smiled and answered the questions of the women before him. He didn't take his feet off the chair where they were resting. Not a good sign for battered women.

I wondered if I was going to cause any heart attacks among friends, shocked to see me in drag. I turned my foot and the little diamonds on the ankle winked at me. If anyone noticed I would take aim and still any heart attack with a tiny beam of light.

But no one noticed me; they were too busy feeling the axe on their necks while trying to make a good impression. I walked from table to table until I came to the Glassman Foundation. A very bored white woman in her thirties was falling asleep behind a stack of typewritten mimeographed sheets. She had a shiny blonde pageboy and a balanced number of small gold pieces sprinkled on and around an emerald green cashmere sweater set. She looked like an understated Christmas tree. I fiddled with some of her papers.

'Is this a list of the guidelines and procedures for approval?' I asked.

'Yes, the title's right there.' She nodded vaguely in the direction of a lot of fine print.

'But this is three years from now.'

The funds have been dispersed.'

'But your annual report here says that two months ago you had assets over two hundred thousand.'

'The Glassman Foundation doesn't like to do a lot of bandaid social service. They fund something, they fund it to the hilt.' She levelled her eyes at me.

'So if it didn't go into bandaids where'd it go to?'

'To the Blackstone Women's Clinic. Made public three days ago.'

'Gees, I didn't figure Glassman funding any feminist causes,' I began. Christmas Tree sighed. I didn't think she'd care if the money went to support elephants going to the moon. Maybe feminism seemed just as unworthy. She was looking distractedly at her fingernails, they were all the same length, long.

'Must be a drag sitting here on a Saturday night,' I tried.

'Say that again,' she muttered. She was looking at the blonde Jonathan across the room. He'd stopped talking to the Battered Women's Shelter women. It was going to be hard to get this girl's attention in any positive way. I was not only the wrong style, I was the wrong sex.

'Cute guy, isn't he,' I said to her and tried to keep my stomach from turning.

'Yeah,' she drawled. A hit.

'That's Jonathan Menck. He's the president of the Private Fund Foundation. He helps organise and coordinate the different funders. Is the Glassman Foundation part of the PFF?'

'Hmm.' She looked at me, tearing her gaze from the slim figure.

'I'm sure he has some membership forms with him tonight. Why don't you go ask him for one?' She looked at me and then at the table. 'I'll watch your table.'

'I've got to pack up soon,' she said, almost complaining.

'Go on,' I urged. 'I'll start organising some of these papers. Oh, yeah, while you're over there, would you ask Jonathan for his phone number? Tell him Emma Victor lost it.' I managed to catch Jonathan's eye and gave him a wave. I turned to the Christmas Tree woman, 'He's got Roman numerals after his name and he's as available as a dress off the rack.' I didn't mention that his last two lovers had moustaches. 'Go on,' I urged her, 'I was just born to fold tables.'

She stood up and I saw her green and black houndstooth plaid slacks. She had on pantyhose underneath, ending in some suede shoes with golden buckles. She turned, and fluffed her hair and showed me her twitchy ass as she headed for Jonathan Menck. I started being helpful, packing and stacking the various meaningless pieces of paper about the precious Glassman fund that wouldn't cough up any money for three years. But I was glad that they'd given a women's clinic the dough. Maybe the Battered Women's Shelter could apply in three years if they could hold on that long.

I was still being helpful when she returned, and had neatly sorted all the papers into boxes, and piled them on the floor. I was just turning the table on its side when she looked at me a little curiously.

'Do you know the Glassmans?' I asked.

'Yeah, sure.' She was recovering from her encounter and started gathering up the papers. I didn't have much time.

'Well, I've always wanted to see their house.' I waited. I waited because she owed me. 'Listen, I'm an architecture major and I did the walking tour of the city last year with our class. We couldn't get into the Glassman mansion, of course. But did you know that the hallways are hand-painted Mayan Velásquez?'

'Who's that? Oh, never mind,' she said, and bent over some books.

She stopped for a moment and looked at me. 'You can come along and help me unpack this stuff if you want,' she said. 'I'm going to the Glassman house tonight. They're having a party.'

But I already knew that.

I was hoisting the large table up and felt my biceps folding the table legs in. The edge of the table caught my dress and a screw nearly reached into my stockings, but I saw it in time and saved them.

'If you pull up the car I'll put everything in the trunk.' I said.

'The car's not far. Here.' She handed me a cardboard box with more papers and I tried to keep her lacquered nails from grazing along my skin.

'Follow me,' she said and took us to the parking lot.

She led me to a big piece of Lincoln Continental. Her slacks swished as she walked; they must have been lined.

'Nice car.' I was starting to feel a bit like Pollyanna over thirty.

'It's a hunk of shit.' She fluffed her hair back with one hand and turned the key in the lock with the other. She got in and reached over to let me in the other side of the car.

'I'm Emma.' I introduced myself.

'Hi. Patricia.' She drove the car slowly through the streets and a lot of untimed stoplights. We pulled into a rich section of town, that got richer and hillier and greener with every block. She chewed her gum and looked at me once nervously, as if she had just noticed me for the first time. I looked like a weirdo, even to myself, and she was providing the entrée. It was too late to change her mind. Maybe I molested girl scouts in my spare time.

'I just want to see the hallway,' I said. I sounded pathetic even to myself.

'They're having a party,' she said again. So she was nervous.

I had read in the paper that Glassman was having an Auduban Society fundraiser at his mansion. Save the Seals, or something. I remembered Stanley was into utility politics. It was an interesting mix. Price of admission was three hundred dollars and probably a black tie. I didn't have either, although I would have been much more comfortable in a black tie.

'I won't be in the way. Besides, I helped you move that heavy table, and I nearly *ruined* my stockings.' I smoothed out my dress, crossed my legs and flashed my heels at her.

We pulled up into a big driveway and Patricia drove the car around the side of the house to a garage. We unloaded the boxes and the table. I was glad for the exercise, I had left my leather jacket in my car. We walked towards the back door of the house. Even the back had a formal appearance to it. A small porch had been windowed in by leaded glass panels, the back door itself had stained glass and everything was freshly painted. We walked into a bustling kitchen, caterers returning with empty trays and full ashtrays, leaving with a variety of hors-d'oeuvres and cocktails in beautiful crystal glasses. Amidst the bustle one woman was still. She caught us just as we walked through the door.

'Hello.' The tall woman got a stuttered response, coolly lifted her eyebrows and looked at me. Her black cap had a white frill on the top, and her black uniform encased a perfectly proportioned broad framed body. Her hands weren't on her hips, but they might well have been. An arched eyebrow and the large nostrils about did me in. I knew it wasn't kosher to shake hands with the help, but she was an exception.

'I'm Emma. I was helping Patty bring the stuff back from the funding fair.' I reached out my white hand and received her strong brown one in response.

'Emma. Nice to meet you. Have a drink.' The stress was almost on the 'a'. She made her point and then she turned to one of the caterers. 'There's three more trays to get ready. And I want those omelettes ready by twelve on the button . . .'

'But, but,' he stammered and some glasses slid around on his tray. 'No excuses.'

I broke from Patricia and headed towards the swinging door. On the other side I was hit with a wall of heat, smoke and babble. I lifted my heels, turned on my toes, shoulders back and ass in. I pranced into the room.

I heard a lot of foreign language, mostly about wallpaper patterns and extra television sets. I heard bracelets clinking and the high sound of female laughter that had a purpose. I saw one elegant woman in a tube of black silk called a cocktail dress. Her breasts were hoisted high and made a soft pillow with a deep crack in it. She wasn't talking to anyone and she was blowing great smoke rings.

There was a tweedy folky crowd that must have been representing the seals' interests. Their rustic yacht had probably brought them over from Beverly Farms. The men had corduroy sport coats with designer name ties and the women featured early primitive art necklaces on tanned and freckled necklines.

I stopped a waiter and grabbed a drink off a tray. The drink had an olive in it. It was a martini. I don't like martinis and this one tasted like gasoline. They all taste like gasoline. There were some nice paintings and some bad paintings on the walls, where I could see the walls through all the silk and smoke and chatter. The maid was against one wall by a corner, unnecessarily putting one long gladiolus stem slightly to the left of another. It was a peculiar time for the help to be arranging flowers.

I searched the room for the right woman with the right body. And there she was under a painting that showed a scene of some people's idea of a nice Saturday afternoon, chasing little foxes and wearing red jackets. The woman standing next to the painting looked like she did other things on Saturday.

She was on a great side of fifty, with bobbed white hair, a mahogany tan under a simple green silk shift and muscles in her arms and calves that made her a matronly Hercules. She also had a voice like an air raid siren.

She was laughing and pouring wine into the empty glasses of some friends, despite the presence of the help. Her friends were not embarrassed by her, she was just a happy, healthy, rich woman and just on the hysterical side of a happy, healthy, rich middle age. I ditched my martini, found an empty wine glass and lined up.

'Hi, there. Do I know you from somewhere?' She was still smiling and all her dental work looked very white inside a heavy Florida tan.

'It's been a long time since I've been on television,' I said modestly.

'Oh, don't tell me,' she screeched. 'You're Suzi Swanson, you did that vegetable programme on Mona Jenkins' Morning Hour Show. You were great! How come you went off the air?'

'Oh, things just kind of . . .'

'I know, you got married. Happens to the best of us, doesn't it. Well, I love my husband, but sometimes he is a nuisance.' She sipped her wine. 'You remind me of my daughter. Such a cute girl and that girl really has talent. I hope she's coming home for spring break. We didn't see her for the holidays this year, she had a rehearsal or something. But you've got to make practical choices in your life. That's what I keep telling her. Everybody can't be a concert pianist.'

'Or a professional golfer.'

'That's right, why if I'd gotten out on the course thirty years ago – well,' she chuckled. 'I'm too old now, and I've raised a family.'

'Allison Glassman wasn't too old. She was a pretty good golfer,' I said.

'Oh, you knew Allison, did you?' she lowered her voice, 'now that gal could drive a ball down the middle of a fairway like a guided missile.'

'Nice analogy.'

'My son is with the Pentagon.' She showed me her teeth again and two fine little scars in front of her ears. 'Terrible what happened, don't you think?' She raised some plucked eyebrows.

'Yes, really awful. Tell me, did he make her give up golf? The last year, I mean?'

'No, I think he liked it when she played. He used to come down to the club to pick her up. They were a darling couple. I don't know what she was doing with a lot of old biddies like us.' She sipped her wine and rolled her eyes. 'Boy, could that little gal get a ball out of a sandtrap, though.'

'You don't look like an old biddy to me.'

'Well, thanks, dear,' she put her hand on my shoulder and smiled. 'You are so cute, you remind me of my daughter. She's in her third year now at Barnard. She's got a nice boyfriend who's interning at the State Department. I told her to give piano a rest for a little while and get that man! Bring him home to meet your family. But you know how gals are today. You can't tell them anything.'

'Could you tell Allison anything? Did she talk to you about her problems?'

'Honey, I didn't really know her that well. You know, we all have problems with our husbands.' She lowered her voice to a stage whisper, 'and I know Allison was having some problems, but she never really talked about it. She said she was interested in other sports. I guess that was a problem; I can't imagine being married to a guy like Stanley Glassman and then risking it for an outside interest. But you gals are different from our generation. We didn't have anything to prove.'

'Maybe Allison didn't have anything to prove. Maybe she just wanted to do,' I coughed, 'other sports.'

'Hmm, oh yes, listen, there's my husband. Would you like to meet him?' She cocked her head at a man with a very high, very round stomach.

'No, thanks. I just realised I have to talk to Dahlia Meyer; do you know her? Oh, pity. She's a *fantastic* arc welder and I haven't seen her in ages.'

'Well, Suzi, it certainly was *nice* meeting you.' We both burbled goodbye and percolated ourselves back into the party.

'It's Suzi Swanson, the Green Grocer Gal from the Morning Hour, remember?' I heard her screech from a distance. o

Then I spotted Stanley Glassman, recognising him from the society clippings. He was softly chuckling with some other men in grey suits and he put his hand on the back of one, lowered his voice and said something that must have been funny because they all drew back and laughed after he said it. Soon his eyes stopped on a woman in pale blue brocade and he guided her to the group. The grey men turned to the brocade woman and uttered small mouthfuls of compliments. I could see that they were compliments, because the woman looked each man in the face and nodded with the appropriate lowered eyelids. Very soon it was time for her to glide off and the men resumed their low-toned conversation. One man listened closely to Stanley's words. I was looking closely at his head. Stanley Glassman had thick, wavy blondish hair. He probably had styling gel, a blow dryer and heat lamps in an electronic bathroom upstairs. The man listening to him was familiar. He didn't have any hair at all. He was the recently elected District Attorney, ever so liberal. They huddled closer and made cosy mumbling sounds. Another man with small greased hairs arcing over his bald head strolled up to the pair. I heard Stanley make introductions saying, 'It's not often that we get a DA who is so good on social issues.'

The maid glided behind the group and swooped up two crystal martini glasses that were busy making stains on a beautiful piece of mahogany tabletop. She took a tiny white cloth and ran it over the moist rings. Then she very slowly took the moisture off from the bottom of the glass stems. She ran the damp cloth over the finish again. She stooped down to pick up something that she hadn't dropped. Stanley's group edged to the left and she paused to wipe the table again before she returned to the kitchen.

There was an open door behind Stanley; I could see a beautiful library with leather bound books on the walls. Just then a thin blonde woman came to Stanley. From her clothes and actions it was difficult to place her, somewhere between employee, family and close acquaintance. I decided she must be a kind of hired hostess, not to be called 'help' but definitely filling some need, the need that Allison Glassman left behind. Rent-a-Wife. I noticed Stanley had a black armband on, it was his only symbol of mourning, but these are times where symbols and mannerisms of mourning are hollow and the way to express grief is in a workshop. I'd even been to a few myself.

Rent-a-Wife spoke to him in a quiet voice and he placated her with some remark that didn't quite seem to make her happy. She pleaded with silent eyes, the other two men politely looked away, and then he excused himself from the group and went walking off. I watched her progress across through the room. She gave a rather sombre nod to those who noticed and then Stanley quietly captured himself another group. I watched Rent-a-Wife walk towards the hallway. She walked past me into the hall. She wasn't wearing perfume.

I went into the study which had been carefully decorated in early Sherlock Holmes. Everything was plaid, leather and reeked of furniture polish. The party kept spinning outside the slightly parted door, like a wheel that glittered in low and tasteful tones. I walked over to the leather-top desk, admiring all the gold plated utensils handily available to help open letters. There wasn't a scrap of paper, a speck of dust on the waxed surface. I pulled a gold handle and slid open a drawer. Tape, pencils, a bank stamp. So the desk lived after all. The big drawer in the middle revealed a leatherbound chequebook. I opened the cover and started leafing through the history of Glassman's recent purchases including men's haberdashers, two jewellers, the yacht club, a Mrs Rachel Geller for $700 and Sue Martinez for $5,000. Apparently somebody else paid the utility and telephone bills.

I raised my eyes to a photo on the wall. It was a photo of Allison, a studio shot with plenty of the fuzzy dreaminess of rich, teenage adolescence. It was the photo that made the papers before the engagement, before the biceps and the cleated shoes. I looked up to the party and saw Stanley shift from foot to foot in the other room. He was going to conversationally disengage any second. I slapped the cover of the chequebook shut and slid the drawer back. Stanley nodded and turned. I turned too, and saw a door architecturally designed to hide its secret. I stepped into the white tiled interior just in time. I flushed the toilet, and in a moment of inspiration wrapped some toilet paper around my hand a number of times. I pulled it off and it looked just like it held a bloody Kotex, or what the sanitary bags called 'a soiled menstrual napkin'. I was just pretending to have trouble fitting the bloody thing into my purse when Stanley came in the room.

He walked into the room the way you'd expect twenty million dollars to walk into a room. On two legs, and embarrassed at finding a woman emerging from what twenty million dollars would call the powder room.

'Hi, Stanley, how *are* you?' I watched him run through his mental file of faces that don't have names. He glanced quickly at the toilet paper object disappearing into my bag. Then he looked away. I fluffed my hair, a lesson from Patricia. The toilet gurgled and he didn't bother placing me.

'I was just noticing this picture of Allison,' I said, looking at the picture of Allison. 'I'm so sorry, what a tragedy.' I made suitable clucking sounds. 'Why, I saw her just a few months ago at a Junior League Geranium Gala. Oh, and she looked so alive.'

Stanley looked less than alive. 'Falling off the boat, terrible, terrible.' We stood together looking sombre. He gave a polite cough. 'You knew her?' he said.

'Oh, we weren't close. But that night I bumped into her. Just as she was running away.'

'What running away?' He looked at me, and I was happy for the black opaque lampshades which gave the low light and indirectly saved me an expensive tailor.

'From the Geranium Gala, of course.' His face loosened and he let out a longish alcoholic breath.

I went babbling on. 'She said she felt queasy, of course it was the morning sickness. I had it terribly with my first, after that I couldn't eat anything except clams and garlic. I smelled so bad my husband wanted to lock me up in a closet.'

'I'd rather not talk about my wife,' he said. His face was playing a nice game of tennis. First he had me on one side of a court, then he had me on another.

'I'm sorry.' And part of me did feel sorry, the part that wasn't scared.

98

'I didn't catch your name,' he said.

'Stanley, how could you forget?' A buzzer by the phone rang and saved me. Stanley lifted the receiver and I lifted my glass, blinked twice at him and sashayed out the door and back into the party hall, weaving my way through some heavy perfume.

Then I saw Stacy Weldemeer. Of course she'd be in attendance. But would her better, scientific half be there? I doubted it, Frances' occasional leather style might freak out the seal-saving set.

But Stacy was in correct form, a yellow figure etched against a brown velvet curtain. Her hair was brushed to a tawny shine and swung about her shoulders and a mustard yellow mohair sweater. The sweater had diagonal gold stripes running crosswise along her chest. She was wearing mustard yellow satin pants and underneath them were suede dress-up cowboy booties which curled their toes. Stacy Weldemeer, head of the Blackstone Clinic, now receiving two hundred thousand dollars from the Glassman Foundation: I almost felt in awe of her. She had captured a man from the corduroy coat crowd and I shocked myself by feeling so inadequate with a fellow sister, a comrade, a media star, a woman in yellow satin jeans.

She seemed to look quickly my way; it was unlikely that she remembered me from Jonell's party. People who weren't in need of tax shelters probably would remain out of her focus at this party. Unless she mistook me for the TV vegetable girl. I felt the onset of ego deflation. Stacy was there on legitimate business; I was a snoop, coveting her yellow pants and the nerve to wear them.

Meanwhile she had a man in a Ralph Lauren sport coat laughing and waving his leather patched elbows around. They started walking across the room, when Stanley, emerging from the library, almost ran into them. Stanley mumbled something at Stacy and they did a little side-stepping dance. He couldn't figure out the right combination of steps to walk past her. She couldn't figure the right combination to let him pass. They laughed nervously and eventually Stanley strode by. Two people dancing who'd just passed nearly a quarter of a million dollars between them.

I was afforded a glance of Rent-a-Wife walking down the hallway custom-padded with something expensive from the far east. I saw her open a small door at the end, she had to crouch and then I heard the short careful steps that mean a small steep stairway. Just then the maid I'd met in the kitchen sailed past me. She let me know I'd been seen. She unobtrusively watched the caterers doing their thing and returned to the kitchen. She also glanced at the little doorway at the end of the hall. It sure was attracting a lot of attention in a mansion where most of the doors were as big as ping-pong tables. Rent-a-Wife emerged from behind the door looking tired and I watched her put on a new face as she entered the crowd. Her laughter was in the correct pitch and she had a smile to go with it if she needed it. And she did. Glassman sent her a questioning glance and her nod was barely discernible when they both dove back into their respective conversations.

The hallway was empty and anyone could see it if they cared to. No one cared to. The party was stepping up. The voices got louder and the jokes didn't need to be funny any more. I walked to the end of the hallway and opened the small door. There was the dark narrow flight of stairs that I knew would be there. My high heels were tacky, and not the right gear for a quick and subtle descent.

Seventeen

It was a hallway to a basement, but it had been elaborately remodelled. Heating pipes had been covered by wallboard, thick carpeting had been added with etchings on the wall. It was too dark to see what they were about.

At the end of the hallway leading down was another small door and another hallway to the left. It looked scruffier going further down the hallway; that part was a basement that wouldn't pretend to be anything else. I heard soft music coming from behind the doorway in front of me and I knew that was what I'd been looking for.

I opened the door and stepped into a long, narrow L-shaped room. At one end huge plate glass windows had been installed, offering a view of downtown, complete with blinking skyscrapers and the Charles River twinkling in the distance. I could even recognise the John Hancock Tower. It was a wonderful thing to do with $150,000 and a cellar.

The walls had some old-fashioned posters on them, from the days of psychedelic maidens with neon spaghetti hair, running the long expanse of white wall on one side. The floor was covered in thick hand-knotted Persian carpets, the edge of one casually overlapping on to another. The floor threads alone could set someone up in a reasonable retail business for twenty years.

A marble coffee table stood in the middle of the room across from a black leather sofa with red grosgrain piping. It was actually a large glass box. It was closed on all sides, which was a good thing. Inside was a long barren stick and a snakeskin. The skin was twisted around the naked limb. A small mirror was leaning against the limb. A live Black Widow spider was not looking into it.

Over the couch was an MC Escher print. It looked like it was signed in pencil on the bottom, and numbered. It was hung up with thumb tacks. It was the Escher print about the stairway that went up and down at the same time.

The soft music came from a massive stereo installation taking up one end of the wall. Its lights blinked uselessly, noting the high and low pitches in case someone was deaf. Enormous speakers, tilted upwards on both ends of the postcard window, disgorged their sound at a chaise-longue. There was smoke rising from the end of it. The smoke had a sickly sweet smell.

After accepting the view through the window I could see what was reflected in it. There was a man on the couch and my form was clearly visible in the doorway. I closed the door.

'Hello.'

'Hello.' Not entirely disinterested, but disinterested enough not to be surprised.

'I'm a refugee from the cocktail circuit upstairs.' But I knew I didn't need to explain myself, not to what what happening inside his head. I walked toward the couch, looking at the reflection in the window.

'Yeah, a big party.'

'It's just a matter of time before they have fun. Maybe another hour or two.'

'Yeah.' Chuckle. 'Party.'

'Maybe never. Mind if I pour myself a drink?'

'Uhuh.'

'Want something?'

'Uh, yeah, um . . . whisky.'

'Neat?'

'Sure.'

I walked over to a small bar and got out two pony glasses. I filled them each close to the brim. Then I walked over to the chaise-longue and looked at the little man lying on it. I gasped involuntarily. He was beautiful. Tiny golden brown ringlets framed a face that wasn't lean. Two small blue eyes had black lashes thick as a paint brush. A mouth that curved upward without effort, a full lower lip topped by a thin upper one with a notch cut sharply into it. He would have a fat face later, but now he just looked like he floated on a lily pad and spent his days sucking pollen from flowers. He had a Walt Disney complexion, which wasn't getting marred by the sticky black opium he was rolling into small balls and putting in a long thin pipe.

It was Hugo Glassman.

'Want a hit?' he enquired. I held out my hand for the pipe. I sucked on the pipe but blew it all out my nose as fast as I could. I had had opium once. It only inspired me to wash dirty underwear.

'I came here with Patty.'

'Patty's gone. They're all gone tonight. All the little babysitters.' He gazed at me as if he were looking at me through a window, or seven windows, or a two-way mirror.

'You a babysitter too?' He was amused.

'No, and I don't want any babies.'

He laughed, or made a sound that caught in his throat and faded away into some oblivion.

'Well, I always get some kind of babysitter, these days. I keep telling her she can play with my arachnids, but somehow she hasn't taken me up on the offer,' he laughed. 'She's scared.' He looked at me. 'You're cute.' He twisted a small golden curl around a finger.

'I'm old enough to be your aunt. And you've got nicer eyelashes.'

He rolled his head off the couch on to my lap. I was sitting on the floor so it was a rather awkward thing for him to do, but his long supple neck didn't seem to care, his head just sort of bobbed on the edge of the chaise-longue. I lifted the large curl-covered object and placed it back on the satin pillow.

'I want some other music.'

I got up and found some digital recordings but I didn't know how to put them on the state of the art digital turntable. Hugo wasn't watching. 'How do you work this thing?'

He raised his stubby body from the couch and put his feet on the floor, I envied his aqua silk pyjamas only briefly. He looked at the carpet for a long minute. Apparently it wasn't speaking to him. Then he stood up, and balanced his short torso on two stocky legs and stumbled towards the wall that housed the system. His pudgy rounded fingertips pushed the glass cover off the turntable and he threw the digital disk on the turntable. Then he flopped back on to the satin couch.

'I'm going to sleep now,' he declared. Then he turned his head and looked at me. 'Sure you no babysitter?' His brows knitted a second and then a small stream of drool left one side of the rosebud mouth.

'Honey, babysitting you would be like watching TV. It looks like life, but it's not.' But he was already in that funny land where you stand up and walk around in your own dreams. I prodded him.

'I'll come back tomorrow night. I'll bring a nice present with me. We'll have a real party.'

'Party,' he mumbled like an echo.

'We won't let any babysitters in, will we?'

The room had a sliding door through the plate glass windows but it was locked. I walked through the Persian padded room. There wasn't a key around anywhere. The Black Widow spider noiselessly followed my shadow from within her glass cell. I turned off the light. I walked into the little hallway and followed it away from the stairs. This hallway had wainscotting and more historical etchings. I could see they were of long gothic churches. This led into a real basement with cement walls and an honest looking washtub. The washer and dryer nearby were not new. The very rich don't need fancy appliances and showplace kitchens. They never use them. A small door led to a garden. I tried it but it was locked. There was a small skeleton key hanging on a nail next to it. The key was rusty and dirty. The door was jammed in its frame and when I got it open it pushed a wedge of dirt and leaves in an arc pattern on a cracked tiled patio outside. I hung the key back on the nail and pushed the door tightly closed.

I shuffled leaves and dirt back against the bottom of the door and erased the circular mud pattern from the tiles.

It was foggy and damp outside. The nylon dress provided no warmth and my bare arms were getting goosebumps. I felt sorry I had worn stiletto heels as I sank into the marshy lawn. The panty hose were beginning to sag and the crotch felt like it was around my knees. I tried to pull them up by the waistband but the crotch remained stubbornly low. My legs were getting shorter with every step. I looked back at the house and saw coloured shapes moving against the steamy windows. Hugo's downstairs apartment showed only the small digital lights of his stereo, scampering back and forth in a slitted line cut out of the fine stainless steel. It wouldn't do to be found absorbing the lawn moisture, so I hurried toward the street through the mist. I took a last look back at Hugo's room and saw a light go on and a tall figure walk to the chaise-longue. The light went off again. I stood on the lawn and thought about all the rich people upstairs and the goofy cherub downstairs, taking a one-way trip into oblivion. The moisture from the lawn was soaking through the panty hose to my ankles. Suddenly I felt a round wetness poking into my legs. I turned and saw a large golden retriever nuzzling my ass. I bent down to say hello, but it bobbed its head and ran away. Its long droopy tits meant that it had had puppies not long ago.

I tried to remember the direction we'd come from in getting to the Glassman's. The neighbourhood only offered big green fronts of shrubbery and iron gates. I arbitrarily chose to walk up a hill, at least that would make me warmer. So, I set off in my best hiking attitude, the mist sneaking under the nylon dress and the panty hose crotch sinking lower and lower.

I saw a car and decided to try and hitch to the local bar. Whenever local became appropriate. But the car turned around a corner and drove in the opposite direction.

It was a long unpleasant walk. Vehicles would drive by on the bumpy brick roads and my presence on the sidewalk usually caused the drivers to speed up. I got a good view of rich townhouses with brass letter slots. The houses became narrower and narrower and I was cold and shivering by the time I reached a commercial street. A package liquor store was handily situated at one of the boundaries of the neighbourhood, where the hired help could bring in alcoholic supplies and the rich wouldn't have to cross into the more dangerous zones of the city. It was unhandily closed thanks to Boston's stringent liquor laws. I would have to settle for a late night grocery store, ablaze with lights and security systems, a commercial fortress that sold milk in the wee hours, or what to Bostonians would be wee hours. I thought again about moving to California someday and approached the late urban trading centre.

I pushed open the heavy plate glass door and saw a nervous middle-aged woman behind the counter. She had a video screen, reflecting my damp black nylon presence with a face shape above the dress. She probably also had a gun underneath the counter; I would if I were her. I asked her if she would call a cab for me. She looked at me with suspicion, but how suspicious could someone calling a cab be? She picked up the phone and didn't look too close at my goosebumped arms, for which I was grateful.

The cab arrived and I slid quickly into its warm interior. The driver wanted to make conversation but I wasn't in the mood. He grouchily shrugged at my silence. We arrived in the parking lot outside the gymnasium where the funding fair had been and I had him take me to my car. I was glad to get into my mobile home. I sat in the front seat of my car and cried, I'm not sure why.

Then I drove through the city and back to my house. I looked at my front door and grasped my car keys in my fist like a clenched ball with metal prongs. I arrived at the door without event. I went upstairs and got some vanilla ice cream out of the freezer. Then I poured cognac over it. I walked into the living room and turned out all the lights. I lit the liquor with a match.

As the flame went out the room darkened and then I saw some little lights on the hillside, opposite my house. It reminded me of the John Hancock Tower, the little man on the couch. Where had I heard the John Hancock Tower mentioned before?

105

My mouth went dry. Sandy's dream, the hunchback and his slimy gums. The John Hancock Tower and my introduction to the little man. Sandy had heard my name. Victor. Victor Hugo. The Hunchback of Notre Dame.

I split the melting ice cream with Flossie who stayed behind to lick the bowl. I went to bed but I didn't go to sleep. I laid awake and wondered if anyone was using their bones for telephones. I was spooked to the tits.

Eighteen

Sunday morning promised a better day. For one thing the sun was shining and you could feel the whole city waking up to enjoy the breezy Boston Sunday. I stayed home and did a load of washing and hung billowing sheets in the fresh air to dry. It was hard to believe in opium-smoking boys in silk pyjamas who put original Escher prints on their walls with thumbtacks. The spider hadn't bothered me.

I looked at the blue sky, its few clouds were racing across the surface. I took a chance and drove to Frances' house. I walked up the many cement steps to her front door. I rang the doorbell. The red jeep was not in sight.

I heard skipping footsteps down the stairs, I hoped the skip was for me. She opened the door and she didn't act disappointed. The ends of her wispy hair met the looped ends of a fluffy white bathrobe, like two species of velcro that couldn't mate with each other.

She kissed me and left her mouth open, dusky and sour with sleep.

'You could do that some more,' I said.

'You wouldn't want to; I'm expecting company.'

'Oh, anyone I know?'

'Keeping up on your feminist health care public relations?'

'The health care part is okay, the other part bores me to death. Here, I brought some orange juice.' I took a jar out of the paper bag and set it down on the counter of the little kitchen. She had a new collection of dirty dishes and the remains of a salad that looked a few days old. I hoped she was a vegetarian, otherwise her messes would not only look bad.

'I also brought croissants.'

'Ah, the gentrification of our fair city,' she sighed. 'French bakeries, quiche corners, Italian coffee shops . . .'

'We can almost pretend we live in Europe.'

'With the raise in rents I could pay for a trip to Paris every year.'

'But you want croissants more often than that.'

She walked over and hugged me. I stuck the croissant in her mouth, and made a small tray with butter, saucers, jam, and I put the juice in two wine glasses.

'So, what kept you busy last night?'

'Same thing that's going to keep me busy tonight,' I said.

'Guess I better not ask for tonight off.'

'Unless you have something better to do.'

'I don't.'

We sat there like two grinning fools over our orange juice. She looked at me curiously; she was also busy chewing on her croissant. I thought they were a little hard.

'Keeping yourself busy?' I enquired.

'Business is booming, couldn't be better.'

'I assume you mean curing crabs and dealing out diaphragms.'

'Don't knock diaphragms. I could never get one in. Besides that's not the business I mean.'

'Fill me in.'

She sat back, folded her hands and looked like the great scientific mother of us all. Who knows, perhaps one day she would be.

'We're making babies upon babies upon babies down there.'

I sat there wondering what it must be like for her; presiding at the moment of conception with a stainless steel tool (what *did* they use anyway?), shooting sperm into women all week. It made me jealous, but I didn't know of which party.

'Some of our babies aren't even . . .' she stopped suddenly as the door opened. Stacy Weldemeer walked in with her big white teeth. She had let herself in with a key at the bottom of the stairs. She was wearing tweed pants ironed to an unbecoming shininess. It reminded me of used cars and the people that sell them.

Her face wasn't visible, but her carroty curls took up a lot of space as she walked right past me to Frances. She leaned over and gave her a kiss, the details of which I couldn't see. I did notice a tattoo of a rose drawn among the freckles upon her ankle. A convent education probably made Stacy a very discreet and esoteric lover. She squeezed some extra flesh on Frances' hip. Then Stacy Weldemeer turned to me.

'Hi, I'm Stacy,' she announced. I had the feeling that she wasn't happy with my presence, but she'd arranged her face into what we all hoped we'd get, pleasing lines.

'You're Stacy Weldemeer,' I corrected her. 'Anyone who can take on Luke Kelly in front of six million late night viewers becomes well known. Anyone who takes him on in a bad mood and wins becomes a media hero.'

'Well, it's not so difficult, really. The man's underwear is just too tight.' I laughed at the line she'd probably said a thousand times since she'd made her debut on the tube. In front of six million viewers she'd made Kelly not only look like the silly little boy he sometimes is, but she'd kept him on her side too. Stacy looked at her feet, which ended in maroon leather loafers with little tassels.

'We've met once, at a party,' I reminded her of our introduction, but she was distracted. Surely the Glassman affair had wiped out all vestiges of Jonell's humble bash. Only her fans showed up there.

'Oh, yes?'

'You called me Nancy Drew.'

'Did I?' she cocked her head and reached up to twirl a red curl around her fingertips, thought better of it and stuck her hand in her pocket. She turned her back to me and was busy with something on the counter.

'I hope you didn't take offence,' she said. 'What were you doing that I would be calling you Nancy Drew?' She put something down that jangled on the counter, took off her tweed jacket with the leather piping and put it on the back of the chair.

'A friend of mine died last week; I've been looking into the circumstances around her death.'

'It takes a long time to accept loss,' Stacy counselled.She leaned over and filled a small orange plastic glass with water from the tap.

'She was shot on the street,' I said.

Stacy took a long sip and looked at me through the orange wavy plastic and swallowed. 'Frances, we should open your schedule to allow time for you to distract your grieving friend here.' Then she put down the glass and beamed a smile at both of us from behind her capped teeth.

'What did you say your name was, again?'

'I didn't. It's Emma. Emma Victor.' She smiled. I smiled. We were both as false as two overworked airline stewardesses in first class under the gaze of a supervisor. And our styles were alarmingly similar.

'Look, I don't want to disturb a meeting . . .' I made leaving noises and I thought about Frances' bathrobe.

'Oh, that's not necessary,' Stacy smiled. 'I just came by to discuss our work schedule for next week, Emma.' Repetition of first names was public relations course 1A.

'Gee, you guys have a schedule? I thought you just camped out down there at the baby farm.' They turned around together and looked at me. Then they walked outside.

I walked over to the kitchen and looked at the dirty dishes. Frances had also left burnt out matches here and there. I saw a cluster of keys. I watched Frances and Stacy on the little terrace outside the glass windows. The sunlight bleached Frances' face; she was smiling. Stacy gave her a managerial pat; they had a mutual laugh and walked in.

'And Stacy, for Christ's sake, let me know where you can be reached. Use your secretary and your answering machine; half the time I can't find you when I need you.' Frances put her terry cloth arm through Stacy's, her sweet terry cloth arm.

Stacy nodded an assent, glanced at her watch without numbers and seemed to look into a future filled with important appointments. Her work here was finished. She quickly said goodbye to us but she didn't forget to smile. She picked up her jacket from the chair and I saw why she'd taken it off. Her tweed sportcoat with the leather piping was very thick. Her blouse showed a large, wet arc at the underside of her right arm. Stacy O'Malley Weldemeer was sweating like a pig. She turned and walked down the stairs. I heard the front door close.

I turned to Frances.

'Now where were we; talking about babies.' But I was thinking about what was underneath that robe. I walked towards her and hoped she wouldn't resist my untying the belt. She didn't. She opened the front of it herself and everything that was underneath it was mine, at least for a while. I backed her over to the couch and laid her gently on the beige upholstery. I felt her breath on my earlobe afterwards.

'Do I have any competition?' she asked.

'If you mean my date tonight, I wouldn't call a baby boy in silk pyjamas any competition.'

'Oh,' she relaxed her blowing and fussing, 'Babysitting.'

'More or less. But don't forget babysitting is at least as important as making babies. When's our next night off?'

'Tomorrow night.'

'Great. Get the okay from great white mother administrator?'

'You betcha. You don't like Stacy, do you?'

'I don't know. I don't want to give her any big chance. After all, she has the keys to your house.'

'Oh, *that*.' Frances laughed and hugged me, pressing her chest against mine. 'You don't have anything to worry about, Emma dear. Science and funding may sleep together, but only figuratively. You

110

might say, Stacy's just pimping for me, finding the money to buy all those test tubes.'

'And finding all the johns to fill them up. She gives good public relations; it's a style I don't appreciate, but I guess someone has to do it,' I conceded.

'Well, I get a good salary and I don't have to put up with any male bullshit, or any hospital bullshit. I can more or less write my own ticket.'

'Does Stacy help you write it?'

'Honey, she pays the fare. Don't forget, there is a terrific need for good donor screening, services for single women and lesbians who want to have children. Several clinics have even asked Stacy to take over as director.'

'Sounds right up her alley and right up her style. Stacy McSperm,' I said. Frances laughed, 'Well, I told her no go. If she starts a franchise I'm taking a hike. It's hard enough trying to get hold of her as it is. So she's just going to stay with Blackstone.'

'You can put a leash on Stacy Weldemeer?'

'Yeah, I've got a leash. And I can tighten it up anytime I want. We have some different ways of doing things, different styles, and I want to make sure that she doesn't interfere with *my* style.'

'Well, I like your style as much as I dislike hers, and that's a lot.'

'You won't find me on any TV show,' Frances soothed me.

'Good, keep it that way, please.' I said. I wasn't so much against public relations, but it was the way that Stacy Weldemeer vacuum-sealed our lives and sold it on the tube with her cherry lips. It wasn't going to do anything for Harriet Housewife's terror when she sees a nice, muscled woman putting the squeeze on her similarly built mate. But this wasn't a moment to think about that.

I offered her my mouth and we moved to the bed and spent another hour there. I fell drowsily asleep this time, the thrilling narcotic feeling of falling, and again falling, replaying itself as I balanced on the edge of a light slumber. Suddenly I realised it was sunset and jumped out of bed.

'Yow, I'd better get moving.'

'So soon, I don't have to get to work for another two hours,' she pulled me towards her, eyes closed, childishly demanding.

'Hey, you're not the only one with plans, remember? I'm a career girl too.'

'Yeah, babysitting.'

'Uh-uh. Be a good feminist now, or Ms Weldemeer will get you for being politically incorrect.'

'Stacy's not like that. What do you have against her anyway?'

'Just her style, I guess . . .'

'I think you're jealous.'

'You've told me I have no reason to be.'

'No, but you have your own reasons.'

'Oh, yeah. Tell me then.'

'Admit it, Emma. The Hotline job has you bored to tears and sitting at a desk all day long feeling helpless. You rag on about Monica and Stacy but I think the problem's with you. It's not in your character to do social work.'

'Oh, yeah? Tell me about my character. I wish somebody would.'

'Emma, I know you well enough to know you want action, and drama. You don't have that and you don't even feel like you're getting something done at the Hotline.'

'So?'

'So, it must feel like a real change from doing PR in a time of daily demonstrations, sorting through news briefs, organising press conferences. You're tied to a phone, and Stacy Weldemeer is shaking up the world. Of course you're jealous.'

'Oh, is Weldemeer shaking up the world?'

'Yes. She has energy, ambitions, plans and connections. She's really doing something.'

'And I'm not.'

'I didn't say that. You did.'

My words hung in the air accusing me. For a moment I didn't like myself, or Stacy Weldemeer or even Frances. But I would get over it. I'd have to.

Frances was tickling my back with long strokes of her warm fingertips and her eyes said something loving even though my bad character was showing.

'Well, I really have to go,' I said after a while.

'Babysitting? You really have to go *now*?' I'd never heard a doctor whine.

I kissed her goodbye and told her to come to my house at eight the next evening and I'd make dinner. I walked down the front stairs and closed the door carefully, just like Stacy Weldemeer had done.

Nineteen

Hugo Glassman was too unpredictable, if not still too stoned, to take into consideration in my clothes formula. Not to mention his taste. So I dressed for myself. I had some deep plush old rose corduroy pants. They had another year to go before the colour would look trite and silly as it went out of style. I pulled over a darker pink sweater. It was meant to be long, but I tucked it in my pants and bloused it out. Tucked in things feel more in control. Then I put on some dark grey suede short boots. They had a fluffy connotation, but were impervious to mud and gave great traction. So I was warm, treaded, pink and in control. Ten years ago I would have looked real pretty; now I had lost that blank attractiveness. I had experience, three nice wrinkles and a sprinkle of grey hair to prove it.

I looked up the Glassman residence just to be sure of the address and drove over the bridge. I wasn't quite sure how I would find out what I wanted to know; that was because I didn't know what I wanted to find out. I wouldn't know until I found out what it was. And that's the way my head was working when I parked half a block past the mansion.

I walked over the lawn which still mushy. It was a good lawn, carefully seeded with diacondra and it felt like an evenly textured sponge, making kisses and little sucking noises on the bottom of the crepe soles of the grey suede boots.

The big plate glass windows upstairs were blank and still, no cultivated laughter responding to cultivated jokes. In the basement window I saw the tiny blinking lights that meant music.

I reached the small patio and the little laundry room. The door was still unlocked. I lifted the handle up as I pulled it out so it wouldn't scrape on the tiles below. I walked into the laundry room and out into the adjoining miniature hallway.

It looked the same as it had the night before. A slow bass beat was pounding behind Hugo's door and the hall runner still looked exotic and expensive. I thought I heard a noise at the top of the stairs, and I ducked into a little alcove. The noise went away, but I noticed the alcove had a small point-topped door, like a monastery, or *The Secret Garden*.

I opened it and met some musty air and looked down and out on to a moonlit stretch of lawn in an enormous bay window at the end of the room. The trees twenty feet behind it were dark green hands waving to me in the moonlight. I walked in and tried to close the door more softly than my heart was pounding.

After twenty feet of highly polished parquet floor three steps descended to a sunken bedroom, with a bed, a Queen Anne writing table and three large bay windows. There was a small French door set into the large paned window on the right side of the room. A large double bed faced the garden and the big expanse of lawn bordered by tall rhododendron bushes with lots of big oval leaves. A blackish bedspread was pulled tightly around the bed, so tightly around the mattress that no sheets or blankets could get in between.

A Chinese vase lamp with a white pyramid shade sat next to the bed on a little spindly endtable. I walked towards the windows. Going down the three stairs was like walking into the moonlit garden. No other lights reflected on the foliage, the room was a wing off the back of the house, far away from everything, except the impish Hugo.

I went back up the stairs to a series of louvred doors, suggesting a long shallow closet. It was a long shallow closet. Three bulging garbage bags stood to one side. Expensive clothes were trying to escape out of them. I spread the two hinged doors and tripped on an automatic light in the wall of the closet. The closet was empty except for a pink plastic garment bag. Inside was a black silk dress. Below the garment bag stood a pair of battered moccasins, with enough red and blue plastic beads left to describe a stylised eagle. Brown oval heel prints had been worn into the suede soles and I realised I was seeing the negative space of dead feet. I closed the door and counted to twenty seeing little white spots before my eyes. It was Allison Glassman's closet.

I closed the door and the light went off after a moment. The moonlit trees came back through the window and waved some more as I turned and went through the narrow pointed door and out into the hall. The hallway looked bright and cheerful and like a wonderful place to be.

Then a door at the end of the hall opened and there was nothing left to do but walk towards it.

Hugo stood there with an impish smile. He outdid his lounging

114

outfit of the previous evening. Tonight was serious relaxation. He was electric blue and all silk.

'Why, hel-l-l-o,' he said, and stuck out an outstretched palm in my face and slowly brought all his fingers back one by one, to motion me in.

I heard a sudden high whistle sound from behind him, and a little sigh. He stared into my eyes like they were long, dark tunnels. Another sigh ended in a soft whistle and I realised he was playing a tape of whale and dolphin sounds, or words, or language. Some simulated wave effects rushed through the room as I walked in.

'So, we're standing tonight,' I said, relieved that he wasn't throwing me out on my ear.

'Yes, we're standing, and we're floating, and we're going ... do you know where we're going?' He cocked his head, and some porpal intelligence from a speaker tried to give us the answer.

'We're going to sit down and look at my party favours.' I tried to meet his gaze but I was a wipe out facing the cosmic steam roller. He motioned me further in to the L-shaped room, which was choking on its own atmosphere. Someone had let Hugo play with the family silver. He had a dozen beautiful art deco silver candelabra thrown around the room. If they had been his mother's then she had ridden the crest of the wave of early modern high-style doo-dads. What a legacy! Meanwhile, candles were stuck haphazardly in them, the wax floating down all over the streamlined cantilevered stems. A stylised nude held one black candle aloft, it dripped over her arm, an oval bicep. A flock of seagulls screamed and I took in a mouthful of incense.

I chose the leather couch, next to a busy bookshelf and behind the spider, to sit on. I was afraid of sitting by the huge windows showing the skyscrapers and the river. I might just float out. Also the chaise-longue and opium pipe were over there and I wanted Hugo to maximise his vertical state for as long as possible.

'So you want to know what is a wonderful journey? I have the ingredients right here.' He took a draw off a long thin cloisonné pipe decorated with serpents and other tangly things. I put the long thin metal tube in my mouth and I took a draw on it too. I expected to draw in the opium again, but the rousing sweet flavour of hashish filled my lungs. In a minute I felt Hugo's unnerving presence as clear as an air raid siren. I also felt the precise texture of the upholstery of the couch.

'I'm going to get us a drink.' I got up and walked over to the little bar. The bottles were gone and the cupboard underneath it was locked.

I turned around. Hugo was right behind me. I smelled his complicated breath on my shoulder.

'It's the babysitters.' He raised his eyebrows and put his finger to his lips. He motioned me back to the couch, walking backwards and crouching down, with his finger outstretched.

'You're a real Marcel Marceau,' I said and tried for a laugh. He put the pipe in my mouth and lit it again. He was a swell little gent. We looked at his spider, and I tried to think about breaking the ice. I didn't have to come up with any solutions. Hugo bent over a small ebony box and pulled out a folded square of paper and poured some powder out on the glass top of the coffee table. He handed me a little golden razor blade and I chopped the lumpy powder up quickly, leaving many small rocks behind. I handed the glass tube to Hugo who took it with a raised eyebrow and a genuinely happy smile, like a boy with his first puppy.

He did a line, I did a line and then we toked again. We sat back and looked at the ceiling for a while, the whales sang their speeches about life underwater. I was hoping the coke would tone down some of the fish eye effects of the hash. I busied myself with looking about the room.

I saw a wooden box, mahogany with rosewood inlays on the bookshelf. A brass edging separated the different kinds of wood: it looked like an antique humidor. A piece of paper stuck out of it.

I raised my eyes at Hugo. I pointed to the box and looked at him with a questioning gaze. He returned it and we mock tiptoed across the room to the box. It was a classy antique with a glassy French hand finish. I opened the lid with silly ceremony and saw a bunch of photos. The first was of a cart and a boy sitting on it in front of a big fluffy rose bush.

'It's big brother. From upstairs.'

He hissed, and raised his eyelids so that his irises floated in white.

'Big brother is watching you, isn't he?'

'Yes, he is!' Hugo suddenly relaxed and giggled for a minute. I thought I was going to lose him entirely to the outer limits when I found a photo of a young woman and someone that looked like Hugo in more conscious times. He had a guitar in his hand. I started leafing through more photos and began to confirm the story that was shaping up in my head. The flower child of the picture grew up, tried living in the forest, succumbed to a managed social life. The boy kept his silly grin; I was still looking at it. Hugo glided over to a hookah pipe sitting on a low shelf.

The bookshelf had an assortment of magazines and drug

116

paraphernalia, bongs, rollers, elaborate sifters and snorters, and a small band of animal wind-up toys, comprised for the most part of monkeys with cymbals. The higher-up shelves sported more dust. I walked over and got a better view of accumulated grime clinging to the fake fur of the cymbal-toting primates.

Just then I heard a buzzer and Hugo went to a small speaker box set into the wall.

'Would you like something to drink?' the little box said. I wondered if little boxes could hear as well as speak. I felt my bowels move; I put my thumbnail in my mouth, it was thick. Clearly Hugo was being monitored, if not being allowed to bury himself alive in the L-shaped room.

Hugo looked at me. 'Bloody Mary,' I said.

'My friend would like a Bloody Mary, and I would like a, let me see, I want a rum and coke. Yes, that's just what I want,' he reassured himself and went back to sucking on the pipe.

'So, you're alone in the basement these days.'

'Yes, Hugo's alone.' And the statement made an echo in his brain, because it showed on his face which melted a little bit at the corners of his eyes. It was the truest thing I could think of about the little man in the electric blue pyjamas. He was very much alone.

Whatever truth or sanity had entered the room became abruptly reinforced by the maid coming downstairs with a pewter tray and our drinks. It was the same woman who had let me into the kitchen at the party. She professionally registered no surprise; she looked somewhere around the area of my knees, but I knew she knew just who I was, and she didn't like it. I had slipped sideways into the upper class and it was meant to be as closed off as the stairway in the Escher print. She turned and walked briskly out of the room. I heard the swish of her black nylon skirt, her shapely, sturdy legs encased in support hose and sensible shoes.

'Thank you, Vanessa,' said Hugo as she closed the door.

'And you were alone.'

'Yes.' He turned to me. 'But I've been alone for a long, long time. I only have my little furry friend.' He looked at the spider and tapped the glass. The spider scurried about the branch on its bent legs. It was nearly the size of a fist. I sipped my drink a little faster. Hugo passed me the pipe.

'Yes, Allison.' He sighed like her name was a new way to smell flowers. 'Allison just wanted to have a good time. Dancing, laughing, playing.' Hugo had an expression like a cross between Timothy Leary

117

and Bambi. 'She didn't care about anything but *love*.'

'So I gathered. Uh, just what kind of love was it?'

He laughed and winked. 'Love with her sweet friend.'

'On a black quilted bedspread across the hall?' I asked.

'Yes!' he twinkled. 'They were lovely ladies.' The devil crept into his voice.

'Did you watch?' I teased.

'Watch?' A flurry of giggles escaped his mouth and ended with a spot of drool. He sucked it in. 'I want to see everything that's beautiful. But I didn't need to watch. I could feel it through the air, through the hallway, through the *doors*!'

'Was she here very often?'

'No, and they left. They left and left me all alone. The main man came home, and boy did the shit ever hit the fan. He was really, really uptight. And when big brother gets uptight nobody messes with him, man. The guy is a mind-fucker. Allison split. She couldn't deal with all the heavy, hostile vibes. And he didn't go for that. The man is really bad news when he's sore about something. And he had his heart set on keeping her and having the perfect blue blood family. Of course, the blood in our family is more on the orange than the purple side of red.'

'And *your* blood must be checkered,' I said and he laughed. I took a breath.

'So, Allison moved out of the garden room. When did this happen?'

'Oh, a long, long time ago,' Hugo said, but I had the feeling that time and space were totally elastic dimensions for the little man in the blue lounging pyjamas.

'Love,' he said, 'has its limitations.' Hugo tapped the glass and the black widow spider jumped around. 'When somebody gets possessive everybody gets uptight and then the one who is loved just gets sque-e-e-e-ezed,' Hugo leaned over the glass cube and made a little tap dance with his fingernails. Then he leaned back and took a puff and checked up on the ceiling which still appeared to be there. He uncurled his fingers from around the cloisonné pipe. 'But I didn't get her on to that boat. He did it and he freaked her out. I didn't do it. Mind games, mind fucking, *that's* what it was all about.'

'Sounds like a really heavy trip,' I said, checking up on the ceiling. 'There must still be a lot of bad vibes.'

'Yeah, a lot of bad vibes. Heavier vibes than I even thought. People are *still* playing games.' He tapped the glass more slowly and the spider jumped on to a higher limb and then fell down swinging from its own line. I felt a little sick. Hugo looked like he was heading for a heavy fade.

118

'Hugo,' I put my hand on my hip and slid my fingers into the pocket of my pants. It was a tight squeeze these days. 'Hugo, if you feel like you want to talk about the games, if you can remember anything about what happened to Allison and her friend, you can call me.' I put a folded piece of paper in his hand. Then I took it out of his hand and put it in his pocket.

'You can always call me and tell me what happened, okay. About Allison and her friend, that night on the boat.'

'I don't want to talk about it,' his forehead creased and he looked panicked. 'Allison was a good person. Allison loved me. She thought I wouldn't hurt her. She knew that I wouldn't hurt her. She was one of the Real People.'

'What happened, Hugo?'

'Aw, leave me alone. I don't want to talk about it. Everybody is into this, talk, talk. I just want to go where there's nothing happening. I'm really getting bummed out by all this . . .' he was whining.

'Is big brother running more of his games?'

'Oh yeah, and if there's anyone big brother is running his games on, it's me, these days. He runs me.'

'How does he run you?'

'You want to know? You want to know what my brother wants to do to me? I'll tell you. He wants to send me on a little trip to the funny farm.' Then Hugo didn't say any more. He reached into a deep pocket in the harem pants and pulled out a clear glass vial with a browning powder in it. He scooped up a dose, put a little spoon to his nose and sent it upwards. He passed me the bottle and I put a small amount on a fingertip and tasted it.

'PCP?' I asked. He seemed to nod. Animal tranquilliser. The boy was a real garbage head. I drank some more of my Bloody Mary.

'Gees, you shouldn't take that stuff,' I said. 'Why slaughter your brain cells?' But I was also feeling badly about my own brain cells. Hugo didn't say anything in reply but the whales sang a long protracted chorus and I watched his eyes taking an express train to nowhere.

'Okay, I have a game,' I said. 'Say ninety-nine.'

'Ni-i-i-ine-ty ni-i-ine,' he rolled the words over his tongue.

'Now what comes next?'

'Ninety-eight,' I said after a moment.

'What next?' I waited. 'Ninety-seven.' I waited. 'And then . . .' Ninety-six, ninety-th-, ninety-th-, ninety-two.' He looked at me. 'Shit, I can't count!' He said and sort of laughed. Sort of.

I started counting the skyscraper lights myself. I got to see his eyes looking scared just as the lids closed over them.

'Well, who needs to count when you've got babysitters, memories and all this dough?' But I asked the question of no one. Hugo was busy with the ceiling again. I shook my head and my brains sloshed from side to side. The whales agreed; the sounds became as clear as water, the meaning underneath them was easy and I remembered without question that whales had higher intelligence.

'You really shouldn't use that stuff,' I said again as I watched him feed his nose. Then I thought about the PCP murderer now sitting on death row. Came down the stairs and offed his parents with a shotgun and doesn't remember a thing.

Then the porpoises had their say and the room got three shades greyer. I tried to make out the candles, the streamlined lady holding her flame, but everything was getting blurry. I fell far back into the couch and found the cherub curling into my lap. He put a hand on my breast.

Then a dark smoke crept in on all sides of the picture of blue boy, the spider and the skyscraper lights blinked out one by one. Greyness filled everything in and then it was total blackness.

Twenty

There's only one thing I can remember from that long, heavy night. At one point two cool white hands seemed to peel my clothes off, fluttering along the log that was my body.

The next morning I woke naked under some blankets. It was not a particularly nice way to wake up. Some very important wires had been crossed in my brain. I saw a spider jump around, I made out the John Hancock Tower under full sunlight but couldn't connect them together. I knew what I saw, and in another department of my brain I knew why I was there, but the two things had nothing to do with each other.

I had a pounding headache which made being unconscious the only solution. My hands were little strangers; but the thing that was my body hadn't been raped: I felt lean and untouched. I looked over to a chair and saw my clothes neatly folded. The sweater was folded flat, the pants hung across the back of the chair. I stood up slowly, feeling exposed to a thousand skyscraper windows, but I was alone in the room. Then I touched my toes, which was a big mistake. A thousand hammers beat under each temple. So I sat down. After a moment I dragged on the clothes from the chair. I looked around, but I hadn't brought anything else with me; I'd left my driver's licence and wallet in the car. The cool hands would have known me only as a stranger.

I entered the dark little hallway and found the small stairs leading upwards. Placing one foot in front of the other I slowly changed the altitude of my brains. A quick turn out of the little door and I pushed the swinging kitchen door open. Vanessa was by the sink making endless hors-d'oeuvres out of silly little pieces of food. She was busy with bits of pitted black olives when I said 'Good morning.' She didn't answer. 'Actually it's not a good morning,' I continued to her back. 'Seems like I had quite a drink last night.'

She started making flowers out of radishes. 'Do your duties also include drugging the guests?' I asked.

'Seems like the guests do pretty well on their own,' she said without turning around.

'But they didn't ask for help from the help.'

'Yes, *ma'am*,' she said like a gunfire salute.

'C'mon Vanessa. Did you doctor that drink?'

'I don't pour them, I just serve them,' she said with a sigh.

'Did you serve the night Allison was on the boat?'

'I don't discuss staff duties with outsiders,' she said with genuine hate.

'Well, if part of your job includes serving up loaded drinks maybe it's time to hit the want ads.' Then I saw her stuff two hard-boiled eggs like she was ramming a fist down someone's throat. I didn't think the throat would have been mine.

'You'd better think about what *you're* doing here. You crash a party and make friends with the likes of what's downstairs. You pose some pretty good questions yourself, lady.'

'Hugo's not such a bad guy. I think he's okay.'

'The only people interested in Hugo are people who want to take advantage of him. He's sweet, but he's not home. And I wish all you gals would just leave him alone.'

'Oh yeah, has he got such a way with the ladies?'

'I think you'd better be on your way. And I don't suggest that you come back. Or I'll be seeing you to a personal interview with Mr Glassman.'

'I'm shaking in my shoes.' I smiled at her. She turned her back and completed a masterpiece out of cauliflowers, smoked sole and a few of the radish roses.

'Got any aspirin?'

'Sure,' she walked to a pantry. Immediately behind the woodwork was a big bottle of generic aspirin within easy reach. 'You got something to hold on to.' She looked me up and down. 'Don't throw it away on a lot of bad chemicals.'

Just then the swinging door flapped open and revealed Stanley Glassman. He looked into the kitchen like it was foreign territory, and he looked at me like I didn't have a visa. I saw him place me as the nameless stranger from the library, and I saw he didn't like it.

'Good morning,' I said.

'May I ask what you're doing here?'

'Do you always treat your guests with such hospitality?'

Vanessa stopped in the middle of a cheese swirl and laid a cracker down on a tray. She silently slid two newspapers underneath the tray and picked them all up together. She put a flap on her expression, sealed it like an envelope and left the room so quietly it was like she had slid herself under a crack in the door. Stanley coughed.

'Forgive me, I'm not used to guests that come and go by the back entrance.' He pointed his words at me.

'They come and go by the back door because the half of the household that invites them resides in the basement. Your brother *does* have a way with the ladies.' I picked up a filled egg with a shaking hand and chomped off an edge.

'My brother is a sick man. And you have a husband that you need to be reminded of. Now if you'll please leave, Mrs – what did you say your name was?'

'I didn't say.' I figured scarlet women never kiss and tell but I didn't have any real experience.

Stanley clamped his mouth over a few words. 'I think it's time you leave young lady. I don't want push to come to shove.'

'When push comes to shove, people fall off boats, Mr Glassman.'

His face filled with red and his mouth had a little twitch on one side of it.

'What are you, some little garbage rag reporter?' He shook his head in disgust. 'Okay, Miss whatever your name is. I don't believe in blackmail, but that's the newspaper trade these days. You deal in dirt and you are dirt.'

I didn't say anything.

'So, how much do you want?' His voice ground out the words like small sharp stones.

'I don't want anything. I'm not here to put the touch on you. I'm just looking into some things, for a friend of a friend, shall we say.'

'I do not like your attitude.'

'It's not meant for your entertainment.'

'I don't have time for this.'

'I didn't ask you for any. Besides, I was just leaving.' I sprinkled a little salt on the egg. He grunted and clenched his jaw a few times and went through the swinging door, a man with many important things to do. I was no more than a gnat buzzing around his head, and he was a man who had a corner on the insecticide market.

'Goodbye Mister Glassman,' I said, my words returning to me on the little breeze supplied by the door still swinging on its hinges. I took a deep breath and disengaged my fingernails from the flesh in the palm of my hand. It was definitely time to go, before I met security guards, deadly drinks, or, God forbid, the police. Of course, he wouldn't do that.

I looked around at the orderly kitchen one last time, swiped another egg and went out the back door accompanied by my head, which had its own rhythm going. I took it with me down the big expanse of lawn, violently green in the sunlight. I turned around and looked at the curtainless plate glass window in the basement. Last night, with the light on in the room, I must have looked like a big pink stop sign to someone.

Twenty-One

It wasn't until I stumbled into my car that I thought about the time, and the staff meeting at Women's Hotline. There was no way I was going to get through it. I couldn't 'share the reality' of my headache, I couldn't say I was hanging out with blue boy and a black widow spider and someone had slipped me a mickey. I drove to the little food store, remembering the long damp walk of two nights before. Now going up and down the hills I just tried to feel less like a leather bag, stuffed with floating organs and nasty thoughts. Julie Arbeder wasn't good for my health, I decided. I wasn't sure why I was pursuing it except that I was worried. I was worried about my intuitions, and about my ego. I was worried about my own love affair and I didn't like the way Julie's and Allison's had worked out. My potential lover was busy creating life and I seemed to be running around chasing death, hoping that some life was behind it, for me.

I found the little all night store where I had called the taxi. It was still open and the same woman was working there. I hoped she didn't have a late shift and then a day shift piled on top of one another. It was a chain store, not a mom-and-pop affair. I wondered if they had a union. I bought a bottle of fresh orange juice and she directed me to the nearest pay phone. I put my hand in the pocket of the pink pants. Somebody had put the cocaine there. I drove my car another block, which was stupid because then I had to drive another block to park. I turned off the engine and drank the bottle of orange juice, one gulp after another. Then I massaged my temples. I found a spot on the skin between my thumb and index finger and started to massage a little ball painfully in the stretched piece of skin. It hurt. I massaged it harder and harder, until it became a constant pressure. It seemed to relieve my headache for a moment. It also felt so bad while I was doing it that I couldn't think of anything else.

I walked to the phone booth and put in a quarter. I got Monica on the line.

125

'Monica, it's Emma.'

'The meeting's started.'

'I don't have any excuses for not coming or calling. I do have a terrible headache, for what it's worth.'

'It's not worth a whole lot.'

'I figured.'

'But it's not so terrible either. We can handle all the maidens in distress by ourselves. Especially the anonymous ones.'

'Okay, I get it. And I deserve it for not showing up at the meeting.'

'You deserve more than that. But we'll talk about it later. Call back and I'll read you the notes. Also we don't have the mail you took home with you to open.'

'Oh, just some stuff about the funding fair. I went to it. Lots of foundations showing off their goodwill in four colours on glossy paper. Nobody got very excited about anything.'

'Yeah, I didn't think so. Did you see anyone from the Battered Women's Shelter?'

'Yeah, I saw them putting the hustle on Jonathan Menck. But I think they are going to need another rummage sale.'

'They're going to need a lot more than that,' she sighed. 'Call back Emma. Call back later.'

I hung up. I squinted against the sun going back to my car. I had had my eyes closed while talking to Monica. It felt better that way. No sunglasses. I had to look at that light all the way home. I even had to look at the road. I stood by the side of my car. I looked at the little succulent plants, thick and rubbery, climbing up the embankment getting ready to make flowers next month. Then I threw up all the orange juice.

I have never been so happy to see my home before. I couldn't wait to close out all the noise and light in the world. Flossie's plaintive mewing sounded like a gospel singer shouting into my ear. The refrigerator door closing sounded like two freight cars bumping in the dead of night. I took a shower and stepped into my thickest cotton pyjamas with the woven satin stripe in the fabric. They felt clean and cool, fresh out of the drawer, the folds still making creases in the pants and in the jacket.

I made my way through the darkened hallway and laid down on the hard cotton mattress that was my bed. My body wouldn't sink into it. My mind was asking questions, so I sat up and my hands made two phone calls, one with each hand.

'Hello, Lieutentant Sloan?'

126

'Yes?' Mumble, mumble.

'This is Emma Victor. The woman who found Julie Arbeder's body on East Lexington Street.' I made her sound like a stray cat.

'Yes, what can I do for you?' Mumble, mumble, mumble.

'Is the case closed?'

'No, ma'am. Homicide investigations remain active for one year.' He shuffled some more papers some more.

'I have some information that may or may not have bearing on the case.'

'Case transferred.' Shuffle, mumble. 'DA's handling it.'

'Oh, do they have a suspect yet?'

'Can't give you that information, ma'am. Why don't you call the DA's office. Extension 446.'

'Sure okay,' I said. 'But if it's in the DA's office, he probably knows.' After all, the DA goes to the same cocktail parties as I do; but I didn't say that.

We hung up and I laid down on the mattress again. I thought about Stanley Glassman, the little beautiful garden room, Vanessa's skill with radishes and how expensive Japanese mattresses shouldn't ball up in two years, but mine had.

I opened my purse and took out a little notebook that I had scribbled in when I went to the library. I found the number in the phone book and dialled.

'Newlight Halfway House.'

'Hello, this is the District Attorney's office.'

'Yes, what can I do for you?' said an unwilling female voice.

'We're compiling stats on parolees released into jobs in 1979, still employed.'

'Well you're calling at lunch hour and we've got a dinner for twelve also taking up space in the kitchen, and the plumbing broke this morning. Now if you folks could just lend me a hand with a pipe wrench maybe I could dawdle through the files,' she cracked her gum.

'Actually, I have some experience plumbing, what seems to be the problem?' I asked.

'Water won't drain but it doesn't seem to be stopped up.'

'Sounds like a standpipe problem.'

'Yeah?' I heard a smile. 'Maybe I'll look into that.' Crack, crack. 'Oh, wait a sec.' Shuffle, shuffle. 'Here's some folder with yearly stats. Four parolees placed in jobs that year. But I know that one is back in the cooler, and one overdosed.'

'Remember any of the successes?'

'Yeah, that guy Dave. He's still working at a garage.'

'You've got a mind like a steel trap. But there was just one more in '79.'

'Seventy-nine, okay, that was when my kid had colitis. Oh yeah. Just a sec, I'll look it up.'

'I'll help you with your plumbing.'

'Aw, that's okay. Just say hello to the DA and tell him to send us some good plumbers from the pen.' She cracked her gum again and I heard a suspended file drawer sliding out and then rolling back in and crashing, like she'd kicked it. 'Yeah, here it is. Black, female, forty-two, still employed in domestic service. I barely remember her, she was real quiet, stayed in her room and listened to the radio a lot. I mean a lot. Talk programmes. That's how I remember. Who wants to listen to talk programmes in a house full of people? And clean, you have never seen a person so clean.' She cracked her gum, loud, into the mouthpiece.

'What was she up for?'

'Embezzlement. She pulled a six to ten but got off in a three for good behaviour. Very good, I imagine.'

'Thanks. And I will come over and check out the plumbing.'

'Naw, it's okay.'

'Thanks again.' I hung up. Good old Vanessa had worked some books in the past. I wondered how easy it would be for someone to put the squeeze on her. It depended on her plans for the future. But I had a hangover of my own making on top of whatever she served. It was a complicated hangover. It needed sleep, and no more aspirins. Just as I pulled the thick, light, goosedown coverlet over me, the phone rang. It was Sandy, with an invitation to a feminist funny farm, Ova Orchards, only three hours to the north.

'Sandy, it's not my thing. Give it up.'

'Emma, it's not what you think. The kind of thing you're allergic to was what I went to last week. This is just free camping, you can be totally alone, you won't be roped into any workshops.'

'Really?' The weather had been great.

'Yes, you can be your cynical self all day long, without cosmic thought, even under the full moon, if that's possible.'

'You mean just read, talk, walk around on two legs and employ my analytic faculties?'

'Yes, no tarot cards . . .'

'No mushy, beige macrobiotic foods?'

'Bring your meat and potatoes.'

128

It was sounding better. Still it was hard to believe that Sandy would give up on me so fast. 'Is there any special reason you want to put me to pasture?'

'Loosen up, Emma. I'm not going to make a duplicate key to your tent zipper,' she sighed. 'Emma, you may not believe this but I've given up chipping away at your facade. I'm going to study organic goat farming and forget all about our romance.'

'Sounds like an improvement.'

'But I still have a message for you from the seance.'

'Get serious.'

'No, there was this fantastic woman from Dubrovnik at the farm last week. She knows everything about auras; she sees rainbows around people's heads.'

'So do I.'

'She also did some renaming. That's her speciality. She reads your true name from your energy field. You should check it out.'

'I have a personal connection to my own name. My parents gave it to me.'

'Well, yes, of course.' Sandy always became reverent or uncomfortable at the mention of authentic dead people. 'Emma, this is a good name for me. I can feel it.'

'What is it then?'

'Seven Blue Horses.'

'What?'

'Call me Seven.'

'Okay, Seven. And what's *my* message from the cosmos?'

'Just a sec. I'll go get it.' I heard her walk away and then I heard the sound of crumpled paper over the telephone.

'Let's see, here it is. We did a whole series that night, but not to worry. I didn't forget you. I asked specifically if there were any messages for Emma Victor.'

'And what did the universe reply?'

'Here it is. You're supposed to be careful when crashing other people's parties and being rude to the help. Here's the good part: "When you spend the night out remember to bring along fresh underwear. You never know when you might need a doctor." '

'Very funny, is that all?'

'Isn't it enough?'

'More than enough. I'm almost getting ready for Ova Orchards, Sandy. And, well, if you're dialling direct to the Great Spirit, ask her why junkies kiss and don't tell. I'd like to know.'

'Sure, Emma. Take care of yourself.'

'You too.'

We hung up. It was hard to go to sleep. Sandy was making the Oracle at Delphi look like a blackjack dealer.

Twenty-Two

I woke up with a start. I couldn't tell if it was light or dark outside; I had done a good job of sealing out all the light before I went to sleep. I had no idea what time of day it was, if it still was day at all. I remembered that I had promised to make Frances dinner; I hadn't done any shopping and I hadn't thought about food. My mouth was dry, but my headache was gone. I stood up and a glass fell over and rolled against a wooden chair leg. My watch said one minute and thirty-two seconds after six. I pulled on my pants and stubbed my toe against the leg of the bed. I didn't feel like I was going to be a swell cook.

Star Market was crowded and people showed all the symptoms of working. Only unemployed people and that vanishing occupation, the full time housewife, could afford to glide down the smooth, grey linoleum aisles waltzing to the muzak. At six o'clock Star Market had a population of people making traffic situations with shopping cards. All the meat and dairy counters had knots of people before them, and minor collisions occurred on every aisle corner. Children released from school and daycare centres swirled around and in the carts, hoping for parental attention, and doing everything audible and physical to get it. Dads compared prices on soup with tired faces, brothers and sisters fought with the hatred of sibling rivalry and whined like banshees.

I was thinking about dinner; I was thinking about chicken, or perhaps turkey, or perhaps even Cornish game hen. I went for the chicken. I made a route in my mind through the Star Market aisles to get the necessary things when a cart ran over my feet. It was not a good evening for toes. The man behind the cart apologised too much and too slowly. I grumbled something and then felt guilty and tried to be friendly. Then I accepted his excuses and ran away. He was a little creepy, but I told myself that he'd just read in a singles guide how to meet girls at the supermarket. Running over toes was the loser's opening line.

131

Some senior citizens had mistakenly ventured in; a few looked confused and couldn't turn around fast enough to see who had nudged them with a cart. Several children came giggling and laughing up to the counter, threw a few hard, cold packs of meat around, one gave a shrill scream-laugh of excitement and an old man tried to see what was happening, but the children were beyond the reach of his cataract vision.

I turned into the lane of cart traffic going towards the produce section. I picked up an eggplant for no reason at all, some green peppers joined it and I tried to swim over the crowd to the cauliflowers but gave up. I pushed on to the cracker section because it was relatively peaceful. Cracker sections usually are. I headed for the lines going to the cashiers. Whatever I had, it was food, and some of it would go with some of the rest; I just couldn't think of how. Eggplant and eggs? Chicken and cheese?

I perused the carts and people waiting to check out. All the lines were long enough to disappear into the aisles by six or seven carts. I chose the line with more carts but less objects per basket hoping I didn't have an Invalidated Cheque-writer in front of me. There was one couple shopping en route, a young man running about with a list and filling the shopping cart as it slowly rolled towards its destiny. The couple's system of run-and-shop always made me jealous.

The muzak seemed to be turned up louder as we all crawled towards the cashier and the plate glass windows behind them. There were two price checks being called out from the cashier, one for D-con Rat Poison, and another for Kraft Instant Macaroni dinner.

Finally it was my turn. The cashier wore a Star Market smiley face button advertising a game whose goal was a trip to Florida. She was also wearing a paper lei which looked strange against her small frame in the pink nylon uniform. I knew this cashier. She was always calling out in Chinese to the cashier behind her. Unless the manager was looking, the two women would carry on whole conversations while she checked out my groceries. The growing Asian presence was making for some good dialogue in the neighbourhood, at least the sounds were pretty far out. I thought about how Asian languages have tonal variations which change the meaning of the words; if you said 'apple' in tone, a register higher it might mean 'lampshade'. This always caused me to listen carefully to the noises of their conversation and I often thought I heard the same words bounding up and down in tone. I used to look and see if she got any of the prices wrong while doing the vocal gymnastics, but in five years she hadn't missed the sale price of tomatoes or the difference by watt in lightbulb prices.

Tonight I wasn't in the mood; my toes hurt from the stubbing and from being run over by a potentially vicious single person. I was glad to fork out my money and leave through the hissing automatic doors. It was cool, dark and quiet outside. I drove the two blocks home. I pulled up in front of my house and turned off the engine and sat a moment in the car, trying to regain some peace. I heard the second layer of noises, traffic streaming in the distance, a car door slamming a block away, two cats fucking somewhere without much pleasure. It was a symphony, with everything in a different register, just like the cashier language of the Star Market.

I gathered up the thick brown bag in my arms and opened the car door. The bag ripped on the bottom and the milk started to slide out. I held the corner of the carton with my hand, then I shifted the bag to my knee while I fumbled with the car keys to lock the door. Regaining the bag and the carton corner I walked up the stairway to the front door and unlocked it. The lights were all off inside; when I had left sunset was just beginning to make a flash ending. The sunset was over, the house was dark. The windows provided a show outside which included street lights and a corner of a twinkling neon sign. I went to the light over the dining room table which was on a rheostat control. I turned it on and pushed it to the brightest level; suddenly the room was washed with a blinding 120 watts.

My fingers turned the switch down out of reflex, but I didn't close my eyes. What I saw was awful; I had to stick around and watch. My house had been thoroughly trashed.

The first second I didn't notice anything. The house still had walls and a ceiling. I was, after all, standing on the floor. Then I noticed books lying on the floor, one book, two books, leading to a pile of books. Pictures in frames had been lifted off the walls and thrown on the floor, in what must have been a two-handed gesture. The aluminium edges folded and stood up like praying mantis on the floor. One silkscreen print had a big rip in it.

All of this took one second, two seconds to register. I thought immediately about securing the house and ran to the back door. I had to walk carefully in the kitchen. A large can of honey was covered by a milk puddle, the refrigerator door hung open, swinging to and fro; it had been tipped over enough to let all the contents spill out, a cabbage was covered with blueberry yogurt.

I was busy listing things and breathing hard at the same time. Call the police, check windows, basement door, thinking about the best method to get honey off the floor, writing the artist for another print, then I started feeling the panic, like hands around my throat. The someone who had invaded my house was actually motivated to do this, not just rip me off, feeling anger or perhaps contempt for reasons I couldn't understand. I was hated. I thought about this and was glad that it was only food to clean up, no smeared faeces, or spray paint graffiti, suggesting ways to die. I was about to resume my check of the house when I noticed that a bag of sugar was still streaming on to the floor, making a small pyramid of white refined on the tiles. The next thing that happened was that someone must have hit me on the back of the head, because I just saw the whole kitchen melt before me, like a plastic painting getting burned and shrinking up into nothing, leaving a pain as big as a truck in my skull and finally one bright light. I felt my face hit a swamp of jelly and milk before I gave up and sank into the big darkness.

Twenty-Three

I woke up to the sound of music, without hills. I had a small, smooth concerto in my head that had qualities like bubble gum. Then I thought about Pennsylvania, and then I stupidly opened my eyes. I felt the back of my head. My hand reached a portion of scalp long before my skull should have been there. I tried to sit up, but then thought better of it. My cheek made a little splash in the milk pond again, so I decided I had to make a better effort to get off the floor. I'm not sure how my body managed it, but my eyes were finally level with the top of the fridge. Then I made some whimpering noises for a while. It occurred to me that I could call the Women's Hotline. That made me laugh.

I laughed for a few moments. I watched a wall for a few minutes. Then I hugged myself. I was making myself nervous and so I grabbed a piece of skin under my arm and pinched it once, tight. I tried standing up and it worked. I tried walking and that worked too, in a limping, loping way. I went as quickly as possible to the front door and locked it and put a chair under the door handle. Then I checked the back door to make sure it was locked and bolted. It was. I went to the little bedroom where I found an open window leading on to the side of the house, enclosed in shrubbery. I stuck my head out the window, and looked down and saw mashed bushes below. I closed the window and locked it. Standing in the room I noticed the closet doors were slightly open and I couldn't remember if I'd left them that way. I certainly hadn't noticed that I'd opened the window to clear my headache with fresh air earlier. Headache made me think of head, and trying to keep my brains a regular distance from my neck while walking through the house was a full-time job. I stopped thinking about that so I could open the closet door. Nothing jumped out at me; just my clothes were hanging there.

I realised I wasn't sure how I was managing to stay upright. This caused me to sit down on the bed. I felt sure I was alone in this house, so I just let my brains take over, they seemed to be busy wanting to do

135

things on their own anyway, like floating around the high corners of the room. The high corners of the room had just been dusted. So why not?

I shook myself and became upright again, and strolled to the living room. I saw a big screwdriver stuck into the couch, and saw that the someone had stuck it in the middle of a pillow, resting on the back of the couch. It rested there supported by the stuffing; it had gone in at a downwards angle. A replay of the hand that did it and the force it must have taken reeled through my head. I pulled at the screwdriver and tried not to notice the feel of the clinging stuffing against the shaft as it came loose. I put it on the floor and cried for a moment. But just for a moment. Then I picked up the silkscreen print and put it high on a closet shelf in the little front hallway, where it could lie flat. I tried making some books into piles. The books kept falling off each other and out of my hands.

I gave up and sat on the couch. I sat on the couch for quite a while, maybe a century, and certainly a substantial part of my lifetime. Then I noticed the typewriter had a piece of white onion skin erasable stuck in it at a funny angle. Someone had also had frustrations with the machine but hadn't taken time to straighten out the page. They were too busy stabbing my couch, probably. A big crease ran across the bottom of the page where it had entered the carriage wrong. The middle of the crooked page showed only three words, 'stau awau glassman'. This gave me an odd satisfaction; now I knew what the reason was. I could review my activities and wonder what would warrant this breaking in, this totalling of my possessions, this incredible anger, incredible, because it was directed at me. The thing that only happens to other people. The answer took shape in my head, but a large construction crew was busy up there too.

I stood up and walked to the kitchen where I was blinded by a cabbage on the floor. So I returned to the living room and tried to put the image of a screwdriver on the couch together with the little stoned man in silk pyjamas. Someone had some big fears, and the scariest fear was that they could be found out a murderer. Those were the highest stakes I could figure, but I have never been a person of great vision.

My head reminded me of some important physical facts and I laid down on the couch. I thought about a typist who would make the typo substituting 'u' for 'y' in the sentence. I thought about imperative sentences and exercises we used to do in school. 'Go do the laundry. Close the door.' Switch that verb around. Make those typos. Bow to your corner for a grand right and left.

136

The typos made it sound Hawaiian and that reminded me of the cashier at the Star Market. I wondered if Glassman in a different register would mean something else, something plebeian, like 'washboard', or 'haemorrhoid treatment.' I hoped this was true. I found myself irritated that the onion skin paper had been used to give me this silly message. I sat in the dark with these things, and a lot more, in my head. I heard two cats outside fucking and that reminded me of something, but I couldn't think what. I had a pleasant feeling that I was becoming part of the couch. Just so much more stuffing.

A car horn honked outside. I thought about calling the police, walking to the phone, but it seemed like a lot of effort. I thought about giving the whole thing to them, surely they'd take fingerprints. Then I remembered that conversation with the second detective. Here was the Glassman message, the DA sat on it, and I sat on it. I could call the cops; I was only a dyke, with some coke in the house, somewhere, probably still in those pink pants. Yesterday I was taking drugs with a rich psycho, all in a day's work. Emma Victor, Crusader of Hotline Crisis. Call in case of danger.

I looked at the screwdriver on the floor. It had a green plastic handle, I never thought it was tempered steel. But it worked okay on the screws that were made out of mush that I bought at the hardware store. I shuddered. I had a square dance between my ears. I was becoming stuffing again when something happened. The doorbell rang. It took me a moment to remember where I was, where the door was. The doorbell rang again, small streams of thought gathered in my skull in the vicinity of my forehead. They tied themselves into a few meanings. I looked at my watch, it was eight o'clock. It was Dr Frances Cohen, coming for dinner.

I balanced my hand on the wall as I walked down the stairs, and for once didn't think about smearing the latex paint that was so difficult to clean. I looked at the door and thought about what would be behind it and I knew it would demand an emotional response, but I didn't have any. I heard the voice on the other side. It had heard me standing in the hall, thinking.

'Emma, are you there?'

'Yes.'

'Emma, open the door.'

I did and all the screens of thoughts suddenly wove themselves into a big pattern full of knots and ribbons. I registered Frances' face and it looked swell.

'Emma, what's wrong? What happened to you . . . Christ, are you okay?'

The doctor was worried.

'Hello,' I said. It was the most logical thing to say, after all. Then she stepped quickly inside the door and closed it, put an arm under mine and wrapped it around my waist. She sort of carried me up the stairs. She had a beautiful mouth and a worried face. She took me to the couch.

'I'm so glad you're here.' The words sounded stupid, even to me, but the meaning felt big and got bigger by the second. She took my pulse. She took out a small pocket flashlight and looked under my eyelids. Then she hugged me and kissed my neck and not my face which was closer to the thing on my head.

'I think I have an awful bump.' She felt gently around the back of my head. Doctor's hands.

'You sure do.' She took the penlight and peered carefully at my bump. I could see her squinting her eyes in concentration through the living room mirror. She looked scientifically detached. Still the face that came back was full of concern and worry.

'Do you remember what happened?'

'Yes, I think someone hit me.' Frances was just starting to notice the house, housekeeping probably not one of her big skills. She walked to the kitchen and I heard her cry 'Jesus!' She ran back. 'Is there anyone still in the house? Have you checked?'

'I've done the closets, doors are all locked. They got in through the bedroom window. I'd left it open.'

'Did you see who it was?' Her voice had a hollow quality coming from the kitchen.

'No, I didn't.'

A huge lump was happening in my throat and I started crying to get it out. I let myself get carried away into spasmodic sobs, some hyperventilation and finally the hiccup state which always signalled the end. Frances hugged me, stroked me, rocked me. She brought me a box of Kleenex, I had snot running on to my shirt and hers too.

'Were you unconscious?'

'No, uh, yes.'

'Do you remember being bumped on the head?'

'Sort of.'

'What did you see right before it happened?'

'Sugar spilling on the floor.'

'Do you remember walking around, anything before that?'

'I don't want any more questions, Frances, get me out of here. Take me to your house.'

138

'Okay,' she said softly. I went to the bathroom to grab a cosmetic bag and my toothbrush and turned on the fluorescent light inside the doorway. I saw myself in the mirror. I have looked better with a hangover and the flu. I would have looked better dead, having died from a romantic illness.

My eyes were beginning to be ringed with a slate blue. A dark purple streak was smeared under each eyeball accentuating the small bags appearing under each eye. The dappled effects of crying left a splotchy red line above my lip, my nose was engorged with blood, swollen and red. Its usual bulbousness had bloomed into red tomato glory.

'I have an ice pack at home.' I heard Frances' voice behind me. 'C'mon, I want to get you out of here,' she said and I let her take control. Suddenly I remembered Flossie.

'I have to find my cat!' My heart raced for a moment as I hoped that the bastard who had such a way with screwdrivers didn't have a dislike for cats. Flossie may have been a no-good lie-about pile of fluff but she was a good teacher of meditation and an excellent decoration. She was also fast when she had to be. I headed for her favourite hiding closet. I asked Frances for her little flashlight. I shone it up on a top shelf. Flossie had managed with cat levitation to get up on the highest shelf and had pushed herself back into a corner. Only the gleam of her golden eyes let us know she was there.

'Floss!' I began in that silly human voice people use to placate animals. She rightly hissed. I went to the kitchen disaster area and opened a tin of cat food and put it on the floor. I wondered if Flossie would lick up the milk and honey and I would come back and find her twice as large, a swollen furry beast. Then I thought about the screwdriver and let Frances hurry me out the door.

She drove quickly and smoothly, on and off the freeways back to her house. I felt comforted, wordlessly safe in her presence. I let myself feel little against her leather jacket. She had on a light, but dusky, scent. She had a beautiful strong chinline. I watched her face looking concerned as the passing headlights moved over her features and slid downwards across her face. I was the object of this concern and it made me deliriously happy, although it would be sick to say that it was worth getting clunked on the head. Still I hadn't known she'd cared, this much.

We arrived at her house and she risked a parking ticket in a yellow zone, all for me. I felt in rapid danger of sinking into things. I tried to make a pillow around my senses to stop the pounding of my skull, the big black void would soak up all the noise going on in my head and put out all the little explosions. She tried to help me up the stairs and I let her. I concentrated on the steps, the chilly breeze, the steps, one by one, the sidewalk lamp on the front of her house. She opened the door and I went up first on the carpeted stairway. I sat on the beige sofa, then I put my feet up on an ottoman. Frances fussed in the kitchen and came back with a glass of whisky and an ice bag. She put the ice bag on my head and handed me the whisky.

'Drink it,' she said, just like in the movies. I drank it.

She helped me off with my coat. She sat there rubbing my arms, my legs, reminding me of long forgotten parts of my body. She looked very worried and the hazel eyes were sending out little brown flecks of endless concern and understanding. Endless concern and understanding, just for me. Then she changed into another mode.

'Still remember being hit on the head?'

'Yes, why?'

'Just checking.'

'And that you closed all the doors and windows. And you found one window open, which one was that?'

'The bedroom window, why?'

'Remember driving over here?' I nodded. 'That's good. Remember walking up the stairs?' How could I forget? It was the trip of a lifetime.

'Okay.' She turned her back, satisfied for some arcane reason. She walked to the kitchenette. 'Hungry? Want something to eat? Can you handle a pizza?'

'Yes, oh yes,' I said. If she'd given me an arsenic cocktail I would have drunk it. I watched her go to the phone and lift the receiver. I tried to think about the blanket and Frances' ass in tight blue jeans, instead of about my head, which was trying to give birth to an egg. I tried not to think about the message at my house, or Vanessa sporting drugged refreshments or a golfing dyke who looked like Doris Day with biceps sliding off a boat deck or Julie Arbeder, dead on the street. I thought about calling the police again, and tried to imagine men taking fingerprints when I was sure there wouldn't be any. Then I looked on Frances' coffee table and saw a small piece of paper, torn on the bottom side, with a phone number written on it in soft red pencil. I felt a small localised pain inside my stomach, somewhere low. I felt something spin towards the outside of my brain where it bumped against something else. The phone number was 823-6111. It was the number of the Glassman residence.

Twenty-Four

'Olives, anchovies, the works. And extra cheese. Mmm-hmm. Stringy mozzarella.' Frances was ordering the pizza.

I went to the bathroom and threw up, trying not to make ugly retching sounds. I tried hard to remember what I had and hadn't said to Frances over a barbecue on an empty deck at a party. I had spoken of the responsibility towards dead people. I rinsed out my mouth and walked to the living room and found Frances clearing off the papers and books on the coffee table. The telephone number was gone.

'You okay?' she asked looking deep in my pupils. 'Still remember everything about what happened? Didn't see anyone, locked all the doors?'

'Yes, I didn't see anyone and I locked all the doors. Satisfied?'

'Hey, don't get sore. I just want to make sure you don't have a concussion that's all. I need to make sure you're not getting goofed up in there . . .' She walked towards me with that nice face, the big mouth, the straight eyebrows and fluffy, fine hair. She kissed me but I kept walking past her and it landed on my cheek. Her eyebrows were sincere, but the eyes underneath them were shifty. I remembered being warned about shifty eyes from the racist Nancy Drew book *The Secret of Larkspur Lane*. In a certain light, Frances could almost be called swarthy by the debutante Drew who would speed past us in her blue roadster. I wanted to cry again but it wasn't the right mood, the right moment or the right person anymore.

Instead I kissed her on the mouth, hard, I kissed her a lot. I kissed her until she was out of breath, in case she wasn't real, in case she'd melt before my eyes like an ice sculpture in a hot breeze. I had to take everything I could get because suddenly I wasn't sure how much there was, and I still didn't want to lose her, and I couldn't let her make love to me. So I made love to her.

The doorbell rang. We let the pizza in and pushed money outside. We balanced the pizza on wax pieces of paper curled up in our hands

141

and ate. We watched TV. I lost the taste of bile.

When it was time I got up and walked around all the rooms and turned off the lights. I walked her to the bed. I made slow and careful love to her. It felt all right. It felt like a pleasant kind of contact to have. It felt like a history repeating itself.

Just before she fell asleep, she said, 'Aren't you going to call the police?'

'I'm glad you asked that question,' I said, but she had already fallen away and left me with my headache.

I couldn't sleep as easily as she. I got up and walked in a big circle around her room. I went to the wastebasket and saw the number on the piece of paper again. I got out Julie Arbeder's address book and looked under 'Allison' again. It was the same number. I put the ice pack back on my eyes and sat on the couch. The phone number lay in the wastebasket. It could have just been a random collection of seven digits, perhaps in another register it meant 'kitty-litter'.

The next morning I woke up to Frances saying quietly to someone that she'd be late for work. She noticed I was awake and walked towards the bed.

'How're you doing?' She patted my cheek, and looked at my eye in what could have been clinical interest.

'I'm fine and I remember everything that I saw last night.' I was a good patient. 'I'd like some strong coffee.' I got up and tried to still the noisy tenant which had sublet part of my head.

I walked straight to the couch. I couldn't kiss Frances and she noticed. I thought about my home and how I felt unable to walk into it; how picking up the broken pieces of my household was going to break my heart. I remembered my income tax refund cheque due to arrive next month. I was inspired. I would hire a cleaning lady myself; I would hire Clara, the professional. I looked up the phone number in my address book and wrote it down.

'Don't you think you want to call the police?' Frances asked.

'No, actually, I don't think. Well, hell, I guess I'd better call them.'

'After all they'll want fingerprints.'

'What makes you think there'd be fingerprints?' I noticed sarcasm in my voice. 'Don't you think whoever did it had a big interest in staying anonymous?'

'There still might be some clues, I don't know.'

'What kind of clues? Typewritten messages? This isn't Nancy Drew, you know.'

142

She didn't bat a honey-coloured eyelash.

'What are you so huffy about?' she said, after a moment. 'Hey, I'm on your side. You think you're the only one who lives in this lousy city?'

'Yeah, sometimes I do.' I tasted the bitterness in my voice as she tried to talk me out of feeling bad. It tasted lousy. 'Waking up with a bashed-in skull doesn't get my day off to the right start.'

'You should feel lucky you didn't get killed.'

'I should feel lucky, right.'

'Stacy's house just got broken into, and she found the guy with a gun in her bathroom.'

'Hell, I should probably feel grateful. Think I could hire someone to come and do that sort of thing, I mean on a monthly basis?'

'Okay, I'm just trying to put it into perspective.'

'There is no perspective. I just feel rotten, and I don't want to hear about how wonderful and brave Stacy Weldemeer is at the moment. I want to sit here and digest my own experience for a while.'

'Sure,' Frances said quietly. And 'Sure,' she said again, just under her breath.

We sat there for a few minutes as I tried to digest my experience. It went down about as easily as lamb's glands, a dish I had had the unfortunate experience of trying last month. The dreams afterwards were really bad.

'So, what did our mother of conception, Stacy Weldemeer, do after her break-in?'

'She went out and bought a gun and enrolled in a course to learn how to use it.'

'Well, isn't that swell. I haven't graduated to the bullet stage of fear yet. I don't want to live with a gun in my house.'

'Hey, I'm sorry,' she said very softly, very earnestly and looking into my eyes. 'You have had a really rough time. Try and relax now, take it easy, Emma. Why don't you take a little vacation?'

She reached out to me and I let her hold me, but I didn't relax. I got aggressive. I put my hand in the warm corner of her jeans and found the thick seam in her crotch. I rubbed my finger along it and the fabric made a slight vibration as my fingertip ran over the top of the coarse thread. She leaned back and smiled.

'You're still beautiful,' she said.

I rolled my eyes and remembered my face in the mirror. My racoon mask was getting green around the edges.

'Just give me the ice pack and stop lying.' I took the cold pack out of her hands and put it on my head. Balancing it I managed to kiss her. She still had the baby-fine hair and the hazel eyes. How dangerous could she be, even if her sympathy had limits?

I asked her if I could take a bath and she showed me to the yellow-tiled bathroom and a large linen closet. Big fluffy towels were arranged in rows, folded with the edges in, according to colour. A day ago that would have made me happy. Now it was just another detail.

She gave me a light grey towel and her white bathrobe. I filled the bathtub up several inches with warmish water, then I stepped into it. Frances walked out of the room. I got my ass in and my feet out as soon as possible. My feet are never a good indication of temperature; they would usually like the water colder than the rest of me. As my body got used to the hot temperature I made it hotter, turning the cold tap off with my foot. My breasts floated as the water hit my nipples and moved upwards. I picked up a washcloth, scratchy from being dried out in the sun. I scrubbed soap across the terry cloth loops and put it to my face.

The water reached the top of my breasts. I felt loosened. I washed my hair and the heat of the water made my scalp burn. I floated away there for a while. Then I got out of the tub, the steam racing off my body, anxious to evaporate in the air. I sat on a little stool.

Frances came in and quickly closed the door behind her. She put the towel around my body and began patting the water off. Then she rubbed the towel over my head.

'My headache is gone,' I said to her. She smiled. I was happy. Classic doctor/patient illness.

'That's good,' she said absentmindedly. She was rubbing the towel around separated strands of hair.

'I've run into a little drug trouble lately, but that thump on the head seems to have cured the desire for chemical entertainment.'

'You into drugs?' she asked and even the vernacular couldn't hide the fact that it was a question she used in making diagnoses.

'It wasn't something I planned,' I said.

'Nobody does.'

'*Some* people do,' I said but all this was going over her head, and mine too.

'No, seriously, are you into drugs?'

'You think that's what's been happening at my house?'

'I don't know what I think. But you are certainly in some mood this morning.'

'No, I'm not on drugs. Only as the lightest recreation. And I didn't

144

have a drug accident. I didn't have any accident. Don't worry about it.'

'Okay, if you say not to worry about it, I won't.'

She started rubbing my wet hair again. I remember it as something my mother used to do. It was a very motherly thing to do, especially in the current days of hair dryers. She was good at it. I put a hand on her hand and stopped her for a moment. 'We still don't know each other very well, do we?' She started towelling again.

'Let's keep going in this direction. Then we can see if that's a question to be answered. Maybe we know everything about each other already. Everything we *need* to know, that is.'

I didn't know what to say. I didn't know where to put my intuitions about this one. And I didn't think she was on the level. I thought about a little pipeline that must go back through the DA to the Glassman's house. I decided to report the break-in at my house, as a robbery.

'Listen, I've got to get home. Think some things over.' She could tell I'd moved over some boundaries.

'Sure.' She dropped her hands and the wet towel, all of them limply in her lap.

I went to my clothes and pulled them on like old brown bags. I didn't ask her for clean underwear, and she didn't offer. She was busy in the kitchen. Last time I got to discover her panty collection.

'Listen, I'll see you later. I'll call you,' I said and went over to her and kissed her on the cheek.

'Sure,' she said. She'd gone over a few boundaries too. For the moment I liked it better that way.

Twenty-Five

I took a bus home and tried to let my mind float over the outstanding features of the last few weeks. But my mind didn't float, it just bumped and scraped every time I thought that Frances was working at the clinic that was funded by Stanley Glassman, every time I thought about Julie Arbeder. I wanted to see Sue Martinez. I didn't go into the house but got straight into the Plymouth and drove over to Sue and Misty's.

Another window had been broken and replaced with plastic. From the two sides of the door the house had a matched set of lungs. They inhaled as Misty opened the front door. She didn't see me; she was dragging a heavy plastic sack down the porch stairs.

'Need some help?'

Misty jumped, recognised me and jumped again. She said, 'Yeah, sure.' Together we lugged the sack to a pick-up truck with no bumper that was parked by the curb. We left it on the gutter of the street.

'Annual cleanup?'

'No, I'm moving out.' She was panting heavily, her small frame heaving. 'The landlord said if I don't clean out the yard first he'll take my cleaning deposit.' She shrugged.

'And you're doing it all alone?' Natch, one of her roommates just croaked and the other had split overnight. 'How much more is there? Come on, I'll help.'

We walked to the back yard and there were three more bags and some clipping to be done. I took off my sweater and put it in the front seat of the car and returned to start dragging the bags with Misty. Small sticks had made holes in the bottoms of the bags and clods of dirt fell out making a small brown trail over the sidewalk.

We returned and clipped the last bush together, filling a final bag halfway. The smell of leaves and dirt was an antidote to the poisons in my head. It was nice to sweat about something else.

'What happened to the puppy?'

'I'm trying to give it away.' She didn't look hopeful. 'Maybe I'll take it to the pound. It was Julie's.'

'I know. Let me look at the little critter again.'

'Do you think you might want it? That would be swell. It doesn't even have a name yet.'

'Lead me to the little beast.'

We opened the kitchen door and the puppy bounced in with endless enthusiasm like I was saving her from execution.

'I'd love to have her,' I said, taking the plunge and regretting it at once.

I held the dog, made motherly movements, kissed its domed forehead. The dog fell instantly in love with me and promised me that we would live happily ever after. 'Well, that's that, I guess.' I held it close. 'Do you know how I can get ahold of Sue?'

'Sure. She left the name of her hotel. But she made me swear not to give it to anybody, under any circumstances. Just in case of emergency.'

'Oh, but I'm sure she didn't mean me, Misty.'

'Yeah, I guess I could give it to you, huh?' I nodded. Sue would make mincemeat out of her later, but I wanted Sue now.

Misty took the stub of a pencil from her pocket and wrote the name, 'Del Mirago Springs Resort, Yuma, California.'

'I can remember anything,' she said. 'Mind like a trap.'

'You told me Sue was in Tijuana.'

Misty pulled a carrot out of her breast pocket and snapped off the top in her mouth.

'I lied,' she said.

'I'll give Sue your greetings, huh?'

'Yeah, do that.' Misty was still frowning.

'Bye-bye.' I said. She said it too. I wondered if she had even noticed my eye.

I walked with the dog to the Plymouth. I got inside and named the rubbery animal 'Safety'.

I drove to a grocery store and got five dollars worth of change, a box of Milkbones and some canned puppy food. I opened the windows a crack and locked Safety in the car. I walked to a phone booth and got the number of Del Mirago Springs Resort in Yuma, California.

I put in a lot of coins and dialled.

'Del Mirago Springs,' came a chirpy voice.

'Hi, this is Patty Pugliasi from Happy World Travel Agency.'

'Yes?' It was not a happy yes.

'Well, we're making some further travel arrangements for a client that is staying with you.'

'I'm sorry, you must have the wrong resort. Our clients are never booked through travel agencies.'

'Oh, you don't understand, we've booked her further itinerary . . .'

'No, you must be mistaken . . .'

'How could I be mistaken? What is this? End of the Line Resort?'

'Very funny, Miss. Now if you don't mind I'm going to hang up now.'

'Sue Martinez,' I said.

'Look, I don't know who you are or what you want, but you are not from any travel agency. Goodbye!' And she slammed the receiver down with a crash.

The second phone call would be even more fun. I remembered the number by heart. Happy World Travel Agency, 533-0431, as well as I remembered the creep Bo Dimini who ran it.

'So Emma Victor returns my call,' he chuckled through his cigar-stained throat.

'You can keep your hands in your pockets, Bo. I'm calling to collect my airline ticket points.'

'And Emma, you said you didn't enjoy travelling.'

'You never take a hint, Bo. Doesn't your ego ever bruise?'

'Not when there are pretty ladies in the world like you, Emma,' he chuckled like a gravel pit.

'Even if you weren't the wrong species, which you are, you have greasy hands and a personality like chewing gum, thick and sticky. Give it a break.'

He was hohoing now. 'Emma, one day you'll give in.'

'Go sell cars, Bo. Go sell nuclear power plants. Give me my airline points.'

'Where ya goin', Emma?'

'Yuma. Yuma California.'

'Armpit of the state. Who's scoring down there? I know some fella's got you on the line.'

'No, Bo, I'm just writing the ending for a story. You've got a one-track mind.'

'You know, Emma, your time limit's almost up on the use of these points. Why should I give them to you, you're so difficult to get along with?'

'And Marilyn, my replacement, is she being difficult to get along with?'

'All the girls don't throw remarks back as fast as you.'

'But you never seem to catch them, Bo. You keep your hands off Marilyn.'

'Well, the way girls dress these days . . .'

'Women to you, buddy. Remember how I told you about the sexual harassment laws?'

'Yeah. So?'

'Well, I told Marilyn too.'

'Aw, nobody pays attention to that stuff.'

'She did. She said she'd be taking notes. One of your brethren in business just got looped for thirty thousand. Better purify your patter, Bo.'

I called the police and reported the break in at my house. I heard them switch on the taperecorder as I talked, then I heard little beeps throughout the conversation. It wasn't very exciting, and I didn't mention that I'd been assaulted. It would be nice to have a day's vacation in California. A day in California; I must be crazy. I should move there.

I drove back to Somerville and sat in front of my violated home. The house didn't shout anything at me so I let it sit there until the police arrived. I looked at it a lot. Then two officers, male and female pulled up. We introduced ourselves and I showed them the sticky mess that used to be my life style.

I left the Glassman note on the floor where it had fallen among the debris. They didn't notice it. They busied themselves with little brushes and jars. The man asked the woman a lot of questions about procedure. They took my fingerprints. They said the glass jars were all clean. Of course, I'd wiped them all clean with a hot soapy sponge the day before. The culprit had worn gloves. I was getting tired and I wanted them to go away. Eventually, they did. I called up Clara, who was going to clean the house, and told her everything was all ready, especially arranged just for her.

Clara arrived. She made a lot of noise about the mess and hugged me a lot. I was trying not to cry and watched her professionally scanning the honey and contemplating solvents; I know, we have similar minds. I showed her the vacuum cleaner, mops and buckets. I left her surveying the battlefield; it would be one of the challenges of her life.

I got in the car and let the small dog adore me. I warned her about Flossie, but assured her we'd be one happy family eventually. But puppies are just living in their own dynamic. Flossie would be another case.

Then I drove to a park to check out Safety's behavioural genes. They were all in top retriever dog order; she would fetch a stick indefinitely, begging with earnest and frantic expression.

I drew Safety to the car with a magic stick, and quickly threw it outside and closed the car door before the dog could leap after it. It was either that or take the stick with us. It was a habit I didn't want to start getting into, taking sticks and retrievable objects in the car with us. I was starting to feel like mom again. I started the car and drove to another phone booth. I dialled Logan airport and found out that my tickets to Yuma were waiting. Then I went back to the car and drove to the fanciest French restaurant I knew. I wanted to look at peacock blue tablecloths again. With my plastic credit card I bought two hours of eating and drinking. The food was great and the wine kept me from thinking too much about the nasty waiters and how I was supporting the Bank of Boston's tendency towards usury. I had a bottle of very dry California Riesling. I enjoyed the waiters and I thought about how hard I had laughed at them the last time I had company over the peacock blue tablecloths. I munched on stuffed mushrooms; I devoured lamb chops with mint sauce; I became maudlin and sentimental. I ate succulent braised potatoes and as I finished the bottle of wine I praised a chocolate mousse with my lips. Frances always said I had a nice mouth.

I ordered a second bottle of wine, even though I couldn't drink it. When I left I offered the rest to two people at the next table but they acted like I was crazy. I told them it was a great wine and how pleasant it was that vulgar Americans were beating the French at their own game. It felt good to be drunk and boorish, full of food and finally not thinking about much of anything. Especially when I was planning on getting myself into deeper trouble the next day.

Twenty-Six

The first thing I realised when I woke up was that I was the head of a family. Safety was leaping over me on the bed, hysterically happy that I'd opened my eyes. I wasn't so happy. Flossie was backed up on to the chest of drawers, certain the puppy could see and panicked. In a moment she'd be complete disdain. Meanwhile, she hissed with great show and let us know how big her tail could get.

'So, beasts, what shall I do for you? Which one should I feed first, and why? Eh, Flossie?'

She ignored me.

I pulled on a robe and went to the kitchen and opened one of her favourite brands of tinned kitty food. It was not a particularly nice scent for humans, but few scents associated with cats are. I put a mental hold on my stomach and dished out the fishy, greasy lumps that she loved on to a saucer. Then I filled a small bowl with water and brought these things back to the bedroom. I put them next to her on the dresser; she pretended she didn't know me; that was okay too.

'You'll get over it, Flossie dear. We'll have our mornings in bed just like always. After all, one animal cannot fill all my needs, apparently. You'll just have to learn to accept it.' I looked down at the wagging, grinning dog and had second thoughts. Then it made that impatient, personable puppy dog sound, looked straight into my eyes and gave a yap. I swear they all go to professional dog school before they're born.

'Someone bred you to act like this, long ago. Your personality is a creation of our species,' I reminded her but the animal window in her brain would never open up very wide.

I mixed some puppy food with warm water and wondered what I'd do with Safety in Yuma. Perhaps I could bring her along, but what if they didn't allow dogs in a gangster resort? I'd have to leave her in a hot car. I realised again with a sinking heart that I had become a mother. I sat down and the puppy tried to crawl into my lap. I found an old blanket and folded it on the floor for her. The house looked much better, Clara had set it back into its normal clean state. The fact that everything was in a different place gave the rooms a misshapen feeling.

Sitting there in the sunlight, listening to the disgusting sound of Flossie eating, I could almost pretend I wasn't going to do anything further about Julie Arbeder. That my heart was not breaking. I'd only screwed up my life by taking on an adorable pet that would be a constant companion for the next ten years and five thousand dollars worth of pet food and veterinary bills.

I closed off the living room, with an improvised barrier from a table leaf and spread a lot of newspapers on the floor in the dining room. Then I called a neighbourchild, Rosemary, who showed up at my doorstep looking lazy and pubescent.

'Wanna earn five bucks?' I asked.

'What I gotta do?'

The puppy ran up to us, as if on cue. 'This is Safety,' I introduced them.

'You want me to feed her? Take her for a walk?'

'That's the gig.'

'Can I take her home and show my brother?'

'Yup.'

'Ten bucks, and five in advance.'

We settled on seven fifty, but she clung to the five advance and left humming with my housekey.

I turned my thoughts towards my one-day vacation in a sunny clime.

June in the desert in California. A state with seventeen climates and a cluster of commuter airlines just to get around in it. I put a white T-shirt underneath a light sweater in case Yuma didn't get hot until the evenings. I would have to change planes in Oakland, California. Gertrude Stein once said, there is no there, there. But now there were even designer dykes in San Francisco, and thousands and thousands of women-identified-women settling all around the San Francisco Bay. What a pity I wasn't going there. What a pity I was going to Yuma.

At Oakland I dutifully waited in the airport lounge until the little commuter plane took off for Yuma. It wasn't a luxury plane and there weren't any luxury travellers. Mostly there were people going to see relatives, showing off baby creatures newly nestled in their arms, an occasional shiny businessman.

Yuma is not a pretty city; in fact it has all the nightmarish qualities of an unplanned urbanised sprawl, except that it is hotter and a lot dirtier than most. It has brown dirt under it and all around it. Other urban developers figured they could turn the desert into a winter playground for the rich, with only service people to spoil the view. They did that a safe seventy miles and one mountain range past Yuma. Besides the traffic there is mining in the area. The sky was only a concept from down on the ground; the mountains are smudged into a horizon that just blends with the brown soup and swallows all the landscape features.

Del Mirago Springs Resort wasn't listed in the yellow pages but the white pages carried it, in lightface type. I wrote down the address and got a map at the rental car desk. It was just outside the city limits. I rented a car. I used my plastic money and offered some more of my future to the Bank of Boston. Then I slid into the interior of a new blue Chevy styleless two-door sedan. A short drive took me out of a maze of shopping malls and used car lots.

I went along the baseline roads, surveyor's lines in the desert. I went through a scruffy desert neighbourhood, with collapsing cactuses in the front yards. I went through a rich neighbourhood with low brick white walls and big arroyo cactuses sticking their arms out all over the place, arranged by a landscape architect who wore leather gloves. I passed a shack with a crippled washing machine in front of it. The same dirt was under everything. I wondered who decided what dirt would spring up in the rich neighbourhood and which dirt would sit under the poor.

I kept driving, took a left and went down another straight grey asphalt line. I found Del Mirago Springs Resort at the end of the road. Two rustic wooden poles reached up high enough to suspend a sign over my car. The paint was faded. A long circular drive had some very ill and fading palms marching around it. There were small brown buildings scattered around the grounds. It looked like a faded resort from the forties, or a youth camp. I approached a building with a long overhanging roof and found a cool entryway.

I walked into the low, blond-panelled lobby. Old flagstone in irregular shapes covered the floor, a lacquered loop of rope encircled a sign announcing times for meals and activities. The dining room was visible, a rhomboid shaped fireplace was cold. It was a pretty place, built in the time when people thought the desert was an exotic part of the wild west, before the golf carts had arrived.

A young man, in short sleeves that bulged to reveal potato arms which stretched the limits of his cuffs, sat behind the desk like a front line of defence. He had tight little grey eyes, a small skull with a close clip, and a scowl that took up most of the space underneath it. He had a crease in his forehead that told he hadn't completed any courses in hotel management lately. From the looks of the place I didn't think he needed to.

'Hello. I'm looking for a guest here. Sue Martinez.'

'So what?'

'So I'm looking for her, that's enough.'

'Not necessarily. Our guests come here for privacy.' He looked me up, and to give him credit, noticed the rented car. 'Beat it,' he said.

'Isn't that her by the pool?' He turned with me to the low window that showed a woman curled up on a lounge chair in a foetal position.

'I think I'll just go there and announce myself,' I said, but potato arms got nervous, shifted in his chair and started to stand up.

'I'll keep my hands in plain sight, just so you can see what clean nails look like.'

He leaned over the desk a few inches and sneered. Then he started to move around to the side of the desk in front of the walkway that would lead me to the pool.

'You can make all the ugly faces you want,' I said, 'And I can make it your business that I see Sue Martinez.' I flipped open my wallet and showed him a card from Lieutenant Sloan's office. There was no first name on it, only an initial. He scowled some more.

'Lady cop.'

'Where I come from bouncers have to learn to be lot more subtle. Especially with the law.'

He pointed to the aqua square that was the pool. 'That way,' he grumbled. He sat down and picked up a grimy magazine. He put his face into it as I walked past him out on to the tiled, tilted patio and closed the redwood and glass door behind me.

Sue was lying on a lounge chair; she had a tight black shiny one-piece bathing suit on, with pieces of silver thread woven in the elastic fabric. The threads gave off little sparks as her chest rose and fell, they also sparkled over every rib on her thin chest. Her belly was flat and she was sweating lightly all over. Her toes twiddled, hanging off the edge of the lawn furniture.

'Hello, Sue.'

She languidly opened one eye and then the other. Then she snapped them both shut.

'What are you doing here?'

'I might ask you the same thing.'

'I might say it's none of your business.'

'I might wonder about your need for privacy.' I pulled a white metal

154

patio chair towards her and sat down on a yellow and white rubber cushion.

'So, how you spend your time is no business of mine.' She fussed in a clear plastic beach bag and pulled out a flip top box of cigarettes and pulled one out. She extended herself back on the chair and closed her eyes, resting the cigarette by her on the lounge chair.

'It used to be, when you wanted me to run around and check out Julie's friendly enemies at work. Also I went over and saw Misty and helped her move out yesterday. Big job. She had to clean up the yard by herself.'

'So what?' Her hand drifted towards the cigarette; she picked it up.

'So, it's not nice to skip out on your friends sometimes.' I struck a match. The sound made her open her eyes and she sat up to take the light. It was more contact than she wanted.

'She's not my friend.' Sue blew some smoke in my direction.

'Oh, I get it. Just someone you split the bills with.'

'You're breaking my heart.'

'I doubt if anyone could. But my house got trashed and I got a nasty lump on my head looking into your roommate's death. I didn't think that would trouble you too much, sitting down in the sun, but I thought I'd come down here and bother you with it anyway.'

'Sorry, you're wasting your time.'

'You've got some pretty expensive attitudes, I'll bet you've been paying a pretty high price for some of your habits. I just thought you might want to know that you're playing with some tough buddies. I haven't met any of them yet, they kind of sneak up from behind.'

'I'm sorry if you've had some bad times. I'm sorry if I encouraged you, got you into something that turned out to be trouble. But I have my own problems.'

'But that's the kind of attitude that gives you the problems you've got. Your tracks may be melting away with that nice tan you're getting, but it's not doing a lot for your personality. You're going to have to do better than that if you really want to take the cure.'

'So what? I've been into drugs. That doesn't prove anything.'

'Who said anything about proving anything? Do you think I want to prove something?'

'How would I know what you're here for?' The wide mouth became smaller and tighter. She sat up and started rubbing sun tan lotion jerkily on her legs.

'Probably the same reason you sent me on that wild goose chase about the union stuff.'

155

'Aw, hell. They probably *did* do it. Look, I just don't care any more.'

'Sure, you're too busy getting a tan.'

'What the hell do you know?'

She looked daggers at me and if she'd thought of it she would have squirted sun tan lotion in my eye.

'You were broke and strung out; you'd just left your job, or gotten fired. Now you're doing real well for yourself. You made the connection, so now you're sucking a little off the tit of a loaded family up north. You sucked off five thousand dollars.'

'I'm getting clean.'

'You made the connection, you worked the play. What did it take?'

Sue puffed quickly on her cigarette, the still desert air was full of smoke and the smell of Bain de Soleil. 'Sue, you're trying to get clean. Then get clean. I've had my own reasons for going out on a limb, but you helped me along out there. If you're going to try and clean up your act you can take a giant step by cleaning things up with me.' She was rubbing her leg quickly, but the movement became slower. 'Even if you don't owe yourself, you owe me.'

She rubbed the lotion on one leg, palming her calf muscle back and forth. She did it for a long time. I looked at the tropical horticulture, lots of pointy desert things, rocks, cactuses with giant needles pointing at each other and the enormous aloe vera leaves, like curling elephant ears, with thorns as big as your thumb along the edges. The only way to work in a desert garden is armoured. It's either you or the plants.

From afar it all looked very dramatic and showy. At night it would be lit up with a lot of patio lights. Then it would look like Mars. There was a palm tree which had friendly little pansy faces planted around its base. The desert says 'Have a nice day.'

I heard a little noise from Sue.

'Shit,' she was massaging her leg harder and harder. 'Julie never even told me.' Her chin trembled and she squirted a small lake of lotion into her palm. 'A few years ago Julie was my friend, she wanted to move into *my house*. I'd just broken up with this guy, hell, I thought it was a nice idea. Then all of a sudden I couldn't do anything right. Julie was never home, she'd only been living with me for a few months. She was in and out. I got to see a lot of the soles of her shoes as she was walking out the door. We had a fight about it. I think she felt guilty about it. One day she showed up with Misty. It was like she was bringing a pet home for me. She met her in an aerobics class she was teaching. I was broke, and I thought, what the hell, take another roommate. Anyway, Julie brought her in from the rain and that's how we happened on to the wafting Misty.' She finished with a calf and had squirted more lotion on to her palm and was starting on a forearm. 'Julie didn't care what happened to that house.'

'You mean Julie didn't care what happened to you.'

'Hmm.' She had too much lotion on her arm again. 'Listen, I was taking care of everything for a while. The bills, Julie's crying fits, before she found Ms Rich Tits. Then I had Misty. Have you ever lived with anyone who would only use wooden utensils to eat from?'

I nodded but I wasn't really interested in Misty's culinary habits. 'And Julie's relationship?'

'I knew she was seeing somebody, she'd been shooting off her mouth about gay liberation and suddenly I wasn't good enough any more. Hell, Julie even brought her home a few times. But they went upstairs giggling. Christ, it reminded me of a fucking sorority. Then they'd just started going to *her* house, wherever that was. Shit, they could have had me over for a drink, at least.' She blinked.

'So you dealt a little in the leftover goods of the deceased?'

'Look, Julie shut me out of her life because she was in love. I was, I don't know – straight, I guess. But when did I ever make such a big deal about it? Then Julie was dead and I had a habit. And I had to clean up her room. What a lousy feeling.'

'So what was worth the five grand?'

'Hell, I figured that Glassman guy would easily cough up five grand for some letters. While Allison was living with the old man she got pretty hot with the prose. I put it to him this way. I said that I figured that the letters of the deceased belonged to the family. I mean you never know about letter collections. I said that Allison's letters to Julie would make Henry Miller look naive.'

'Glassman must have loved that.'

'Actually, they *would* have made Miller look naive. The letters were really forthright. Athletes.' She stopped rubbing. There was still white lotion left. 'I told him that I had five thousand dollars in medical bills. And,' she started rubbing, 'I did. So what the hell. What difference does it make now? He won't need to worry about the fate of the pornographic epistles from Allison and if Julie hadn't been so fucking in love – well, she would probably be glad I'm sitting here in the sun getting tanned and cured.'

'And you figure it's better to live.'

'You know what it's like to be strung out? First you do it on the weekends, something to give parties a lift, you know. Then you do it a bit, during the week, it's exciting. You break your rule and do it during

157

the day, at work, then it's a midday lift, then it's a kind of maintenance habit and you need more to get high for those parties you used to enjoy. And then, what's really freaky, after a while you feel like you just sort of become the drug. It owns you.' She started rubbing her calf again, but this time it was the other leg.

'I started to take the edge off with a valium here and there. You know, if I couldn't get to sleep or something. Then somebody had some horse at a party. And it was like I got to get the monkey off me, that had been riding my back for months. Then I was married to two drugs.' She looked at me, and I had the feeling she was going to win. 'And don't ever forget, no matter how clean the scene is, it kills you. It honestly does.'

A roadrunner ran suddenly across the clipped lawn.

'Here, give me some of that lotion,' I said leaning forward and extending an arm. We rubbed forearms together. 'You're like a greased pig,' I said, but she was skinny and I could see the ribs flexing underneath her black bathing suit.

'Julie would like to see me get in shape, don't you think?' she said.

'Yes.'

'Hey, Emma.' She stopped me. 'They tell us here we've got to make amends for trashy stuff we've done. I want to apologise to you. I'm sorry.'

'What are you sorry for?'

'Well, I was pretty ugly in the car that night.'

'Yeah, but that's your ugliness, and I don't have to live with it the way you do.'

'It's not just that. *You* know, I liked you, but I really didn't know what to do with it. You asked me out to dinner and I said yes.'

'But you had business to do and you figured it would be better to have me out of the picture for a while. And the surest way was to come on as a steaming Mae West.'

'Yeah,' she blushed under the tan and all that lotion. 'It really worked, didn't it?'

'I couldn't believe it when you said "Don't be like that, honey!" '

'Yeah.' She laughed. Her laughter had a nicer sound now.

'Well, you don't need to protect yourself any more,' she said.

'Pity.' I stood up and got out of the chair, offered her a hand and we pressed our lotioned palms together.

I turned and started walking away. 'You've got really nice arms, you know.'

I walked towards the doorway and looked once back at her. She was lying down with her eyes closed. She'd finished rubbing lotion all over herself.

I walked back through the cool breezeway and into the lobby. I felt very satisfied. I had confirmed a few of my ideas and told Sue she had pretty arms. A woman with a full head of grey hair and a stethoscope was raising her voice ever so slightly to the boy behind the desk. She stopped abruptly and he shrugged his lumpy arms and looked away. The doctor had walked out. I came close to the reception desk. I leaned over it.

'You can hang it out in the breeze, tough boy. She isn't interested in anything you have to offer.' Potato arms clenched his teeth and peered out again at Sue. We both looked. She was smoking a cigarette and looking at the eerie desert landscape. He looked back up at me. 'And next time,' I said, 'ask for a badge, sucker.'

I turned and left with his purpling face warming my back.

Twenty-Seven

I came back to my house the next day. Somerville looked good after the tan plaid bedspread and Gideon Bible of a Best Western Motel. I only seemed to fly over the good parts of California. I opened the front door and walked upstairs. Safety was jumping up and down behind the tableleaf and chair barrier I had made to close off the living room. I saw evidence of Rosemary's employment in a dirty dog food bowl. I let Safety out the back door. I cleaned up one cool yellow puddle in the dining room.

Then I felt the feline presence behind me. Flossie was eyeing me with utter contempt. I fed her some quality sardines. Safety came in, and I fed her too. I was just starting to reap those benefits normally denied to people without issue and yet of childbearing age, when the phone rang.

'How are you feeling today?' My damned imagination gave me a picture of her face immediately. 'Do I get to ask you if you still remember everything, or are we still touchy today?'

'Sorry, I guess I was a little grouchy or something there.'

'You sure were. I was afraid I'd developed the first yeast infection with bad breath.'

'*That* I could live with.'

'What was it then?'

'I dunno. I guess I'm afraid of getting involved.'

'Don't back off. I really think I could make a nice playmate for you.'

'So far I've never found anyone who could play as nice as you that turned out to be a playmate. Once you're in the mood it's not playing any more.'

'Okay,' she sighed. 'Be that way. What makes you so unapproachable anyway?'

'I've got to figure some things out, and company doesn't help.'

'Let me come and visit you, please? Just to show my good intentions?'

'Or your mixed messages?'

160

'I've been busy, Emma. Too busy. But my messages aren't mixed. Just let me come and say goodnight. Ten minutes.'

'You want to come over just to say goodnight?'

'I won't bring my toothbrush. I promise. Let me come over and hold you for a minute.'

'Okay,' I said but it sounded risky. I remembered that I had a new toothbrush in a cellophane wrapper on the bottom shelf of the linen closet in a shoebox.

I put it out of my mind and sat down with Safety and Flossie to read a book. I was reading *A Journal of the Plague Year* by Daniel Defoe. I put it down for a moment to turn on the radio. It competed with the sound of a branch scraping against the window. Defoe described one mode of plague prevention by throwing coins in buckets of vinegar.

After a while the doorbell rang. I walked downstairs and opened it. There was Frances, wearing a raincoat over something that looked like underwear. She opened the coat to show me pale fawn pyjamas.

'Gees,' was all I could say until Safety ran out the door and made a puppy pyramid arching her back in the moonlight. Then I still couldn't say anything.

Finally, I said, 'I'm an animal mother.'

'Actually, I've been feeling a little burnt on beasts lately,' she said.

'What, no doctor's heart of gold, embracing all living creatures?'

'Just creatures that answer the phone all day.'

'Well, I'm on vacation.'

'What's that like?'

'Oh yeah, you wouldn't know,' I said and Frances sighed.

I watched her watching Safety. Safety was playing with an invisible friend and was jumping around in surprised circles.

'I guess you'll have to leash her.'

'No dogs on leashes, no animals in cages,' I said. 'Good thing Golden Retrievers are so smart. This dog is going to be raised politically correct.'

Frances groaned. 'Can't say I'm wild about animals in cages myself.' We started walking up the stairs.

'Maybe it's all relative,' she said. 'I mean it all depends on the proportions of the cage. And the ability to get out when you want.' She sighed. I watched her walk up the stairs, tired, or hesitant. But when we reached the top she stopped and waited. I did what she intended, starting very slowly to undress her.

'I don't want to make love to you,' I said.

'I can't imagine why not.'

'Maybe that's the problem. You enjoy tempting me.'

'What's the matter, got a headache?' She came to me again, but I just couldn't leap over my doubts. I tried once, but it was getting harder.

'Don't end it, Emma,' she said, 'not for a while. Please.'

'You certainly are persistent. It gives a good impression.'

'Oh, Emma, what's wrong with you?'

'I have a headache.'

'Okay. How much time is it going to take you to get rid of it?'

'About as much time as you're busy.'

'Don't make it conditional.'

'I don't mean it like that. We both have something to finish. And neither one of us wants to tell the other what's going on. Or haven't you noticed?'

'I've noticed, Emma. Listen, I'm just sort of sworn to secrecy, it's a long-term project. I'm just waiting for that first step, and then I'll give you the goods. It's exciting. You'll *really* like it.' She gave a wink and laughed.

'Yeah, for you. Listen, let's just finish our business and see where we are at the end.'

'I don't want to lose you, Emma.'

'Frances, try and take "no" for an answer, tonight. Please.'

'Okay,' she said, and went to her raincoat.

'And don't punish me for it.'

'Okay,' a shade softer. She kissed me again and left without saying anything more complicated than 'I love you', complete with tears in her eyes. It had started to rain. I counted to twenty and picked up the phone.

'Jonell, it's Emma. Can I come over?'

'Emma, it's a little late.'

'You going to bed? What are you doing?'

'I'm sitting here not having a glass of brandy and then I'm going to bed as soon as I can get finished.'

'Oh. Can I come over tomorrow morning before you go to work?'

'Emma, what's up? You want to come over at eight thirty before I leave for work?'

'Yes.'

'What's the rush?'

'I'll bring croissants.'

'Yeah, but what's it all about?'

'I'll tell you tomorrow.'

'And now you expect me to get to sleep?'

162

'Think about soft, warm, buttery croissants, all the little light layers rising, rising, softly in the warm oven. And go to sleep, Jonell.'

'Okay. Come at eight and then we'll have time for tea.'

'See you then.'

'Goodnight, Emma,' she said with suspicion in her voice. She had every right to be suspicious. I was going to arrive at her door with butter croissants and a question that would put our friendship on the line.

I hung up the phone and walked to the little kitchen. I leaned against a piece of clean woodwork and looked at the few dishes on the draining board; they were rinsed and waiting to be washed. I drew a hot bath and thought about not drinking, not smoking a joint. I didn't have any food in the house, the groceries of a month had been too recently smeared all over the floor.

After my bath I put on clean pyjamas and had a drink. My head hit the pillow like a brick and I went to sleep.

Much later, out of the middle of the night, the phone rang. I groped for the plastic horn in the dark and a voice entered my ear.

'Oh God,' wailed a voice, 'Emma!'

'Not again,' I said. 'Pleas for help are bad for my health, especially in the middle of the night. And I don't make appointments in dark alleys any more either.'

'Emma,' came a strangled sob, 'I killed her.'

'What? Hugo? What do you mean?'

'It was all my fault. He asked me to invite her to the boat. I knew she would come. She loved me Emma, she trusted *me*.'

'Go on.'

'Don't you see, Emma, I betrayed her.'

'Tell me what happened, Hugo, step by step.'

'I knew what my brother had planned. A little cruise. I didn't know what he wanted from her. He controls everybody, everything. You can't get away from him. I couldn't get away, don't you see?'

'And Allison? She got away.'

'No she didn't. You can't get away from my brother. Allison couldn't get away.'

'He used you to get Allison on the boat that night?'

'Yes, I didn't tell her he'd be there. I was just supposed to meet her there. I invited her in. She said she was really uptight. She told me she was afraid of him. I was afraid to tell her that he was coming. I knew he was there.

'We had some drinks. I don't know how many. She wanted to know what he was doing, if he was going to give her a divorce. I knew he was waiting outside the boat. Waiting. I didn't know why. I was very nervous. So there we were and he walked in. She was afraid, she was afraid of him. He was so cool, so smooth. He acted like it was a surprise. He said he wanted to talk to her alone for a minute. I had a terrible feeling. I knew something awful was going to happen.

'They went into his cabin,' Hugo gulped some air, 'and I heard them talking. Then I heard Allison scream. She sort of wailed. Then he laughed. I heard him, my brother laughed and laughed. Oh god, I have to get out of here. I have to get away from him.'

'And then what happened?'

'I see it over and over again. It was foggy. I felt the boat tip with her footsteps coming up the stairs, running from his cabin. I knew she was coming on deck. I-I-I wanted to talk to her, tell her I didn't mean to do it. I came on deck and saw her. She hadn't seen me. She was startled, I frightened her. She was just coming up those stairs, and she took another step and there was no last stair. It was just air. Then a wave hit the boat and we pulled away from the pier and she just – she just –' he sobbed, 'she just slid off the deck and I watched her. She fell right into the water, looking at me, and I didn't – I didn't even move to help her.'

'But you didn't kill her.'

'I didn't help her. I didn't react.'

'That's not murder.'

He was still crying.

'You're not guilty of murder, Hugo. You loved her. You felt guilty. That's not murder.'

'And then the girlfriend came. It was terrible, terrible. She was so flipped out. I told her everything. But she said terrible, awful things.'

'You wanted Julie to absolve you?'

'Oh Emma, I didn't really do it, did I? Oh, God, I have to get out of here. It's bad, bad things are happening all around me . . .'

'I know, Hugo,' I said. But I was thinking, 'You never get straight enough to stop it.'

He made a sound, a sort of grunt and then a punctuated 'urp' into the receiver. The sound stopped and then it echoed down a tube. I heard some liquid noises and Hugo's footsteps running along a carpeted floor. Some distant retching and the phone was noisily hung up.

'Thanks for upchucking into my dreams.' I said to no one.

164

Twenty-Eight

When the night time was over I went to Jonell's. There was sun everywhere, streaming across traffic, long orange streaks on car hoods threatening to overheat. Borders of impatiens and lobelia lined the sidewalk leading to Jonell's house.

When I rang the bell Jonell answered the door with something less than a smile. Then she yawned.

'Is it that bad?'

'Only when I'm reminded of it.' She looked like she hadn't slept. 'But today I'm starting a short gymnastic course, trying out the body again, see if it can still do that stuff I used to be so good at.'

'Well, you look great.' And she did. She had on a red knitted body warmer and an enormous cream linen overblouse, long enough to be a dress.

Jonell waved me into her sunny breakfast nook, with jigsawed curlicues decorating the sides of the upholstered benches. It had the homey tasteless look of a former owner's Sunday carpentry. We slid on to the benches and sat with sleepy eyes across from each other.

'Oh, I'll get some saucers,' she said noticing the bag with little grease spots holding the croissants. 'I'll make some of the herbal tea. I keep hoping if I drink enough of it I'll get high.' She laughed. 'Actually, that's not true. I'm going to do replacement addiction therapy. I'm going to get addicted to parallel bars again. I'm looking forward to it.'

She slid out of the bench and I heard her putting water in the teapot. She yawned and stretched and touched her toes at the end of the long expanse of red knitted legs. She could put her entire palms on the floor. Former dancers always seem to keep their muscles like rubber bands, no matter how many lines they get in their faces. In a moment the water boiled and I heard the water being poured into a teapot. It was probably the teapot with little red roses on the side. Then she returned and put a ghastly carved tray with two pentagon shaped tea cups and saucers on the little breakfast table. I watched her pour the tea and put

165

the croissants on the saucers. The teapot had yellow roses.

'This teapot is uglier than the last one you had.'

'My Aunt Harriet's,' she smiled.

'You can't be feeling too bad. You look great,' I said again.

'Cut the hot air. What's going on?'

'How's volunteering down at the clinic?'

'You came over here to ask me that?'

'Okay. I'm in love with Frances Cohen. It feels like an emergency.'

Jonell laughed and leaned back on the little bench. It was made for smaller people than her. A streak of morning sunlight hit her face. 'So, Emma's finally fallen for someone. And it's a three alarm fire.' She laughed again and shook her head.

'It's not funny. She's always working at that fucking clinic. And she has an extra job on the side a few nights a week at a lab. But there's something else going on.'

'And you thought *I* was getting into trouble with Stacy Weldemeer.' Jonell snorted.

'Maybe you are.'

'Hey, I'm just having a recreational crush, remember? Speak for yourself, Emma. I wouldn't ask Stacy Weldemeer out for a drink, even if I wasn't on the wagon, and even if I could get into her appointment book. Women in the medical business are heavy news.' She stretched a red knitted leg over the length of the upholstered bench. Her foot stuck over the edge and she touched her toe with one hand and nibbled on her croissant with the other. 'Frances Cohen just works her brains out, that's all, beginning and end.'

'Yeah, but what's she doing?' I asked and Jonell looked at me from over the edge of the pentagon shaped tea cup. Steam hid her eyes. She blew the steam away and put the cup down. 'As far as I know Frances has no extra-curricular activities. Her thing with Stacy is strictly business. She isn't visible a lot. She hides herself out in the back wing.'

'The back wing?'

'Yeah. Where the clinic has a small lab, and all the sperm banks. I heard she used to have a few hamsters out back. She stays out of everybody's way and lets Stacy handle the people stuff.'

'*All* the people stuff? Even four, five months ago?'

'Of course, volunteers do all the reception work and two paramedics do intake.'

'Where's the appointment book?'

'On the front desk, why?'

'So Frances just handles the back room baby stuff?'

'You could call it that if you want to invest overtime emotion into it. I think you've got a clear field. What's the matter anyway, Emma? You've usually got people's numbers pretty fast. What's stopping you if you've fallen so hard?' Jonell sipped her tea and made a face.

'You work at the clinic day after tomorrow, don't you?'

'Yes.'

'Jonell,' I took a sip of the tea. It burned my lips and tasted like brewed potting soil. 'I want you to give me your set of keys to the clinic.'

'What, are you crazy?'

'No, I'm not crazy. Just give them to me.'

Jonell sank back on the bench. She fingered the hem of her shirt. 'Don't you think you're getting a little obsessed about this, Emma?'

'Yes, that's why you have to give me the keys. I just want to look around.'

'Come in the daytime. I'll give you a tour.'

'Not of the back wing.'

'She's really got you going, hasn't she?'

'Yes, she really has me, coming and going. I have to put an end to it. I know the answer is in that clinic. I know it.'

'Come on,' Jonell laughed but not very hard. 'Are you going over the deep end or what?'

'Jonell, I'm not. Trust me. I just need to find out a few things. I need to see that appointment book. I need to see that back wing. Then I'll know. Don't make me ask you again. Just go along with me. Please, Jonell. I won't ask again.'

I watched my friend. Her mouth was having an argument with her eyebrows. I watched the steam rise off the herbal tea. I looked at the yellow roses on the teapot. I looked at Jonell and saw that the eyebrows were losing and the mouth was winning.

'Okay,' she took a breath and crawled out of the bench. She walked to the kitchen counter and fumbled in a beige canvas bag. 'But, christ. Be careful. And, if someone catches you, well, you have to say you got the keys from me. Say, hell, say I have the flu and that I had left some medicine in my desk there. But don't let yourself get caught. I'd rather not have any explaining to do. Especially to Stacy.'

'Thanks.'

'I just hope you know what you're doing. And I hope I know what I'm doing too.' She dropped the two little keys in my hand. I looked straight into her big brown eyes.

'Thank you, thank you,' I said.

Jonell leaked out a sigh. 'You're welcome.' But it sounded a little bit like a question.

'I'm going now,' I said and stood up. She walked me to the door and put her dark, almost maroon hand, on mine. Jonell is the darkest black person I know. I am always shocked by how white and lifeless my skin looks next to hers.

'Take care of yourself, Emma,' she said. 'The little round one is the alarm key.' Then I felt her lips quickly on my cheek, she turned and walked back to the kitchen to finish her tea and get ready for work.

I spent the rest of the day waiting for nightfall. It was a long wait, the sun wouldn't give up, wouldn't fall down and my ironing was over before I knew it, thanks to modern fibres silently creeping into everything. I couldn't bear calling anyone or making visits, playing the Boston-Cambridge Life Summary Game where for one hour you interview each other about current relationships, attitudes towards work and self development. I wished I could have a rousing argument about a third topic, an actual disagreement where I could enjoin with someone in not respecting the sanctity of our emotional lives. Perhaps we could discuss the finer points of the intrusions of computers in everyday life, or the development of film in the forties. I decided that was pleasing, but unlikely to happen. I beamed some suggested conversational topics at Safety but it was beyond the scope of dog brain. Many things would be.

But my scope was not limited for long. Soon it touched infinity. I decided to call Seven Blue Horses.

'Hi, Emma,' said Seven when she answered the phone. 'I'm glad you called. Hard to get used to calling me Seven, isn't it?'

'Not as long as you don't whinny. I presume you have kept the English rose complexion, the green eyes, the other beautiful human equipment you were originally issued.'

'You forgot the big tits.'

'I always forget the big tits, I'm afraid of them remember?'

'What can I do for you, Emma?'

'Well, have you tuned into the white light lately?'

'You mean you want to know if I've played cosmic answering service for you.'

'Well, I mean, if you happened to pick something up . . .'

'Tell me why I should bother, with your attitude.'

'Because I need the advice, seriously, Sandy, I mean Seven. I need it for tonight.'

'Sorry, the great mother doesn't provide escort service.'

'Maybe she does. Come on, Sandy, give me a break. I know you've been coming up with some weird titbits throwing my name out into the unknown. Well, it's *my* name and I want to know what kind of messages you're receiving from it.'

'Okay, Emma, you're right. Ever since my experience in the clinic I have been using your name as a sort of channel, a wavelength to get a response. But you just seem to call down some maternal trip from 1956.'

'Like what?'

'Like the thing about the underpants, "you never know when you might need to see a doctor".'

'Hey, just tell me, have you had any response from using my name?'

'Yeah, I'll get it.' I heard her walk away and then I heard her uncrumple the paper that was my personal telegram from beyond.

'To make an angel food cake,' she read, 'a woman must first learn to separate eggs. An important part of the baking process is to avoid sudden sounds which could result in a fall. In this case your creation may be saved by generous helpings of fresh ice cream from the frozen foods dairy case of your grocer.'

'Thanks Sandy, I owe you a cake. A wholewheat space cake.'

'Sure, Emma. Peace and love of the goddess to you too.'

I couldn't tell if she was being sarcastic and I didn't care. Who was Betty Crocker anyway, to send me messages from beyond? I laid back on the couch; I felt sleepy and I wanted to sleep, just a short quick one with no dreams. But I wasn't so lucky. I dreamt about a colossus, a huge woman sixteen feet high. She was wearing a starched white organdie apron with ruffles at the shoulder and green felt holly leaves appliquéd on to the skirt. She was circling a white porcelain bowl the size of a bathtub in her arms. She was beating something inside it with a wooden spoon as big as a shovel. Then with her burgundy lipsticked smile she leaned over towards me. I saw her two white breasts hanging beneath the sheer material of the apron. She tilted the bowl towards me and I looked into it.

I saw a baby; except it had the head of an adult. The huge head turned its blow-dried hair towards me, the tiny pink body squirming behind it. The face had a leer and probably a hair transplant. The stretched and wrinkled forehead owned utilities. It was the full grown head of Stanley Glassman.

I woke myself up with my own cry. I was glad to be awake; I was glad until I remembered what it was that I had planned for that evening.

Twenty-Nine

It was a moonless night, the leaves made slightly darker shapes against the black sky above. I decided to wear all black in keeping with my adventure and was reminded of all the robbery scenes I'd seen on television with sneakered thieves in black turtleneck sweaters.

I parked two blocks from the clinic. I was sweating already. Petty Shoplifting had not prepared me for Breaking and Entering, and acrylic fibres made me clammy.

I crossed the street and walked past the Blackstone Women's Clinic. It had a small, landscaped lawn. Its forties exterior had thick, wavy glass bricks lining either side of a curved green door. Small bushes on either side had been pruned into leafy ice cream cones. It was a cute building, it wasn't asking me to break into it either.

I kept walking; I walked past it a block and then turned left and walked down another street and left again so I would approach it from the back. I passed a row of houses and could see vaguely through their back gates the small parking lot of the clinic. I thought about how a lot of women drove there with their hopes and dreams of reproduction. I wondered how many of their dreams came true; and I was also curious why Frances and Stacy were working so often at night; keeping the sperm warm for tomorrow's clients? Little test tubes wrapped in pink and blue flannel buntings, Stacy with one on a talk show and Frances with the other, doing what?

So I stood looking at a house with a broken iron gate. It shared an alley with the Blackstone Women's Clinic. I could see a sign painted on the cement block wall of the back of the clinic, 'Visitors of the Blackstone Clinic Parking'. They hadn't hired a signwriter to do it; the letters had an amateurish quality, but they were evenly spaced and the wall was freshly painted.

A light went on across the street and a curtain was pulled back. I realised that stopping and watching a dark house, or the alley behind it, was enough to get someone to their telephone calling the police. In the old days, I guessed, behaviour must have been different. The curious neighbour, opening their door and walking across the street and enquiring about what your business was, in a friendly way, as if you could be Jack and Doris' niece coming down for a surprise visit and not finding them at home, poor girl, do come in for a cup of hot cocoa. Then a few times it would show up in the papers that someone had gotten a belly full of lead for greeting the world like a buddy, or at least not an enemy. I walked on quickly and didn't look back at the dark house. It was a world full of strangers; you assumed people had guns, which was only reasonable, in case they did, which was only smart. A lot of smart people carried guns these days.

Dark trees loomed over my head and swayed back and forth, reminding me of winter in another climate. The wind had a chill that went to the middle of my chest; I saw a man on the other side of the street, passing under the glow of the streetlamp. I quickly stepped into the middle of the street. I walked past him, not looking down, but without looking straight ahead either. I walked by him. I let out a breath. The Women's Safety Game is always trying to think with *their* minds, in case they're the enemy. Someone is less likely to attack you in the middle of the street, away from the cosy bushes, garden hedges and alleyways. So I walked along the middle of the street feeling like an ass, trying to think with the mind of a criminal, who might just have walked past me. I was also trying to think about breaking into that clinic.

I saw a small alleyway that ran behind one house to the garbage cans of the clinic. I was contemplating going into the alley when I saw two figures walking from the clinic, crossing the street and walking towards me. One was practically carrying the other. The one who was the crutch said in a loud whispering voice, 'I said I'd get it for you, now shut up. I ask you to wait five minues in a car and what do you do? You can't go wandering around the fucking street. Christ, stay put, okay?'

I didn't hear the rest because my thoughts interrupted my vision. It was Hugo Glassman who looked bombed out crying on the shoulder of Miss Liberated Speculum herself, Stacy Weldemeer. I ducked behind a tree in a cliché move that always worked in cartoons but the sparse city trees didn't have big trunks. I said a silent prayer to Sandy's goddess, and I watched the little man. For such a case, Hugo Glassman sure was attracting a lot of women these days. Crying on the shoulder of Stacy Weldemeer's red leather jacket he didn't look like a million dollar throwback to Flower Power days; he just looked like a lonely lush.

'Look, I said I'd get it for you. Just wait a second.'

Hugo was holding his stomach and bending slightly over at the waist. 'I don't feel so good,' he said.

'Hold on,' Stacy fumbled with some keys, 'I don't blame you for being upset. I would be too if I'd done what you did.'

'I didn't mean to do it,' he said. 'Stacy, I'm not guilty. I-I just feel guilty.'

'Where'd you get that idea? You're as guilty as if you'd pushed her off that boat yourself. You're a sick person, Hugo. Who knows what else you've done?'

'I didn't, I didn't, I mean it didn't happen that way.'

'How do you know, Hugo? Can you remember everything that happened? Do you remember how I put you on the couch earlier today? You were screaming and yelling crazy things Hugo, and when you woke up you didn't remember any of it.'

'I did? What did I say?' he groaned.

'Hugo, just calm yourself. Get in the car and sit down. Everything will be all right if you let me take care of things. I'll see that you don't hurt yourself any more or anyone else.'

'Take me away. Someone has to take me out of here. If you won't take me away I'll find someone else who will.' He was panicking again.

'You don't have any friends, Hugo. You can't be anyone's friend, Hugo. You are a sick and dangerous person. You don't have any friends but me. There is no one left to trust, Hugo. Just me, Hugo, just me.' She put her arm around him. 'You can trust me, Hugo.'

'Stacy, I didn't do it, did I?'

'Get in the car, Hugo.'

He fought with her a moment, like a child who doesn't want to take a bath, like a child clutching a teddy bear, but Hugo was clutching his stomach. He folded himself up and deposited himself on the kerb. Stacy stood there a moment, she had her hands on her hips and I could see her jaw moving back and forth. She jangled some keys and strode up the little sidewalk to the clinic. She stopped between the ice cream cone bushes and I saw her fiddle with the security lock. I watched her progress through the building, along a corridor, each window lighting up in succession and then each light going out again. She emerged and swept Hugo off the pavement.

'C'mon, let's get going.' She steered him across the street to the red jeep that belonged to Frances. He was a broken person by then, she walked him to the passenger door and shoved him up and on to the front seat.

172

I watched the two people ride away in the car, leaving me on a dark street looking at the dark and unlit clinic building. I glanced both ways and walked directly to the front door of the clinic. I opened the door and turned on a light and found a spotless tiled white hallway. I turned the light out again and closed the door.

The hallway was small, but broader than a house hallway, and still in keeping with a modest business venture. There were fresh flowers on a small table and some literature arranged among some magazines. The waiting room had a white tiled floor too, and a dark ebony set of chairs, squarish with a dusk blue damask covering. The chairs kept the place on the butcher-block side of high tech, but it was smart, a bit fashionable and expensive. I love to see women get what they deserve. I hoped they were only getting what they deserved; I hoped they were only getting service at the tidy and prosperous Blackstone Clinic. Then I found what I was looking for. A tall white reception desk had a small fluorescent lamp suspended on the back side over the working area, I switched it on. The narrow desk surface was cluttered with pencils, paper clip holders, and an assortment of taped messages. A large formal appointment book sat in the middle of it all. It was covered like a Hallmark card in quilted flowered fabric. I didn't think women deserved that.

Inside the bad taste I found names, dates, times and finally I found Glassman, Allison. Then I started counting, twenty-eight, twenty-six, thirty days apart. Once, Arbeder stood next to Glassman. By the last appointment there stood 'SW' and a series of numbers.

But it still wasn't enough. I wanted to know where the invisible wheel was, the tightened spring that kept these people and events turning and turning around each other. I was part of that wheel too.

I found a long narrow corridor and unlocked another door which led to another corridor. I opened a few doors as I went along. I found examining rooms and storage rooms – the examining rooms looked a bit sparse, but everything was clean and organised. It gave me a chill to think about Frances working there. I made a mental note to take Safety to the vet soon.

I kept on doing this, walking down the corridor and opening up doors, there weren't so many doors to go; it was just a matter of time before I opened The Door. I wondered what it would be like, another examining room that was an entryway to a giant casino, or an S and M scene, or something that might tie Frances together with a rich hippie boy or put Stacy Weldemeer in a picture with the woman I could be so in love with.

I found the answer down at the end of the last corridor. It was a large door and it was locked; the front door key slid easily into the lock. I was in.

I debated on turning on the light, but I didn't need to. The first thing I noticed was the humidity and the smells. It wasn't too bad actually. I knew in a minute or two I'd get the noises. I walked into the room and closed the door softly behind me and looked around.

Glass boxes everywhere, filled with crawling plants and crawling things. Snakes slithered over white rocks in an aquarium which held large catfish with long whiskers. They swam back and forth and back and forth behind the glass.

A few chameleons pressed their lime green bellies against the edge of their prisons and flicked their tongues at me. I shivered. Two tanks with slimy grey water bubbled and little monitors blinked and bleeped.

Four furry hamsters were busy at a treadmill. They were the only warm-blooded things in the room, besides me.

So what was Stacy doing? Scoring blood of eel and eye of toad to exorcise Hugo's guilt? And why was my girlfriend spending her evenings with amphibians when she could be spending them with me?

I looked in a few cupboards but didn't find anything. There was another door, thinner than the entryway doors, but it was locked and none of my keys fitted it.

I was about to search for the key when I thought I heard someone in the front hall. I remembered I'd left the light on behind the reception desk and I froze.

I heard a lightweight car door slam. I waited for a few minutes for the engine to start but the car just sat there for a while. Then it started and roared away quickly, with the lumpy thundering of an untuned motor.

I counted to ten and then I ran out, out of the reptile room, down the hallways, through the entryway and out the front door. I ran until I remembered how stupid it was to run, attracting attention to myself, but I could hardly be anonymous; a woman on the street at two a.m. in the morning. I got in my car and drove the hell home as fast as I could.

174

Thirty

     I walked into my darkened living room and sat down on the couch. I sat very still and held on to my elbows. I put my feet together. I had a picture in front of my thoughts. It had a baroque frame around it, because that's the way I think and it was that kind of picture. It showed a pastoral and urban scene, crowded with characters and stories. It was the kind of picture they made in sixteenth-century France, telling stories and trying to explain everything that had gone on in the province for three hundred and fifty years. In between the historical stuff the artist had to put in some religious content, to bargain away the bad conscience of the patron who commissioned the work. Perhaps a guild had ordered the painting, and was obligated to put in the story of a saint in the background to buy them a little spot in the hereafter.

But I was the painter and the patron, so I started with a different emphasis, although I would try to buy my own guilt off later. I put in lots of animals. They were wandering around a parable island with unknown plants. They looked peaceful enough, but reptiles and amphibians, reminders of a former age, crawled over rocks and in crevices. While the animals lazed around in the middle ground I turned my attention to the focus of the work, the group on the left.

It looked like a Dutch textile guild, silent, stern business people obeying Calvinism and capitalism with a twentieth-century public relations gloss. Stanley Glassman was there, holding a small portrait of his wife for the viewer to see. It made an oval spot against his grey flannel suit.

A town official stood paternally grinning behind him; a light shone on his face. In the picture this would be from God, but in real life it was a television camera floodlight. He was destined for a higher office than District Attorney.

Stacy Weldemeer stood before them both in yellow satin jeans and capped teeth. She had a glossy smile that was as hard as the shine on any publicity photo. She displayed a user-friendly speculum in one hand. The other cradled a small globe, probably a reference to Stacy's education within the Catholic Church, and their mutual desire for world domination. The painter added a small clip-on microphone tucked into the folds of her sweater. Weldemeer beamed and flashed a rose tattooed ankle at the attending physician, a woman with babyfine hair. But the physician wasn't noticing. Ethical and removed, she pointed to a bullet wound in a foreshortened body which lay upon a stainless steel table, her gaze saying, 'This is where it entered the neck.'

Before them all stood a colourful figure, the counterpoint of the group, in checkered silk bloomers and little shoes with rolled up toes. He could have been the court jester except for the sable trim around his pantaloons. Under a head of cupid curls the eyes looked glazed or maniacal, depending on how imaginative the viewer was. A small glint of drool could be seen on the side of his mouth, where the patron could have protested and the painter could have answered that it was only a spot of white paint.

Behind the group on the left, slightly before my animal island, was a villa gracing a rolling green lawn. Lords and ladies were visible through a plate glass window. They held tiny crystal glasses. A red golden retriever nursed her puppies to one side of the house, lying on her back.

On the far side of the painting, as far away from the villa as possible, the painter had placed a town scene. A street plan of the town had been rendered tilted up on its side, its walled streets and towers were visible and showed assorted scenarios of desperation. The everyday one-arm beggars in sackcloth plied their woes to a few disinterested burghers. Children played with rats and sewer systems belched up foulness into the streets.

Women wandered through the streets with their hands outstretched, the guild that was the benefactor of women and children had been disbanded. Children roamed the alleys and used a lice comb on each other. Shopkeepers ran after them for stealing.

Crowds gathered where hawkers sold trinkets as saintly relics with specific powers of cure. A splinter of the ankle bone of Saint Anthony was the best bet against arthritis and the plague. Others intently listened and paid gold coin to a man professing he had the secret of alchemy. There was an assortment of inquisitions, a few burnings at the stake and a cliché crucifixion scene.

It was a painting one could look far back into. In the distance behind the town, behind the villa with its lords and ladies, the painter had put a range of misty aqua mountains with snowy peaks. It was an imagined paradise. Above the mountains a few clouds parted conveniently to shed their rays like spotlights from God on different parts of the range.

And then, at the very top, two angels floated in a technicolour heaven, united on the Other Side and playing lavender harps. One had a banner attached to her set of wings saying, 'Gay is Better.' It was a busy painting. I should have let it alone, put ten coats of linseed oil on it and sold it as a fake antique. Instead I sat transfixed looking at the main subject of the complicated piece. A huge romantic nude covered the foreground. Her smile was inviting but self-contained.

It was too romantic to call it an erotic piece; she lay on her side, her body festooned with flowers, small pink and purple petals were entangled in her pubic hair. One breast hung down fully upon another as she leaned over. There were tiger stripes on her hips that rounded out from a tiny round waist. A soft belly revealed a dusky navel, the wonder of chiaroscuro. She didn't need any cherubs with mirrors hanging over her. Her eyes said she knew just who she was and dared me to admit it too. And all along I was wondering, who killed Julie Arbeder?

Thirty-One

I needed time to think. I had the images dancing before my eyes, I was jiggling thoughts about like a cocktail shaker and only getting foam.

The retriever puppy woke up from a nap and discovered me. She was predictably joyous. I let her out and afterwards let her crawl all over me on the couch. She had a soft tongue that even felt pink. But she was a reminder of the nude in the painting, the woman I was dying to have charm and seduce me, the woman I was dying to be willing for. The woman I wanted to use all my own tricks on, in the most friendly and unassuming way. All the terrible ambitions and faults of the figures were etched sharply before me, sticking up like the peaks on the horizon, but none had looked scary or big enough to turn into murder.

The naivety of the puppy adoring me was too much; all the weaknesses of our species had been invested into making that sort of personality. The dog emotions mocked my own hopes. I needed more time.

I needed to get out of the house. I needed to walk around a street with life, any kind of life, even low life. I got in the car and drove along Mass Ave, over the river until I got to the place with all the neon lights, the hustlers, the last, sad tourists looking for a last, sad piece of action.

I parked the car with difficulty and too much money. I walked among the thinning crowds, I got hawked at and passed a lot of photos of women. Eventually the crowds got thinner and the signs blinked less furiously. I felt calmer myself. I saw a small door painted yellow. A sign above it said, 'The Yellow Door' and photos outside promised Latin music and a floor show. I walked in; I hoped it would be the loud and flashy spectacle I needed to keep me from thinking, not trying to put the pieces together. It was definitely a new experience.

The population of the nightlife is never appealing to me; the division between workers and non-workers is always too clear. If anything is pretending to be art or entertainment I prefer that it doesn't ply its wares in any way I'm aware of. That goes for museum walls too. The club I went to made it all too obvious, but I needed something else, for a while.

The place was designed like a cave and you had to pay green money to get to surrender your coat. The floor was crowded with little tables and big people. I took a spindly chair and waited as the lights went dim.

Some heavy driving disco music thundered out of four speakers and five young, very young, Asian women went through assorted dance routines that made me think how much their bodies resembled each other. Their costumes were mostly of an orange, pink and reddish hue. Little plastic circles embroidered on to the outfits made small noises, just audible in between the bass beat of the disco tune.

The youngsters went backstage to catch their breath and a very bored band came out. The singer didn't sing very much, mostly she waved a tambourine around a little and didn't tire out her wrists. The drinks cost a fortune, and I had no idea what I was doing there. I was getting tight. I had decided this in the place in the mind that thinks about alcohol not subconsciously, or consciously, but in some nowhere-zone in between. Maybe the Massachusetts liquor laws had a point. Mostly I took that point to mean that I'd better order my last two whiskeys fast. I did and dropped them down.

The tinny tambourine stopped and some canned music blared out of two speakers.

A small fat man walked over to my table. He was preparing to plant his ass on the velour seat next to me when I put a hand on it. I hoped he would notice my hand there before it was too late. 'I came here to drink alone,' I said. He shrugged and walked away, a man used to women saying 'no'; a man who always keeps trying. Some woman would say 'yes' sometime. I was irritated at having to defend my privacy.

I diverted my attention to a very bored looking couple to my right. They looked like they hadn't said anything new to each other in twenty-five years. The canned music stopped, the lights went out, except for a spotlight on the silver curtain. A beautiful woman stepped into it. She wore something red, shiny and see-through.

I watched a group of men leaning forward and literally breathing harder at the sight of her, fully covered and full of promises. She had a tight, high-breasted body, now wrapped in the full length peignoir, trimmed with something long and red and furry at the cuffs and hem. A feather boa floated and twined around her.

She slid over the floor waving her arms and suddenly the boa was lying there, in little red heaps, on the ground. She paused to pose, walking in place. Her nipples became visible under the filmy material as she turned in the light. She turned around, running her arms up and down her sides, the feather boa was dead on the floor. She twirled around very slowly and with one move the peignoir came loose and started to melt right off her.

The music picked up and she was dancing there in a see-through G-string and tiny bra. She teased the boa with a quick foot, then she moved her leg so that the boa seemed to be snaking its way up her thigh of its own accord. Then she was into some kind of rhythm and the boa found its way over her breasts as she was moving her shoulders, and long red feathers were waving at the men leaning further and further over their tables. She turned around and raised her buttocks, sticking her ass out at the men and moving her stomach muscles.

She moved her ass in a way that made you think about a penis moving in and out of her vagina. Certainly the men thought so, they were on the edges of their chairs. I was hoping one would fall off.

She got busy with the little spaghetti straps of her bra, sliding the long lengths off her shoulders and turning her back as she peeled off each cup.

While the men were busy with her back, she was looking me squarely in the face. Her eyes gave away her surprise at seeing a woman, sitting alone directly in front of her. Our two faces glowed, but she had all her moves down for the johns behind her and I watched her decide what to do with me. Our mutual realisation was making me fall into a well growing between my legs. She kept going with her routine, putting the feather boa between her legs for the guys behind her, turning around and looking me in the eyes as she drew it through her crotch.

Then she turned to give us all a side shot, she bent over and her breasts hung down, her butt thrusting into the space behind her. She imitated being fucked doggie style. It only made me think of Safety and how I would have to get her sterilised.

I was getting into a biological frame of mind. It was after all, a movement of procreation. Seeing the men behind her, leaning forward, like children for candy that's just out of reach, made me think of conception and took me back to the painting, the women and children begging in the streets. The men watched her ass, I saw their eyes travelling up to the hanging breasts, her ass rose again in a shivering motion.

Of course these men didn't want babies. Dressed in their business suits and paying five bucks a drink to watch a strip tease had nothing to do with babies. Babies got saved for the good girls, the ones who wanted men for marriage. This made me think about a big time businessman who would kidnap his wife and her unborn child that wasn't his. Except that he wouldn't.

The stripper was frontal to the men now; her ass to me was a bunch of contracted muscles, making little wrinkles in the flesh as she humped at the men at the table.

I went back to the babies. I was wondering if men ever actually had ejaculations watching stuff like that, and I wondered what they would do with the mess. The stripper gave a rather weak whoop, meant to simulate the excitement of a climax, but she was a dancer, not an actress and the orgasm fell flat and died somewhere in her throat.

The thought of little cells meeting each other and making a miniature complete biological system made me think of Frances and the animals at the lab. At the same time it made me think of Misty and her sentiments about Julie's death.

Things were becoming very clear, except that I was getting very fuzzy. The stripper had loosened her G-string and was pulling that back and forth across her cunt. She turned again in my direction, giving the boys her ass before she presented them with living pubic hair. She'd nearly forgotten about me, I could tell, but her eyes got stuck on mine and I actually saw her put her hands across her breasts for a moment, nearly dropping the G-string in the process.

I got out of the spindly chair and made my way towards the exit. I got into the car and realised I hadn't paid the bill. That was because my mind was really somewhere else, and it was getting there fast and clear. I had the feeling that someone was in big danger, and I remembered Sandy's ghost with her Betty Crocker advice. I hoped I wouldn't be too late again.

Thirty-Two

I drove in that concentrated way, to prove to myself that I wasn't drunk; that meant I was. I hoped the scene I was going to, with the skyscraper background, wouldn't be gruesome.

I crossed the damp lawn and slid open the small patio door. It opened easily this time, the hinges had loosened through my own secret use. I found the room at the end of the hallway and opened the door.

He lay on the chaise-longue, facing a forest of tall, blinking buildings, a pinball machine of civilisation. His aqua pyjamas were silk and would have matched his eyes, if his eyes had been open. Scattered about the floor were green flakes of marijuana, like Hansel and Gretel's crumbs. They made a path that ended in death. The gruesome still life consisted of a candle burning, a blackened spoon, a small broken glass vial, and a syringe. I walked towards the figure; he was a beautiful man, lying small and limp, laid out before the Boston skyline. There would be no bloated face, swollen with water, drowned off the deck. His thick eyelashes rested on his cheek like little bird wings, swooping over a pink satin pillow. His chubby hand curled slightly around a silk tie, that was partially wrapped around a pyjama'd arm. The little sculpted mouth opened to let a pearl of dew show, and his head rested in a nest of sandy ringletted curls. A high baroque painter couldn't have done it better.

I put my hand on the short neck, he was cool; I couldn't find the artery. I put my ear to the beige silk on his chest; I thought I could hear, far off in the distance, a beat, like Hush Puppies treading hesitantly down a corridor.

I turned my back on the little man and walked out of the room. I ran up the stairs and into the kitchen. Vanessa stood there with her mouth open and her hands stirring a pan of milk on the stove.

'I don't have time to explain,' I explained, 'call an ambulance. Hugo's overdosed.'

182

I couldn't have looked too good myself. My black pants were short and tight, showing dirty white socks. My tennis shoes were caked in mud, my black turtleneck smelled. She stared with her mouth open.

'Call an ambulance!' I said again and this time, without taking her eyes off me she walked sideways to the telephone. She still had on her uniform, but it was a worn blue cotton one, and she hadn't buttoned it all the way down the skirt. A white flannel triangle showed at the bottom.

'Oh my God, this is horrible.' Then she stopped herself. 'I hope you're right about this.'

'Hugo's got enough different stuff floating around his head to make him a garbage brain any second. That is, if his heart holds out.'

Vanessa's face cracked a little on one side, she was shaking, but she picked up the phone without taking her eyes off me. Then she dialled and gave an address.

'What keeps you up so late?' I asked her.

'It's none of your business. Who are you anyway, coming into this house, bringing all this trouble . . ?'

'I just show up at clean-up time. After all, I thought that was what the help was for.' I heard my voice rise. 'Seems to me the trouble got here long before I did.'

'Well, I've got nothing to do with it. And neither did Hugo.' She turned her head sharply away. She was a woman who liked to hide things. 'That's what the help's supposed to be for,' I thought I heard her say under her breath, without bitterness.

I heard an ambulance siren. It was still far in the distance. Soon the kitchen would be filled with the panic of white-coated people. But I didn't think it would be of much use to Hugo. I thought I saw Vanessa wipe her eyes, and her rib cage expanded with a deep breath.

Before she went to the door she turned to me and planted her feet on the same linoleum squares I was occupying. They were large squares, but not large enough.

'There's been a lot of trouble and a lot of drugs going through this house. You'd be better off just getting out of here. Your presence makes it harder on you, and harder on me.'

'I don't really want to complicate *your* story, and I don't even have a story, yet. But what's the problem for you? What's with the silent maid act, wiping tables at parties and arranging flowers too many times? What are you getting out of this anyway?'

Her face clouded and cleared. 'Okay, I'll tell you, then will you get the hell out of here?'

I nodded.

'I'm learning more about funds, mergers and commodities than a business Ph.D, and I've got more inside information than a stockbroker with a seat on the New York exchange. I've got myself a little legal capital and I'm going to make a fortune that nobody can take away from me. But I got a history, honey, and this scene does not fit into my plan, so just blow yourself away.'

'Okay, Vanessa,' the sirens were coming closer. 'I guess this is goodbye.'

'That's right, or you can visit me on the Riviera next spring. I'm getting out of here, this place is crazy!'

The doorbell rang twice quickly in succession. 'I'll keep a lid on it,' I started to say, but she was already pushing me out the back door. Suddenly I was outside.

I walked down the wide back stairs sliding my hand along a curly iron railing. I glanced along the back of the house. A light went on, flooding the green grass. Then it went off again. I walked along the side of the house, past Allison's darkened windows. I walked over the lawn clipped like a crew cut, a great place to hit little white balls with sticks. Around the corner was the cliff, with all the skyscraper lights twinkling behind it. The mist was slowly creeping up from the bay. Soon it would wrap itself around the tall buildings and fall off around their ankles with the morning sun. But that would be tomorrow.

I turned the corner and looked into Hugo's room. He wasn't peaceful anymore. A lot of white coats were making busy with the silk-covered body. After a while they all stepped away and left the body on the chaise-longue facing out the window at the skyscraper lights.

'Well, you can call off the wagon boys,' someone said. I watched the blinking lights and the fog that moved between me and them. Emma Victor to the rescue, a little too late. I turned around and walked back over Allison Glassman's putting green.

Thirty-Three

It was three-thirty in the morning and the mist had rolled over Somerville too. Fog hung over the grass, and fog hung over me as I ascended the steep stairs towards Frances' house. I let myself in and walked up the stairs and heard no sound at all except a heavy deep breathing, getting louder and louder as I went up. What I saw next was better than any fantasy and erased all my doubts. She lay on the couch in her white bathrobe. The tie was loosened and one breast had fallen out, capped by a brown quiescent nipple. Her mouth was open, the heater was on, the room was hot and she was snoring to shame a diesel truck. A bottle of champagne sat on a glass coffee table with many dark red roses stuck haphazardly in a tall vase of cut crystal. I tiptoed over to a table in the corner that showed scraps of paper and her address book.

I looked up an address and jumped when a sound from the dark corner by the door responded. It was a squeaking, but not of metal. Something softer, like heavy cardboard. It squeaked some more and I saw a corrugated box shift slightly on the floor. There was a deep, throaty tone. Another sound joined it. The box shuddered and I walked over and peered in. Something hit the top of the box, again and again. I closed my eyes and stuck my hand in. I felt something slimy and wet which wiggled and pushed to get out of my grasp. With great effort I did not scream. It was a frog. Frances was drinking champagne with frogs. The reptiles were winning over me; Frances was a pervert.

I walked to her side, she leaned over and her shoulder rustled in the deep cushion of the couch. Her eyes opened and registered me under sleeping lids.

'I love you, my Jekyll and Hyde,' I said.

'Ha, ha,' she giggled in the champagne way. Bubbly. 'Jekyll and Hyde, that's funny. I guess I've been a bit of a bitch lately. And I love you so much.'

'Let's find out if that's a lot of expensive champagne talking. C'mon, let's sit up.'

She wobbled, pulling herself upright. 'Only doctors can use the first person plural when ordering other people around.' She planted a wettish kiss on my neck.

'And kindergarten teachers, and anyone talking to a drunk,' I said. 'You're pretty soused. You aren't a closet drinker, are you? And what's with the frogs?'

'I've been trying to get hold of you all night. I called you at eleven-thirty, and then twelve, and one and two and three. Emma, are you holding out on me?'

'Not any more. What was the three alarm fire?'

'Here. I've finally finished it and I couldn't find anyone to celebrate with, not even Stacy. Oh, but we can still have a party, can't we? I'm so happy.'

'When did you give birth to tadpoles?'

'Early tonight. Boy was it a long wait.'

'You were present at delivery?'

'Honey,' she stood up. I saw her white underpants under the robe. She was wearing green socks. 'I was present during conception!' She bent over, I got another sloppy kiss, and tried not to think about frog conception. 'So, we've both become pet mothers!' she fell on the couch and draped two loose arms around me and smiled sort of goofy into my face.

'Don't talk about that just now. It gives me the creeps.'

'It's a big night for me, I want to celebrate.' She curled her bottom lip. 'Oh, but I'm so tired.'

'Frogs are cute, but they're not worth champagne and roses,' I said. I noticed a huge broad grin that was eating up her face like the moon coming up over the horizon of Ova Orchards. 'Oh yes they are. I've been working at this for three years, at Geno Corp, even before I met Stacy Weldemeer. Shit, I couldn't even get hold of Stacy tonight. She'll probably make a big press thing about it, and it was my idea, and my research. Anyway, I hope she at least shares the credit.' But she was still smiling. I wondered later how often women have gotten to sit with a history-making smile.

'What's going on, anyway?' I asked.

'Lesbian frogs,' she said, leaning back on to a cushion and gave me that goofy drunken smile again. Then I realised what she'd done. Frances Cohen had just generated life from two female frogs. And I knew what that meant for the future; because I knew Frances Cohen's

186

primary interest wasn't frogs. Her eyelids were dropping and she giggled a little as I kissed her for a few moments, and held her and finally had a little celebration with her. It didn't last long. She fell back into the champagne stupor for which she'd pay dearly tomorrow.

'Like they say, it'll be one for the history books, baby,' I said to the sleeping body. 'And I'll do my best to make it a happy ending for you.'

I left her house to go clean up. It was time to visit Stacy Weldemeer.

Thirty-Four

The street was dark and I hung back standing on the pavement and looking at the neat wooden house. Wood siding is unusual for Boston. There was a tidy little porch, with two thick barrel pillars at either end, and a small bench wedged between them and the house. A climbing wistaria rested on a vine support to one side of the porch. I walked up the little driveway and touched the hood of the red jeep that was parked there. It was just warmer than the night air. A light went on in a window upstairs. I rang the bell and soon a movement occurred in a brass peephole set into the centre casing. She didn't open the door.

'Stacy, it's me. It's Emma Victor,' I said. No response. 'It's important. It's about the clinic. I've just come from Frances.' The door knob moved, I saw a chain stretch out in a black space, and then the chain fell. Stacy Weldemeer stood there in a long maroon woollen robe, and a freckled mask on her face. She registered no surprise; she registered nothing.

'Where's Frances?' she asked, pulling the tie on her robe and tightening the knot.

'Frances is indisposed. I came alone. I think we'd better talk.'

'About what?'

'Let me in, Stacy, you want to hear what I have to say. It concerns the future of the clinic.'

There was a moment in her face and then the moment was gone; I was pushing the door open and she followed me as I walked into a long room, with a fireplace and a big mirror at one end and lots of Danish modern furniture which was busily trying to be simple in a stick-like way. There was a looped white carpet stretching across the whole room.

'It seems Frances is keeping rather hysterical company these days.' She tossed her head, the curls were springy, unflattened.

'What were you doing tonight?'

188

'You came to question my social life? Look, this is all very exciting and dramatic and everything, but I have to get up and go to work this morning so why don't you just go play with some poison bats? Christ, it's four in the morning!' she yawned. 'I'm going back to bed.'

'You haven't been to bed, Stacy, the hood of your car is still warm. I know what's been going on at the clinic.'

'You think you know what's going on? Go back to answering phones, honey, you got the wrong number, or you wouldn't be here.'

'I know about the experiment Frances is doing,' I said. Stacy looked at me and past me. I saw anger and betrayal, but just for a moment.

'I suppose Frances told you. Well, no harm done. You will keep our work quiet, won't you? You wouldn't want to screw the whole project with premature press coverage?'

'You mean you wouldn't want me to spoil your credit?'

'Charges of elitism went out with downward mobility. You said you wanted to talk to me about the future of the clinic, well talk. But I hope you have the common sense and integrity to put your emotions aside and think about what is good for our community, what is good for women.'

'What is good for Stacy Weldemeer.'

'You said you wanted to come here to talk to me about the future of the clinic. It seems you don't have a lot to say and it's getting late . . .'

'I wanted to talk with you about how you paid the bills at the Blackstone Clinic. Your recent grant. The Glassman Foundation.'

'It's public record.'

'It wasn't public record four months ago when you were first promised the money. And I think you paid an interesting price.'

'I don't know what you're talking about,' she said and turned her back and walked towards the low white brick fireplace set into the wall. She lifted a box off the mantel. It was too short to hold a screwdriver and too small to hold a gun. She opened the lid and pulled out a thin cigarillo.

'Even your cigar won't make me leave. Come on, Stacy. Let's not play cat and mouse.'

'Oh, tell me, is that what we're playing then? I thought you were a confused person wanting to make her mark with some inside information. I hope you're not one of these dangerously delusioned people.'

'Thinking of calling the cops? Go right ahead. Or shall I?'

'Sit down, what was your name again?'

'Emma Victor. Look, how long do you want to go on with this?'

She put the little cigar on a big glass ashtray which took up a lot of room on a low blonde coffee table. She twirled the tip around. 'I want to know what you have to say. And then I want you to get out,' she said.

'I want to know how you happened to inseminate Allison Glassman with her husband's sperm,' I asked and sat myself down in the deep bowl of a butterfly chair. Stacy rearranged her face quietly and sat down too.

'Where did you get that idea?'

'I guessed. If I want to find proof I know where I can get it.'

Stacy looked at me for a moment. The cigar was not so smelly for a cigar. She licked her lips. She slowly twirled one foot in the air. It ended in a rose tattoo and polished toes. She appeared to think for a moment. She appeared to think for several very long moments. Then she said, 'Emma, I'm going to tell you how this happened. I am going to take you in my confidence. But what we are talking about is not you and me, or the petty lives of people around us, lives that will really mean nothing when we are talking about generations.' She leaned forward and looked closely at me. 'Do you understand?'

'No.'

'We are sitting under a sentence, in a matter of time the biogenetic possibilities are going to have overwhelming consequences for women. The sentence we are sitting under is death; death after the coming generations,' she twirled her cigarillo and looked at me. She was impressive. 'Only if you believe this to be true, can I entrust you with this information.'

'I won't pledge allegiance, but I've been around, Stacy. You don't need to test my credentials.'

'Emma, it was one of those rare, freak opportunities and when there is an opportunity like that we must take it. Emma, we have no time, you must understand that. There isn't one moment to spare that can't be used to make our future. Here was one woman with one appointment. Maybe I didn't know what it would lead to at the time, but I had to try every possibility that came along.'

'How did you get Glassman?'

'I don't think I got him, I think he got me. He's not a very nice man. But we both wanted something badly. And we both got it. It wasn't really too difficult to arrange.' She recrossed her legs and looked somewhere just past my left ear.

'I remember the day so well, because it meant the beginning of the future. It was a hot, October heat wave. I came to the clinic early in the

190

morning to do some paperwork. I got there about six, I walked in, and decided to look through the register. I don't always do that, usually I start with administration and only review files of clients selected by the para-meds, or Frances. Business had been slow and I had been out milking all my sources trying to line up the second half of next year's budget. The clinic does all right, but it takes constant funding efforts. I get tired, Emma. I get discouraged. And I can't afford to get discouraged.' She drew her feet up and stretched them out on the coffee table. 'I'd been going after the Glassman Foundation for six years. There wasn't any way in with his political ambitions. He's trying much too hard to be Mister Clean. A women's clinic wouldn't really make a hit in the press.

'Then one day I look in the register and there is it "Glassman, Allison". My key to all that money, at last, after years of visiting middle-class bridge clubs, and giving interviews. I was starting to think the only way I could get press coverage was to marry Princess Caroline.'

'Go on,' I said.

'Well, there wasn't too much to it, I got in touch with the man, he wanted to give me the money.' She smiled sweetly, like she had only followed the Lord's path. I thought I had seen the same expression on Jehovah's witnesses.

'It wasn't that easy.'

'Emma, I was thinking about the clinic. I called Allison Glassman at home. Not there. I got sort of a strange response. A message was taken but I had the feeling she wouldn't get it.' Stacy looked at me, 'You get practically psychic about these things.'

'Go on.'

'Well, then I asked for Mr Glassman, I asked him point blank, since his wife was now making use of the services of the Blackstone Clinic perhaps they would like to review our grant proposal of last year. I went on about our day-care placement and then he invited me to his house. That evening.'

'Pretty fast response from Mr Big.'

'And I went for it. Believe me, after six years I made fast tracks for Mr Glassman. So when Mr Money invited me personally out to his house I took a cab. We had a friendly chat and then he said he wanted a sperm count done at the clinic, privately.'

'So he got a very expensive private appointment.'

'He didn't talk about money at first, but he mentioned the Foundation. He told me his wife was very neurotic. He told me that she had given up on the possibility of conceiving with him. He said it was pure neurosis. I could see for myself that his sperm count was normal.'

'You fell for the good husband with the neurotic wife routine?'

'He offered me four hundred thousand dollars, first payment immediately and the second payment after two years.' Stacy looked at me. 'I saw our future, Emma. It was there, I could see it.'

'You couldn't turn it down.'

'I didn't want to turn it down.'

'And the consequences?'

'Could be dealt with.'

'Had to be dealt with,' I said.

'So now you know, it has been a nasty business, especially when the poor woman slipped and fell off the boat. Accidents do happen.'

'Especially when people find out that their bodies have been used.'

'Emma, what does it really matter now? I understand it's upsetting for you, but try and put your personal feelings aside.'

'And Julie Arbeder's? And Hugo Glassman's?'

I watched Stacy; I had the feeling I was pushing her towards a cliff. And I didn't know what she'd do when she got to the edge. But I didn't have any choice any more.

'I don't know what you're talking about,' she said, 'I've told you everything I know, and I hope that you have the good sense to respect my confidence. Now if you don't mind . . .'

'The last appointment with Allison. Julie Arbeder was there.'

'I don't know what you're talking about.'

'Your initials are in the book. Next to their names.'

'I suppose, I don't really remember . . .'

'Surely you remember Julie Arbeder. She played a big role in this thing.'

'Listen, I don't know about this other person. I don't know what you're talking about.' Her eyes travelled around the room. They landed on a bureau in the hallway.

'Oh, but you will, you will tomorrow morning,' I said.

'You seem to know so much. Fill me in.' Her face was getting whiter and she started scratching at one spot on her wrist.

I was tired of sitting. I raised myself out of the bright yellow butterfly chair. It was difficult. 'I might not have found out anything, if it hadn't been for a woman named Sue who was also putting the touch on Glassman.'

'I don't see what this has to do with me.'

'Her ideas weren't so grandiose, she was just trying to save her life, comfortably.'

'What?'

'It's just one life, nothing that you'd bother with. You killed Julie Arbeder, because she came after you with cannons ready to tear your clinic down brick by brick for what you'd done. And how did Julie know? She went to Hugo who felt so guilty about luring Allison on to the boat he couldn't wait to blame Stanley. So he told her the same thing he told me; what a ruthless fucker the guy was. He also must have mentioned how Stanley planned this little trip for his family. "Family" wasn't just his estranged wife, now a lesbian. So Julie figured he'd planned to kidnap Allison and her unborn child. But how did he know that Allison was pregnant? Julie must have realised in a flash that Glassman had bought you off. No, she didn't go after Glassman. She went after *you*; the woman that betrayed her trust, who used a feminist health clinic for her own ends, and was in some way responsible for the death of her lover.'

'I don't know what you're talking about.' That seemed to be the only line Stacy could think of anymore. Maybe it was the only line she could believe in anymore.

'You killed Julie Arbeder because she said she was going to blow your clinic. Then you tried to kill Hugo Glassman, because he was too close to the truth, and answering too many of my questions.'

'You can't prove anything.'

'I don't need to prove anything.'

'Good, then we can both go back to bed and get a good night's sleep.'

'Hugo Glassman's not dead,' I lied. 'Tomorrow morning he's going to wake up and he's going to tell the world that you tried to kill him.'

'He's not dead?'

'And I'm going to corroborate his story.'

'I don't believe you.'

'Call the hospital.' I picked up the telephone receiver and waved it at her. She looked bad.

'Emma, you have to help me. You understand now. The work we are doing is so important . . .'

'You killed someone.'

'I had no choice. You can help me keep this a secret. No one will believe Hugo, he is demented already. We don't have to say anything, don't you see?'

'Stacy, you committed murder.'

193

'No.' She was outraged. 'No,' she said again and I started to smell the fear emanating from her body. 'You can't mean it, Emma. You see how it all happened. That woman was following me around, calling the office. Why, she was hysterical. I couldn't reason with her. She kept threatening me about the press, she said she had a connection with someone.'

'How did it happen? What were you thinking?'

Stacy's voice became quieter, and word by word, emotion left her voice.

'I followed her, I drove behind her car and then I saw her get out on East Lexington. Then she ducked into an alley, out of the street lights. I approached her and she backed farther into the darkness.

'She started yelling at me again, she was like a rabid dog. She was totally out of control.' Stacy looked at me with some strange kind of justification. 'She was like a wounded animal, she had snot running out her nose, and she'd actually torn her skin up with her fingernails. She looked awful. And she said it was all my fault.' Stacy stared at me. 'She said I had killed her lover.'

'I tried to reason with her, but she said she would choke me on my own ideals and she said by the time she was done with me I wouldn't be able to raise a dime for a pay toilet.

'She was yelling at me, hissing at me in that alley. She was backed up against those bushes and she was goading me, telling me how she was going to ruin me. She was almost *enjoying* it, Emma. She kept saying it over and over. I was standing there, listening and I knew that it had to stop. She had to stop saying all those things. She could not do what she planned.' Stacy turned to me. 'She was crazy, Emma.'

'What happened next?'

'I didn't even think about it, I reached into my purse. She was still saying all these crazy horrible things and then I just came at her, my arm was in the air, I had a gun. I pointed it at her. I pulled the trigger. That was all there was to it.'

I heard a drunk outside on the street. He was singing something. I heard the electronic whine of a police car far in the distance. Stacy was looking at the ashtray with the cigar in it.

'Then suddenly everything was quiet. I stood there and looked at her. I felt sorry for her, not because she was dead, but because she couldn't see the importance of what was happening. She couldn't see that she was only playing a role. She didn't realise the importance of it.' Stacy fingered a curl of her hair, twirling it round and round her finger. 'We are all playing roles, Emma, you too.'

194

'The next role you're going to play is going to be very nasty,' I said.

'No, Emma, we can't make this public,' she was smiling, slightly.

'But it is going public, Stacy. It has to. Because I don't want to carry your crime around with me. I think the story goes something like this: You've killed a person and all the rest of your life it's your baggage and it's heavy. And every person that knows or has some part of the story will carry it too. And every person is a bomb that can blow up your life. These people will sit and fester in your mind. And the possibilities will drive you crazy, Stacy. You will always be wanting to know what they know, and what they will tell. Your future, your life will be at stake with every word they might say. And you won't be able to let it rest. Just as you monitored Hugo, just as you broke into my house to try and warn me off the Glassmans, some loose end will always be asking for your attention. And loose ends have a way of trailing off and unravelling. And for every loose end you solve there will be six others hanging loose. You can't win.'

'Emma, you cannot jeopardise the future of women's health care.'

'You mean I cannot jeopardise you.'

'Emma, you can't be serious. These things are practically accidents.'

'I think you're asking me to cover up murder.'

'You don't understand.'

'*You* don't understand. I'm sending you over, Stacy. I can't be your accomplice, I can't cover for you, and if I did I'd never be sure of you when the night is dark and I'm alone and you feel panicked and I become an object in the way of your future. No, Stacy, I'm sending you over. It's the only way.' I walked towards a bright yellow pushbutton phone. 'I'm going to call the cops, now.'

'Emma, you're a misguided person.'

'How would you know?'

'You're playing with the future of women.'

'Maybe the future of women isn't safe with you. Certainly my future wouldn't be. No, Stacy,' I looked at her. She looked sick.

'It's either you or me, and I'm afraid it's going to be you.'

Her face fell and fell and the marrow in her bones seemed to soften as she sagged further into the couch. Suddenly she stood up. Then she thought better of it and sat down again. I looked in her eyes and it was like watching a traffic accident. She sat very still for a few moments. I didn't pick up the phone. Her head bent low, it sort of hung in a space over her legs.

'Do you have a lawyer?'

She laughed a second; her shoulders shrugged. She looked up at me.

'It's worth our lives. I don't want you ever to forget that,' she said to me. 'Even if you don't seem to understand it.'

She stood up and adjusted her bathrobe, pulling it closer around her. I felt paralysed, unable to move. Stacy walked past me into the hallway. She opened a drawer. I ducked behind a wall but Stacy didn't turn around. She went into a small door set in a space underneath the stairway.

I heard the little bathroom door close, I heard the taps turn on and off. There was silence for a few moments. And then I heard the splintering sound of a shot going through Stacy Weldemeer's skull.

I reeled backwards with the sound. I stood there. I looked at the telephone receiver; I stood in the same silence that Stacy Weldemeer had stood in when she had shot Julie Arbeder. It is the sudden, total stillness after the sound of a panicked and pained soul taking a quick exit out of this world.

I heard no sounds from neighbours, no windows being opened. I looked outside, no darkened curtains had lit up. No one knew what had just happened.

I didn't want to break that stillness with police sirens, and detectives with little pieces of chalk and flashbulbs illuminating the body of Stacy Weldemeer.

I thought of Stanley Glassman, the man who used a woman's own body against her, and laughed. He would read about it in the morning paper, and only the ink on the newsprint would soil his fingers.

I backed across the room and wiped any object I might have touched. I backed out of the house. I left by a back porch doorway. I got in my car and drove away.

I would return to Frances' house. I would lift her off that couch and hold her through the remainder of the night. I would nurse her through her champagne hangover and then later over the information that her boss had committed suicide. I didn't know what other facts there would be coming and I would probably never know the consequences anyway. Four people were dead and there was no one left to prosecute. Even if somebody might take the trouble to do so, the file would probably still be making a nice cushion for the DA. I reminded myself to get the keys back to Jonell. I reminded myself that the women at Blackstone Clinic were smart and capable and would know how to deal effectively with the press. Generous helpings of ice cream. The future of the Blackstone Clinic, and the future of women's health care in Boston would depend on it. But not the way that Stacy Weldemeer had meant.

I let myself into Frances' house with her key and walked up the stairs. She was still lying on the couch exhibiting her breast. She was still snoring. I was trembling with the shakes that a busy, sleepless night and two dead bodies give you. I had never had those shakes before.

I went and laid down on her bed at the other side of the room. The high mattress with the puffy white coverlet facing the little valley, was the perfect place to collapse in. It was hard to fall asleep. I looked outside.

The trees were waving their summertime leaves in a pre-dawn restless breeze. The sky was clear and I heard some birds waking up. The cardboard box jiggled on the floor. I was tired.

I looked at the tree and saw one branch that had died, and a brown winter leaf left over from last fall, still hanging on it like a dirty rag. The branch had moss growing along its skinny length. I stretched out as a cloud, pink with the dawn, floated by.

I fell into a restless sleep with dreams filled with quickly-moving colours and lights. There were voices but I didn't know what the voices were saying. What they were saying probably wasn't important any more.

I heard Frances get up and stumble into the kitchen. A bag opened and small hard coffee beans slid out into the metal cup of a coffee grinder.

I heard the frogs jump in the cardboard box. It was ten o'clock. I looked out the window at the tree and the leftover leaf of last season. I waited for the phone to ring.

- Lesbian left wing activist - detective
Women's issues   (Women's Hotline)

Procreation + lesbian relationships
female murderer invested in power
structure

"Sue" uses lesbian letters of Alison
Glassman to get money

"Stacey" uses Alison's body to get
money, kills Julie (who wanted tell)
to keep funding in name of research